PRAISE FOR TRACIE HOWARD AND DANITA CARTER'S
REVENGE IS BEST SERVED COLD

"A rich story that puts you in the heart of the city, with a sexy set of characters."

—Keith Clinkscales, CEO and Chairman,
Vanguarde Media

"A sexy, stylish, and sophisticated glimpse into urban culture."
—Antonio "L.A." Reid, President, Arista Records

"A must read. Carter and Howard have written a witty novel with caché and heart. It is highbrow yet earthy, serious yet funny. A new dynamic duo is on the scene."   —Yolanda Joe

"Consistently compelling."   —*Booklist*

"Tracie Howard and Danita Carter have a ball chronicling the lives of several New York strivers from Wall Street to Park Avenue in this glitzy romp."   —*Essence*

Tracie Howard

WHY SLEEPING DOGS LIE

NEW AMERICAN LIBRARY

New American Library
Published by New American Library, a division of
Penguin Group (USA) Inc., 375 Hudson Street,
New York, New York 10014, USA
Penguin Group (Canada), 10 Alcorn Avenue, Toronto,
Ontario M4V 3B2, Canada (a division of Pearson Penguin Canada Inc.)
Penguin Books Ltd., 80 Strand, London WC2R 0RL, England
Penguin Ireland, 25 St. Stephen's Green, Dublin 2,
Ireland (a division of Penguin Books Ltd.)
Penguin Group (Australia), 250 Camberwell Road, Camberwell, Victoria 3124,
Australia (a division of Pearson Australia Group Pty. Ltd.)
Penguin Books India Pvt. Ltd., 11 Community Centre, Panchsheel Park,
New Delhi - 110 017, India
Penguin Group (NZ), Cnr Airborne and Rosedale Roads, Albany,
Auckland 1310, New Zealand (a division of Pearson New Zealand Ltd.)
Penguin Books (South Africa) (Pty.) Ltd., 24 Sturdee Avenue,
Rosebank, Johannesburg 2196, South Africa

Penguin Books Ltd, Registered Offices:
80 Strand, London WC2R 0RL, England

First published by New American Library,
a division of Penguin Group (USA) Inc.

First Printing, November 2003
10 9 8 7 6 5 4 3

 REGISTERED TRADEMARK—MARCA REGISTRADA

LIBRARY OF CONGRESS CATALOGING-IN-PUBLICATION DATA:

Howard, Tracie.
Why sleeping dogs lie / Tracie Howard.
p. cm.
ISBN 0-451-20977-X
1. Triangles (Interpersonal relations)—Fiction.   2. Manhattan (New York, N.Y.)—
Fiction.   3. Illegitimate children—Fiction.   4. Women journalists—Fiction.   I. Title.
PS3608.O94W48 2003
813'.6—dc21   2003008320

Set in Sabon

Printed in the United States of America

PUBLISHER'S NOTE
This is a work of fiction. Names, characters, places, and incidents either are the product of the
author's imagination or are used fictitiously, and any resemblance to actual persons, living or
dead, business establishments, events, or locales is entirely coincidental.

I would like to dedicate this novel to three people (. . . and a cat) who always share their home and hearts, and most especially during the writing of *Why Sleeping Dogs Lie*: My sister Alison Howard-Smith; my brother-in-law Donny Smith; my niece Chelsea Smith; and the four-legged feline-fetale KittyMan!

ACKNOWLEDGMENTS

If you are reading this, hopefully that also means you have embarked, or you are about to embark, on a journey peopled with characters that I love, and situations that I find fascinating and intriguing. For that, I am very thankful. It is a blessing from God to be able to share my thoughts and fantasies (however twisted) with you.

For making that possible I thank my wonderful family, starting with my mother, Gloria Freeman (who doubles as one of my publicists), and my stepfather, Edsel Freeman. My sisters are always an inspiration to me, Jennifer Freeman for her amazing vocal ability and her resilient spirit, and Alison for her creativity, focus, and deep compassion. My nieces are a great source of love and pride. Chelsea is everything that I would be if I could do it over with a script! She's a brilliant Harvard undergrad, an athlete, and a beautiful and charming young lady. Korian is sheer genius in a nine-year-old's body! My aunts Opal, Maryland, and Virginia, I thank for always supporting me in whatever I do. I'm also eternally grateful to my cousin April, her husband, Ted, and their son, Saxton (who is the namesake of a character you are soon to meet), for opening their home and hearts to Scott and me when we are in Atlanta. Margaret Mroz and Robert Folkes are also people who've made my sanity and peace of mind possible.

There are others who are like family, and those special people include: Rose Salem, who is like a sister; Imara Canady, who is such an incredible, caring, and considerate person, aside from being the best publicist ever; Vanessa Baylor and her groom, Bill Johnson (welcome to the family!); Karen, Oswald, and Zoe Morgan; Juan and Judith Montier; my attorney and friend Denise Brown; Julie Borders; Mike and Diane Frierson; Tony Smith, Florence Johnson, Eula Smith and Sandra Folkes. To my fellow authors and friends, Danita Carter, Veronica Chambers, and Harriette Cole, I say, "Keep it coming!" I also thank Roy Johnson, Keith Clinkscales, and Len Burnette.

On the business end, I thank my management company, UnZipped!, and I am always grateful that my editor, Audrey LaFehr, continues to adopt my characters as her own and helps me to raise them. Blessings to all African-American bookstores and thanks to the Atl 4 O'clock Bookclub. And to Kristina Matesa: You are a jewel for helping me and UnZipped! design the BOMB Web site (www.traciehoward.com)!

Erin Holvey and William Young, life wouldn't be the same without you both. And, always and forever, I thank my love and best friend Scott.

To my uncle "L.M.": Your words did not go unheeded. Rest in Peace . . .

1

ACCIDENTAL ENCOUNTERS

Mallory Baylor loved the boundless energy that surged through Manhattan. Often she thought of it as one big glorious playground. Only this playground was ten miles long and full of adventure seekers looking for fame, fortune, or simply a good time. The city's vibe seemed especially strong to her during the fall, when sexy little T-shirts and barely there midriffs gave way to chic designer sweaters, swanky hats, and sexy ankle boots.

She was walking fast this morning—on her way to her first real assignment. Her dark hair was cut in loose layers, spiky at the top, with tendrils framing her keen, exotic features. She wore a black calf-length knit skirt over a pair of black suede lace-up Marc Jacobs granny boots, and a black cashmere TSE turtleneck. She looked every inch the stylish, chic reporter. So why had the prospect of interviewing Saxton McKensie reduced her to such a nervous wreck?

The evening before, Alan Randolf, the lead features writer for *Heat* magazine, had taken a nasty tumble while sprinting for an out-of-bounds ball on the tennis courts at Chelsea Piers. Hospital tests revealed a broken ankle. It was a classic case of good news/bad news for Mallory. It was great that she would finally get to write a feature story. But the subject was the last person she wanted to see.

The minute she arrived at *Heat*'s office that morning, she had been called into Chad Williams's lair.

"How would you like the opportunity to interview Saxton McKensie?" Chad was the editor-in-chief of the urban fashion and lifestyle magazine.

Mallory stood in the doorway with her jaw ajar. The surprise announcement certainly pierced her usually unflappable cool. "Me? Interview Saxton McKensie?"

"Unless you don't think you're up to it . . ." he challenged. Chad leaned back in his desk chair, straining the tight springs, his arms folded across his thin, if not puny, chest. He was close to five six, which put him below Mallory's eye level whenever she wore any size heel—which was most of the time, since she was in committed relationships with Manolo (as in Blahnik), Jimmy (as in Choo), and Walter (as in Steiger). Furthermore, Chad suffered from a Napoleonic complex, so he avoided standing close to her at all costs.

She bristled at his insinuation that she couldn't handle a feature article, particularly since she was a better writer than most of those at the magazine who held the prestigious title, including Alan. She was sick and tired of penning the tiny tech pieces and the short "what to wear" blurbs that came with her current job as staff writer. When she first accepted the job as staff writer for *Heat*, Chad had assured her that it was only a stepping-stone, and given her credentials, she would be a features writer within a year. That was over two and a half years ago. So Chad was also a liar, among other things.

"Of course I'm up to it," she insisted.

"Then it's settled," he announced, leaning forward to make a note on his editorial calendar. "Be at his office at eleven sharp." He looked at his watch. "It's nine o'clock now, so you don't have much prep time. You'd better get a move on."

Should she tell him about her past history with Saxton? she wondered. *Definitely not*, she quickly convinced herself. Chad would only make a big deal over it, and might even decide to do the interview himself. "Did you tell him that I would be stepping in for Alan?" she asked. She wanted to know if Saxton would be expecting her.

"I had Angela call first thing to tell him about Alan's accident, and since we were lucky to get on his calendar to begin with, I told her to assure him that the interview was still on, even though I wasn't yet sure who the writer would be." He leaned across the desk, reaching for the four-line phone. "I'll have Angela call him now."

"Don't bother," Mallory said instantly. "I'll call myself." She turned to leave.

"Don't forget the story angles we discussed in last week's editorial meeting. I don't want the typical celebrity-couple fluff piece about his engagement to Deena. I want to tell our readers what they don't already know—especially about him."

I won't have to interview him at all to nail that story, Mallory thought to herself.

"Take a look at Alan's notes, and the file of press clippings. That'll give you some good leads."

Saxton's fiancée, Deena Ingram, was one of the most recognized women in America, with a highly rated television show and a glossy women's magazine in development. She was a media darling. But *Heat*'s editorial angle was to focus on the thirty-seven-year-old Harvard-educated attorney Saxton McKensie, who for the last five years had orchestrated her meteoric rise while building a multimedia empire to be reckoned with.

As she headed back out the door, she heard Chad say, "You owe me for this one."

Right, she thought. The only reason he was giving her this opportunity was because all of his feature writers were either out of town or buried deeply under tight deadlines. Besides, they had only two weeks to close the story, leaving precious little time for it to be written, edited, fact-checked, top-edited, and copyedited.

Mallory reached the Madison Avenue address with an inward groan. Of course Saxton would have to work in the sleekest building around. She avoided looking up to see how high the skyscraper soared.

"Hi, I'm Mallory Baylor with *Heat* magazine. I'm here to see Saxton McKensie," she informed the guard who manned the imposing desk in the building's marbled lobby. Her nervousness idled just beneath the surface of what she hoped was a cool veneer. There was a lot at stake here. Personal feelings aside, this interview was the break that she'd been waiting for since coming to New York. Chad, had proven to be a passive-aggressive male chauvinist, so the only writers he'd ever promoted to feature status were fellow members of his own good-ole-boys club, plus a lone female writer, Devon Brown, whose true talents lay elsewhere—more specifically, on Chad's office couch.

Barely peeping over his fanned-out newspaper, the guard droned, "Sign in here," before calling upstairs to announce her arrival.

A minute later, he sent her to the bank of elevators with a building pass and directions to exit on the fifteenth floor. On the elevator ride up, she took several long, deep breaths to help steady her shaky nerves. At least fifteen wasn't that high up.

"You must be Mallory Baylor," a freckled-faced woman sitting behind the reception desk said.

"I am."

"Please have a seat, and I'll let Mr. McKensie's assistant know that you're here." She picked up the phone attached to a switchboard that looked like the command post from the starship *Enterprise*. "Cindy, Mr. McKensie's eleven o'clock is here. The writer from *Heat* magazine." Just then two other phone lines lit up with sharp rings. "Hold on a moment." When she switched back, she said, "Her name is—" On cue the phones once again lit up. "Hold on."

Before she could depress the HOLD button for the second time, Cindy said, "I'll be right out to get her."

While she waited, Mallory surveyed the reception area, taking in its rich decor. Obviously, Mr. McKensie and his wife-to-be were doing quite well. Even from the lobby she could hear the sounds of success resonating from the office beyond: the continuous hum of phones ringing, the ambient buzz of faxes and printers, and echoes of various conversations. This was clearly a place where things happened, as the plaques of recognition and Emmy Awards that lined the walls bore testament to.

A few minutes passed before a heavyset woman topped with long sun-bleached dreads appeared in the lobby. "Hi, I'm Cindy, Mr. McKensie's assistant."

"I'm Mallory. Mallory Baylor."

"If you'd follow me, Ms. Baylor, I'll take you directly to his office. I have to warn you, his schedule is very hectic today, so you won't have much time."

Mallory followed the sound of the woman's thighs as her panty hose rubbed together—*swish, swish, swish*—down a long hall, past several rows of modernistic cubicles and several increasingly large, plush offices. The last one dominated the southwest corner of the floor, offering a commanding view of the Empire State Building. Cindy knocked on the door once before announcing Mallory's arrival.

"Mr. McKensie, this is Mallory Baylor from *Heat* magazine."

A look of amazement replaced the canned nice-to-meet-you face he'd started toward the door sporting. As Saxton reached out to shake her hand, he looked as though a vision from a dream had suddenly materialized during his waking hours. "Mallory?"

She tilted her head, pinning him with a firm look. "Mr. McKensie," she said with a seed of sarcasm.

"Wh-wh-what are you doing here? Are you with *Heat*? Where have you been?" His handsome face searched hers for answers. Saxton McKensie was strikingly good-looking, with butterscotch skin, honey brown eyes, and dark eyelashes so thick and long they never should have been wasted on any man. The years since she'd last seen him had only accentuated his irresistible good looks. *Why couldn't he be fat, with a receding hairline?* Mallory thought.

Before Cindy retreated through his office door, she too was puzzled, looking back and forth between the writer and her boss. When the secretary was safely out of earshot, Mallory dropped Saxton's hand and said, "I'm here to interview you, so yes, I am with *Heat*. And where have I been?" she asked, shifting her weight from one foot to the other. "Let's just say *around*."

A frown crept across his brow. "Listen, Mallory, I'm sorry about what happened. It was just a very complicated time."

"I'm sure that it was."

They had met in Atlanta when Saxton was in the city for an extended stay to facilitate a joint venture between his law firm at the time, Brown, Stills and Riley, and the Southern powerhouse the Pegasus Group. It had seemed like love at first sight. They'd had a torrid affair, which had fizzled inexplicably the moment he'd returned to New York. Mallory had been devastated by his rejection.

She looked different to him now. Her hair was shorter, and the girlish charm that had captivated him six years ago was suffused by a woman's self-assuredness. Along with the flow of memories of their time together came an overpowering rush of embarrassment. "I am so sorry," he said. "For everything."

Anxious to put the fake sentimentality aside, Mallory got down to business. "I know this is a little awkward, given our past relationship, but I'd like to pretend that it never happened and proceed with the interview."

Without waiting for his response, she sat on the suede couch opposite his handcrafted mahogany desk. She opened her Prada satchel and pulled out a tape recorder and a legal pad, adroitly switching from the hurt ex-lover to the consummate professional.

"Sure." Saxton settled down next to her, fighting off a storm of emotions. He'd been apprehensive about the interview to begin with. He was doing it only because Deena had begged him, thinking it would help her public image. She and her publicist were convinced that the concept of the two of them as a power couple would boost her ratings with Middle America.

Saxton was also deeply ashamed of the way he'd ended his affair with Mallory. He'd let his head rule his heart in choosing Deena over Mallory. To complicate things further, he found himself strongly attracted to Mallory, just as before. He longed to touch her and hoped that she felt the same way, but her brusque demeanor told him otherwise. Besides, he was engaged to Deena now.

"So tell me," Mallory asked, anxious herself, positioning the handheld tape recorder like a barrier between them, "how did you and Deena meet?" She forced a fake smile.

He leaned in closer, wanting to explain what he'd done all those years ago. "We met about seven years ago at a cocktail party in the Hamptons. Before I met you."

Mallory wished he hadn't sat so close to her. His jacket was open wide, affording her a broad view of the muscular chest that strained the fabric of his Brioni dress shirt. She could smell the teasing fragrance of his cologne. She found herself drawn into his piercing eyes while studying his full, sexy mouth, smooth skin, and well-toned body. As he continued speaking, his words were mostly a blur to her. She loved the way his top lip wrapped around a good-size divot, forming a perfect bow. Thank God—and Thomas Edison— for the tape recorder, since her own recollections of the interview would probably include volumes of details on what he wore, his scent, and the sexy way that he licked his lips when deep in thought. Not quite the makings of a serious feature story.

The urge to simply lean forward and melt in his arms was

almost too strong for her to resist. The attraction between them seemed otherworldly, as though she was powerless to do anything to prevent a reoccurrence of the passion that she could still recall by simply closing her eyes. Then she heard the word "Deena" and quickly came to her senses. Even aside from the fact that he was engaged to another woman, and that he had dropped her cold, there was one other good reason that she should have nothing more to do with Saxton McKensie.

After fifty minutes, his private line buzzed, announcing a call from Cindy. He reached for the receiver and held a finger up to Mallory, mouthing, "One minute." He listened to her brief message, and when he hung up the phone, he stood with both hands stuffed into his pants pockets. "I hate to cut this short, but I've got a twelve o'clock waiting in the lobby. Maybe we can meet later to finish," he suggested eagerly. The question hung in the air, like a lightning bolt just before finding its target.

Mallory took a deep breath. "I'm sure that I have enough," she said as she began gathering her things. "I'll call if I have more questions." She had to get out of there. It was all she could do not to show the trembling she felt inside.

"Hopefully you'll stop by to bring me an advance copy." He flashed that smile that should have been outlawed in fifty states.

"Thanks for the interview," she told him curtly.

Before she turned to leave, he pressed into her hand a card with his numbers elegantly embossed: private office line, cell phone, and home number. "I hope to hear from you soon," he said in a husky, but sincere tone.

For a moment she was taken aback, but quickly recovered. "Good luck with your engagement," she responded firmly.

During the taxi ride back to the office, she let the events of the past hour rewind in her head as though watching a reel of an old movie. No matter how she looked at it, certain scenes remained unscripted. During the interview with Saxton she wasn't inhaling his handsome features only out of physical lust—she'd been there, done that—but instead, out of a long-ing and a curiosity that haunted her. Did her son have those same honey-colored eyes and thick lashes? And what about that warm caramel complexion? Was he tall for a five-year-old? And was he as smart as his father, who just happened to be Saxton McKensie?

2

LETTING SLEEPING DOGS LIE

"You interviewed Saxton McKensie?" Nikki's face registered pure shock. "You have got to be kidding!"

Nikki and Mallory had been roommates since Mallory arrived in New York. Mallory had found Nikki's cell phone in the backseat of a taxi and, after scrolling through the phone's telephone book feature, came across a number labeled MOM. After Mallory left her number with the woman who'd answered the phone, Nikki called back within minutes. As luck would have it, she lived only blocks from the apartment Mallory then shared with two ex–college buddies. They met at the Wet Bar in the W Hotel, on the corner of Lexington Avenue and East Thirty-ninth Street, and hit it off right away. They decided that Mallory would move into the second bedroom that Nikki had been planning to rent after her current roommate moved out.

"I wish I were," Mallory said, shaking her head. "The whole thing was pretty surreal." She had previously confided in Nikki a few of the details about her past relationship with Saxton. One night Nikki saw him on TV escorting Deena to the Emmy Awards. She started going on and on about how fine he was, and Mallory told her the story of their aborted affair to shut her up. Living in the same city as Saxton was difficult enough, but to have Nikki carrying on about him was too much to bear.

"I can't believe it," Nikki said, popping an olive into her mouth before taking a sip of her dirty martini. "I hope you cursed his ass out good."

They were in the upstairs bar of the Four Seasons Hotel on Fifty-seventh Street. It was a cozy home away from home for successful businessmen—not the traveling salesmen type, but members of the C-club: CEOs, CFOs, and COOs—as well as locals from the neighborhood. Of course, considering that the neighborhood was just off Park Avenue, they weren't the typical "locals." There was always a smattering of celebrities thrown in as well. It was a hangout for the music mogul L. A. Reid, since Arista Records was just across the street, and Derek Jeter also held court there during baseball's off-season, as did Bono, Mariah Carey, and Jay Z, among others.

"That wouldn't necessarily have made for the best interview," Mallory answered. She swirled her glass of merlot while reflecting on the improbable turn of events. Though she'd never wanted to see Saxton again, the random twist of fate was just the sort of thing that she loved about being in New York. Every day there was the possibility of adventure—whether good or bad.

"Girl, what happened when you walked into his office? I want details." Nikki settled deeper into her lounge chair, ready for a dramatic tale. Unfortunately for her, the best parts of this one would forever remain Mallory's secret. No one, except for the adoption agency involved, knew that she had borne a child and given it away. After Saxton disappeared and she began to show, Mallory left Atlanta, pretending to do a six-month internship in Philadelphia. Not even her family knew the sordid details, and as far as she was concerned, it would forever remain that way.

"It was no big deal. Once the shock wore off, we simply got on with the interview."

Nikki squinched her face into a tight scowl. "I can understand wanting to get the story, but you shoulda also set him straight. He must have been seeing Deena when he was dating you. And to just dump you like that . . ." When details of verbal warfare weren't forthcoming, she folded her arms. "Don't tell me you still care about him?" Nikki questioned, ready to pounce. She was a first-class drama queen, so she savored a good story, and as far as she was concerned, this particular one was ripe. It had sex, rich people, and deceit all rolled into one juicy bite.

Mallory affected uninterest. "No. That was a long time ago. I don't know if he and Deena were seeing each other or not, but we certainly weren't married or even engaged. So it's really no big deal."

"I doubt that she would see it that way."

"Fortunately, there's no reason that she'll ever have to know," Mallory said, fixing Nikki with a firm look.

Her roommate's appetite for drama was still far from satisfied. "Girl, you're a better person than I am," she hissed. "If it were me, I'd be calling the tabloids as we speak."

"I'd much rather let sleeping dogs lie." And she meant that—even if sometimes the restless ones insisted on getting up and roaming around anyway. She was haunted particularly by thoughts of her son. After giving birth, Mallory had seen her baby only for a few precious minutes before he was taken from her arms forever. Though he was physically gone, and she'd moved on with her life, she still thought of him often, whether she wanted to or not.

Nikki tried another angle. "Did he try to hit on you?" she asked, holding her breath.

"No, he was very professional." Mallory remembered their last exchange and blushed. It was obvious that he wanted future contact, but she had no intention of ever seeing him again.

Sensing an opening, Nikki popped forward in her chair eagerly. Instead of a model, she should have been an actress, Mallory thought. "He did hit on you. Didn't he? I know his type. Even though he's engaged to Deena Ingram, he's still got to have a piece on the side."

Nikki had never been known for her tact. Although she was Mallory's roommate, she could be obnoxious at times. And this was definitely one of them.

"It was nothing, really, but he did ask me to call him, which of course I won't."

"Why not? You should do it, and let him get caught fooling around by his famous girlfriend."

Shocked, Mallory said, "You've gotta be kidding."

"It would serve him right."

"I'm not interested in serving him anything."

Nikki couldn't believe it. "That dick must have been dipped in gold!"

Mallory shot her a scathing look that said, *Mind your own business*. "It's over, Nikki, so forget about it. I have."

Their waitress approached the table looking a little sheepish. "The gentleman at the bar would like to buy you and your friend a drink," she said to Mallory. She tilted her head in the direction of a handsome white guy sitting alone at the bar, nursing a scotch.

"We already have drinks. But do thank him for the gesture," Mallory replied.

"What nerve!" Nikki exclaimed. She was always pissed when Mallory got more attention than she did. After all, she was the model, wasn't she? What was worse was the cavalier way that Mallory played it off, as though it were no big deal, just her due.

As if reading Nikki's thoughts, Mallory said, "It's really no big deal."

"It is. Doesn't he see that we're having a conversation? It's just plain rude."

Mallory ignored her ranting. "How are things going with you? And by the way, where were you last night?" She peered at Nikki over the top of her glass. Though they didn't monitor each other's comings and goings, they usually left notes or messages if an overnight stay was in the cards. But last night Nikki was nowhere to be found—nor was a note or message.

"Just out getting my groove on." Nikki winked.

"Well, I'm glad somebody is," Mallory mused, taking a sip. "So who's the lucky guy?" she asked, even though she knew how secretive Nikki was about her love life.

"Oh, no one important, just someone I met a few months ago," she answered evasively. It was clear from the glow she radiated, though, that this was more than just "someone she met a few months ago."

Mallory rolled her eyes. "Well, that narrows it down to a couple of hundred people."

Like Mallory, Nikki was an avid party girl. She hung out at the trendiest places with the most beautiful people in fashion, magazine publishing, and entertainment. She was also a big flirt, known for going after what she wanted. She was not supermodel material, but you couldn't tell her that. She was five foot ten, with a deep ebony complexion, chiseled features, and a svelte figure that bordered on boyish.

Nikki's cell phone rang, and she dug it out of her Hermes backpack just before the final ring put the caller through to voicemail. She checked the phone's caller ID, then answered, purring, "Hi, baby."

Mallory figured this was the mysterious "someone" calling because Nikki cooed into the phone for over five minutes, leaving Mallory to survey the scene in the Four Seasons bar. It was business as usual. Aside from the usual high-rolling execs and celebrities, the room was full of white guys out to prove to the world how cool they were. She watched one Wall Street crew as they puffed cigars and blew smoke up one another's asses.

Finally Nikki whispered into the phone, "Gotta run, but I'll see you a little later tonight. Glad you can get away." The call had put her in a very good mood.

"Someone's obviously happy," Mallory teased.

"A few good orgasms will do that for a girl," Nikki laughed. "What about you? If you don't start dating soon, I'm gonna buy stock in Eveready batteries. You and Bennie are getting way too close." She had bought a butterfly vibrator for Mallory for her birthday, and Mallory had promptly named it Bennie.

Mallory laughed. "A girl's gotta do what a girl's gotta do."

"I hear ya."

"I can't sit around waiting for Mr. Right." Truthfully, since Saxton, the birth, and the adoption, Mallory had been gun-shy about nurturing any long-term relationship—except, that is, with Bennie.

"It would help if you returned phone calls, you know, and disavowed your two-date policy." It also secretly pissed Nikki off that Mallory had guys fawning all over her and she had the nerve to simply ignore them. She hated the way Mallory pretended to be oblivious to her beauty. Some people were so full of themselves, she thought.

Not wanting to hear any more of Nikki's advice on men, Mallory reached for her wallet. "I've got to pay a visit to the little girls' room. Maybe you can settle the tab while I'm gone."

Nikki held her palm up, ending the debate. "No. Remember, this is my treat. I insist." Nikki had offered to take Mallory for drinks to celebrate her first feature story. But Mallory was hesitant to let her pay, since her modeling jobs were few and far between. She never knew how Nikki paid the bills each month, let alone how she financed the likes of that nine-hundred-dollar Hermes backpack. "You don't have to do that."

"I insist." Nikki gave her a don't-argue-with-me look.

"Okay, thanks." Mallory stood up to head downstairs to the ladies' room.

When she was out of sight, Nikki reopened her phone and quickly punched seven digits. "Girl, you're not going to believe what I just found out."

3

THE TROPHY WIFE

Saxton was running late. He was supposed to meet Deena, who was tonight's honored guest at the Women in Media awards, and had neglected to have his assistant order a car and driver. Spotting a taxi as it cruised to a stop in front of a middle-aged white man, he dashed to the driver's side and opened the door before the poor man could get his hand affixed to the handle. To placate the jilted passenger and the scowling driver, Saxton tossed them both twenty-dollar bills, converting their frowns to smiles.

"Thirty Rockefeller Plaza," he instructed the driver.

"Yes, sir." There was nothing like a big tip to instill a bit of enthusiasm and respect, even from surly New York cabbies.

As they rolled by another pedestrian who happened to have seen the episode unfold, the bystander sneered in contempt at Saxton's aggressive tactic. Hey, it was a dog-eat-dog world, as far as Saxton was concerned, and he was nobody's puppy. As the president and CEO of Ingram Enterprises, he'd expanded the company to two hundred twenty million in revenues, and it wasn't because he stood curbside. Besides, as Samuel L. Jackson could attest, a curbside wait for a black man in New York could be a long-term affair.

Settling into the backseat of the cab, he whipped his cell phone from the breast pocket of his Armani suit. After dialing, he held the phone close to his ear. He didn't get an answer, so he left a message. "Hi, honey, it's me. I'm running a little late. The conference call with the publisher went on forever—haggling over the last three basis points on the publishing deal. Anyway, sorry, but I think it'll be well worth the haggle. I'll see you in a few." He knew how important it was to Deena for him to be at her side for these events, but he had to take care of business also. Under his guidance, Deena had grown from a local television anchor on Channel 7 to a multimillion-dollar media brand. That happened because he did take the time to negotiate the last basis point on every deal.

Before the taxi came to a full stop in front of Thirty Rock, Saxton bolted out the door after tossing another twenty through the driver's window. "Keep the change."

When he reached the expansive lobby, he straightened the hang of his cashmere evening coat and leveled his black bow tie. He'd had to dress in a hurry back at the office, and he hoped his appearance did not betray his haste. He needn't have worried. At thirty-seven, he was six foot three with a body remarkably similar to the one he boasted while playing college football at Notre Dame. His square jawline and thickly lashed eyes meshed perfectly well with a set of even, pearly white teeth and full, kissable lips. And his clean-shaven head only added to the handsome hunk's overall package.

Not breaking stride, Saxton caught one of the elevators going up to the Rainbow Room just as the doors were beginning to close. Once on board he stared straight ahead, quietly willing the elevator to ascend even faster. His fellow passengers, two elegantly dressed women, both eyed him intently as though he were the main course at their last meal.

"Excuse me, what time do you have?" the one to his left asked, making sure her diamond beveled Hublot was well hidden under the sleeve of her evening coat.

Without making eye contact, Saxton smoothly slid back his monogrammed cuff to reveal an elegant Piaget wristwatch. "It's ten after eight."

"Thank you. Hey, don't I know you?" She was now flashing a brilliant Colgate smile.

Saxton was accustomed to women hitting on him, all day, every day. "I don't think so, but it's a pleasure to make your acquaintance. I'm Saxton McKensie." He politely extended his hand. Women in New York were often as aggressive in matters of love as the men were in matters of business.

Maybe not all of them, reflected Saxton, thinking of Mallory. He hadn't been able to get her out of his mind since the interview yesterday. One of the things that had attracted him to her to begin with was her effortless elegance. She had none of the brassiness that tarnished most of the women he met in the city. Maybe it was true what they said about Southern charm.

Unexpectedly, the woman grabbed his hand, holding on a little too long for his comfort. "I'm Lisa. Lisa Davis."

Before she could segue the conversation into the direction of exchanged phone numbers, the elevator door opened, giving Saxton an out. "Have a pleasant evening, ladies," he said, standing aside as he motioned for them to exit ahead of him. After checking his coat, he made his way to the head table, taking the empty seat next to the guest of honor, Deena. Leaning in to kiss her cheek, he said, "Sorry I'm late."

She shot him a less-than-warm look. "No problem," she said through a fake smile. He could tell that she was fuming at his tardiness. But the three other couples at the table saw only the beautiful Deena Ingram with her handsome fiancé.

Deena was one of those bourgeois black women who grew up believing the "princess" part of the title BAP, Black American Princess. She was from one of the few old black Boston families. Her father was a prestigious judge and her mother a socialite who reveled in the pecking order that Jack and Jill, the Links, and other assorted African-American social clubs established. They raised Deena to be perfect and successful—those were their only two requirements. And for the most part Deena was everything that they dreamed she would be—except for one little secret that Judge Ingram's hoity-toity pals in Martha's Vineyard would be shocked to learn.

Rather than attempt to thaw the iceberg by way of explanation, Saxton decided to go for suave. "You look gorgeous," he said, reaching over to cover her perfectly manicured hand with his own. Her hair was swept elegantly into a French chignon, and she wore a stunningly simple black Calvin Klein evening dress with a plunging yet tasteful neckline and a figure-flattering bodice. At her throat was a double strand of Mikimoto pearls, and on her ring finger sat the impressive three-carat engagement ring that Saxton had "surprised" her with over a month ago.

"Thank you." She smiled, and this time it was genuine. Compliments never failed to work on Deena. She accepted them graciously as her due. "Saxton, meet Jonathan and Emily Greenberg, David and Samantha Williams, and Ronald Jones and Yvette Boynton. This is my fiancé, Saxton McKensie."

They all greeted him warmly. "Deena was just telling us about the publishing deal that you are working on with Condé Nast. That'll be quite a coup." The compliment was from Jonathan Greenberg.

"It's not quite a done deal yet," Saxton cautioned. He also wondered why Deena would discuss the deal publicly at this point. That is, until he remembered that Ronald Jones, seated to her right, was the editor-in-chief of the *New York Times*. She was undoubtedly drawing him in to make a play for national coverage.

"The ink may not be on the papers yet, but it's all but done, thanks to Saxton," Deena said. "He's just being modest. And of course a tough negotiator."

Deena leaned over and made a show of straightening his tie affectionately. Since when was Deena ever focused on anyone other than herself? he thought, realizing that her little show of affection was more for the benefit of his tablemates than for his own. She smiled superficially without comment before patting his hand and turning her attention back to the group at large.

Formal presentations hadn't yet started, so dinner was still being served. The buzz of conversation swirled throughout the spacious grand ballroom, which was filled with an impressive representation of New York's top media players, business leaders, and politicians. Tonight's dinner was the hottest ticket in town—the place to be and, more important, to be seen. Particularly since the event would undoubtedly be highlighted in the society section of tomorrow's *Times*. Being seen at the right event in New York was a sport worthy of Olympic stature.

Saxton and Deena's dinner partners would definitely be medal contenders. Jonathan Greenberg was the CEO of Arch Ventures, a top investment firm on Wall Street. The Dow and NASDAQ averages often reflected his daily moods as he wielded the fortunes of the truly wealthy individuals and companies that were his clients. David Williams was the famous labor lawyer who'd recently settled an eight-hundred-million-dollar class-action lawsuit against Microsoft, and Yvette Boynton was a powerful, well-known, and well-connected nationally syndicated gossip columnist.

They were soon all engaged in a lively debate about what went wrong with the AOL/Time Warner merger. Deena weighed in her opinion. "Though Ted Turner was a visionary, he undoubtedly lacked the finesse to run a Big City company like Time Warner." The look she bestowed on her dinner partners said, *Of course you all* do *know that.* "Then you add what was at the time the new-age economic engine, an Internet company—it was a disaster waiting to happen, particularly for a born and bred Southern boy." Saxton cringed inwardly. As savvy as Deena was about some things, there were times when she was too impressed with her own opinions to figure out that they need not always be shared with others.

"Are you saying that Southerners are ill-equipped to run 'Big City' companies?" Yvette asked, flipping a cluster of dreads over her shoulder. This question was asked with an even tone, though it didn't take a rocket scientist to deduce that a designer-clad toe or two may have been stepped on. Saxton shifted uneasily in his seat. Yvette Boynton was known for her scathing articles, dicing up one celebrity after another. She was New York savvy, but Saxton detected a trace of melody to her accent. He quietly prayed that she was not from the South.

"Of course not all of them," Deena offered, still not fully understanding the thinness of the ice upon which she trod. "But certainly many aren't up to the high-stakes pace of big business in the city."

"Do you suppose this is a geographic or a genetic handicap?" Yvette asked with dripping sarcasm.

Deena was taken aback by the response; then she scowled. Saxton held his breath. The last thing she needed was a catfight with Yvette, especially given their history. But before claws could be sharpened, the president of the awards committee opened the evening's program.

The rest of the night was a breeze. It was all about Deena. She graciously accepted her prestigious award before delivering a rousing speech encouraging others to mentor young girls, particularly minorities, so that one day there wouldn't be the need for a special award for *women* in the media. This philanthropic appeal played well to the audience and to the press, even though in reality, Saxton knew, Deena would never have considered spending time with anyone who couldn't further her own cause.

Holding her trophy victoriously in the air, she invited her future husband to join her at the podium. "Without Saxton's strength, support, and Harvard law degree," she joked, "this would not be possible." Saxton reluctantly took the stage to give her a hug and a kiss on the cheek. Everyone in the crowd—with the exception of Yvette—applauded the newly appointed power couple.

After making their way from the stage through a sea of admiring well-wishers, Saxton retrieved their coats, anxious to bring an end to the four-hour dinner.

As he strode through the throng of people he heard a familiar voice say, "Without Saxton's strength, support, and

Harvard law degree . . ." It was his best friend, Greg Donner, mimicking the end of Deena's sappy speech. It was no secret that Deena was not one of his favorite people.

"Hey, man, what's up?" Saxton said. The two greeted each other with a fist shake. Greg was accompanied by a young woman dressed inappropriately for the sophisticated event, in a glittery gown with a plunging neckline that revealed cleavage as deep as a vast cavern. Saxton turned to introduce himself. "Hi, I'm Saxton McKensie," he said, extending his hand.

Greg looked as though he'd forgotten she was there. "Oh, I'm sorry, Saxton. This is Tannesha," Greg said as an afterthought.

"It's Tammy." She eyed him accusingly before extending a limp hand toward Saxton.

"Are we still on for the Knicks game this weekend?" Greg asked.

"Bet," Saxton said. "I gotta run," he added, seeing Deena approach.

The second their feet hit the curb, Deena's car promptly rolled to a stop, and the driver of the black Bentley hopped out to open the door for them to get in.

"Ms. Ingram, are we heading to the apartment this evening?" he asked, ready to serve as always.

"Yes, Charles," she answered, flashing her celebrity smile as she pulled the fur-trimmed collar of her coat up around her ears. She and Saxton had moved in together three months ago, and she still glowed from the idea of them going home as a couple. They were one step closer to the altar—which had been her final destination since she first met him.

Saxton reached forward, pushing the privacy button to bring down the custom one-way glass partition that separated them from the driver. "Why don't you let me keep you warm tonight?" he whispered in her ear.

After he'd drunk a few glasses of wine and champagne, the thought of a hot session of sex appealed strongly to him. He reached over to pull her closer, then nibbled on her ear and trailed kisses along her neck. She responded by turning to give him a hot, steamy kiss that quickened his blood, sending his hands roaming beneath her coat. Her hand traveled south, landing on his already stiff penis. It had been a few weeks since they made love, and Saxton was eager to get her between the sheets.

Lately, her interest in sex had been cursory at best, not that she'd ever been highly sexual to begin with; so he planned to take full advantage of any interest on her part. Theirs hadn't been the most ideal physical match, despite Saxton's highly charged libido, but she'd assured him that once they were engaged and living together that she'd feel better about giving herself to him completely. So far, though, her desire seemed to have waned.

When Charles pulled up to their Upper East Side apartment building, she cut Saxton's attentions short and began hastily fixing her hair and coat, making herself presentable. As the driver held the car door open and the doorman opened the heavy glass door to the building, they swept into the stately lobby. Saxton's coat barely covered the tent that had been erected in his pants. He pushed the elevator button three times, anxious to get upstairs.

Once inside their apartment, he quickly removed his suit, shoes, and shirt and hurried into the bathroom for a quick visit. A few minutes later he walked back into the master suite, wearing only his boxers and a proud erection. He found Deena already in her striped cotton pajamas, under the covers feigning sleep. He didn't need a crystal ball to tell him that she was no longer in the mood.

He crawled into bed frustrated and wondering—not for the first time—if he was doing the right thing by marrying Deena. Then he chided himself for even wondering, because at the end of the day—or night—it didn't matter. Their relationship was now inseparable from the business empire that he'd built. Rather than a marriage, if the truth be told, he was simply negotiating another merger. As cold as that sounded, it was fine with Deena, who really felt the need to seal the deal.

All of this analysis did little to alleviate his mounting sexual frustration, which Mallory's sudden appearance had only sharpened. She had stirred emotions that he thought were put to bed. Long-buried images of their hot, passionate sex teased his memory, taunting him with snippets of the desire that he couldn't help feeling while she was in his office. Though Mallory had worn a protective suit of armor that day, he could still feel the heat from the strong attraction that they had shared.

As he tossed and turned before finally drifting off to a restless sleep, he knew he had to see Mallory again.

4

ONCE UPON A TIME

Mallory sat at her desk in the corner of her bedroom in the small Murray Hill apartment. On the one occasion her mother had visited her in New York, she had been shocked by the size of Manhattan dwellings.

"Why, this is about the size of my master bedroom," she'd drawled in a light Southern accent. And she was right. Mallory's parents, Dr. and Mrs. Edgar Baylor, owned a spacious home in the most exclusive black enclave below the Mason-Dixon line: Southwest Atlanta. It was where most of the city's black politicians, lawyers, and doctors lived. Mrs. Baylor's worry abated significantly when she realized that Mallory had transformed a kitchen pantry into a shoe closet, completely categorized by color, style, and season. This proved to her that the city hadn't changed her youngest daughter too much.

As small as her space was, Mallory still preferred to write here instead of in the office, where there were always a million distractions, ranging from the latest hot artist stopping by to drum up publicity to the frantic buzz that descended on the staff right before closing the magazine each month. Pulling a magazine together had been described to her by the veteran editor Roy Johnson as being a lot like making sausage: the end product might be tasty, but you really didn't want to see the actual process. It always amazed her when all of the disparate pieces—artwork, editorial, layout, and captions—seamlessly came together at the eleventh hour.

When she settled in to begin her article on Saxton, she pulled out her file, Alan's file, and the tape recording of the interview that she'd conducted yesterday. Though she and Saxton had dated for several months, the interview showed how little she really knew about him. She could not help but think that formal interviews should be an integral part of the dating process. She learned more about him in that one hour than in all of the time they'd spent together in Atlanta.

It was clear to her that he had always been accustomed to being the big man on campus. He was handsome, athletic, sexy, and smart. From birth, he was the kid who was destined to be cast as the high school quarterback, the most popular student, homecoming king, and the boy who melted the most hearts. During his four years at Notre Dame he did, however, manage to grow beyond the confines of his pretty-boy exterior. No longer a big fish in a small pond, his adjustment was a tough one. Overnight, he went from being the small-town, movie-star-handsome football hero to just another good-looking athlete on a very big campus. From being the captain of the football team, he found himself sitting on the bench as a third-string rookie. Late in his sophomore year, he figured out that life was more than a string of victories and defeats played out for spectators every weekend. There was a world full of other challenges that had nothing to do with locker rooms, cheerleaders, or an oblong leather ball. Once he made that discovery, with the help of a particularly patient professor, he also lived up to his promising but often ignored academic abilities.

During Saxton's senior year, the team's starting quarterback was expelled following a fraternity hazing incident, leaving Saxton to lead Notre Dame to a triumphant victory at the Rose Bowl. Afterward, a college booster impressed with his athletic and academic acumen took him under his wing and mentored him through Harvard Law School, and later into a coveted position with one of the leading law firms in the country.

It became clear to Mallory that Saxton's quest to build a multimedia empire was in many ways just another field for him to conquer. She wondered, sadly, if that was what she'd been to him as well.

While she reread her notes and listened to the interview again, the article began to take shape in her mind, and over the course of the next few hours found its way onto paper as an excellent first draft. It had a formal yet personal tone, ultimately painting a picture of Saxton as the Wizard behind the curtains in Oz, deftly pulling the strings to create, animate, and capitalize on the brand known as Deena.

The article was strong work, Mallory told herself after polishing it several times. As she put away Saxton's file, though, her thoughts turned to another, much more painful one. She could not think of him without thinking of the secret that lay buried underneath her sweaters in the last of her chest drawers.

Though hidden from sight, the thin file marked THE BROWNS loomed larger than life at times. As it had so often, it beckoned her to the chest of drawers, under the clothes, until her fingertips pulled it free. The file was the only tangible evidence that she had of her son's existence. It contained her copy of the adoption papers, the last known whereabouts of the Browns—the family who had adopted her son—and a picture of a cheesing three-year-old with as much ice cream around his face as in the cone that he held up toward the camera.

An attorney in Philadelphia who had handled the private placement assured Mallory that she would know the name and address of the adopting family and would also receive pictures and updates at least once a year. But after the third year all correspondence from the Browns came to a halt. Mallory later found out that they had moved suddenly and also changed their names. She was devastated by the news. It was as though her baby boy had been taken from her arms for a second time.

Since then she'd continued her search using the Internet and by staying in touch with Bill Starks, the lawyer who'd handled the adoption, though to no avail. A month ago she'd taken the process a step further and hired a private investigator to find her son.

A part of her reasoned that their disappearance was for the best. Better for her to finally let go of the child that she had given up parental rights to, and perhaps even better for her son, who more than anything needed a stable environment. But she could not help but wonder how stable it really was. What kind of family moved in the middle of the night and changed their names? Taking a deep breath, she placed the contents of the file back in the folder and tucked it snugly under her sweaters, back in its hiding place.

The muffled sound of Mallory closing the chest of drawers traveled through the thin walls of the small apartment. Nikki's vanity backed onto the shared wall between the two bedrooms, where she sat diligently studying the lines of her face. Her career as a model was threatened more and more as time went by, pushed along by an influx of younger, prettier models each day. Many of them acted as though it was their right to take plum assignments that should have been hers, which angered Nikki and reminded her of another time in her life when she was forced to even the score.

To Nikki Adams, life was a serial movie in which she was the director, producer, and lead actor. No matter how her ever-dramatic plot evolved, she was quick to rewrite the story line, and improvised brilliantly to make sure that her scripted ending was never compromised. Nikki had grown up an only child in Philadelphia with her mother, a dancer whom she called Bette. In elementary school Nikki boasted ad nauseam to friends and enemies alike about her mother, the professional dancer. In her fertile imagination, Bette starred on Broadway under bright lights, wearing fancy costumes and bowing to a chorus of applause. Not until her sophomore year in high school was Nikki confronted by the fact that her mother's dances were actually done in low light and cheesy costumes before an audience of men only.

Nikki was humiliated when her nemesis, Wendy Thomas, broke the news to her—and the audience in the crowded school cafeteria—that her mother was actually a low-class stripper. She and Wendy had a festering rivalry that dated back to the sixth grade, when Wendy transferred to Nikki's school and, unfortunately, landed in her homeroom class. Nikki would probably have hated Wendy on G.P., since she was now, hands down, the cutest girl in school; she had long curly hair and cute dimples and wore freshly pressed clothes each day. A long line of preadolescent boys drooled over her incessantly, and every girl—except of course for Nikki—idolized her. She was sick of the fuss everyone made over Wendy, so minutes before the other girl walked onto the stage to star in the school's spring production of *Cinderella,* Nikki "accidentally" spilled grape juice all over the front of Wendy's white ball gown. Since that day they were like Israel and Syria—no chance of peace in sight.

So, when Wendy prissed past Nikki that day in the cafeteria, tossing a five-dollar bill at her, she could not wait to drop the bomb. As the crumbled bill floated to the table, she said, "Give that to your mama for one of her cheap five-dollar lap dances."

The room fell deathly quiet. The students all stared, frozen in anticipation of a clash of the titans, while Nikki stood to confront Wendy. "What are you talking about? My mother's a professional dancer." It was the same line she had delivered with aplomb since she could formulate a complete sentence. Only, today it came out weak and pleading.

Enjoying Nikki's moment of weakness, Wendy snapped, "Yeah. At the Kit Kat Klub." Wendy had overheard a couple of her uncles talking to her dad about seeing Bette Adams stripping at a local club. Though the men were whispering as they sipped from bottles of beer while tending to the barbecue grill, Wendy stood just on the other side of the screen door lapping it all up, so that she would later be ready to dish it back.

Nikki felt as though she'd been physically pummeled. "Liar!" she yelled as hot tears streamed down her cheeks.

Now that she had a rapt audience, Wendy was not about to leave the stage. She reached into her jeans pocket and pulled out another five-dollar bill. "Oh, here's one for you, too," she said, tossing the bill at Nikki's feet. "You know what they say: like mother, like daughter." She flung her hair over her shoulder, almost slapping Wendy with the thick, long ends, as she turned to execute a dramatic exit, stage right.

Normally Nikki would have snatched her back for a good old-fashioned cafeteria brawl scene, but she was too devastated to do anything except grab her bag—along with the remains of her crushed ego—and walk out of the cafeteria with her head hung low. The intense hatred she felt for Wendy was more blinding than the tears that stung her eyes. Though she was humiliated by the sordid revelation, she wasn't exactly shocked. The always-late nights that left her in the care of a string of baby-sitters were a dead giveaway. Not to mention that Bette certainly did not live the life of a Broadway diva. Their small apartment was a two-bedroom unit with a tiny kitchen and a den. But now everyone knew that her life was nothing but staging; the curtains had been yanked up to reveal the awful truth.

By the time the retelling of the cafeteria drama made its rounds through the school's grapevine, Bette was not only a lap dancer, but had descended to the depths of whore as well. Nikki hated Wendy more than anything imaginable. She would sit for hours transfixed in her room absently applying her mother's stage makeup, while she developed a repertoire of nasty scenarios to exact her revenge on her mortal enemy. Those moments when she was free to orchestrate the girl's demise over and over were all that sustained Nikki for the remainder of the torturous school year.

During the last play of their senior year, Nikki was finally able to get her pound of flesh. She managed to mix a healthy dose of lye into the cold cream jar that Wendy used to remove her stage makeup, and the once-beautiful girl's face was permanently disfigured. Though there was an investigation, it was never proven that Nikki was the culprit. If nothing else, she knew how to cover her tracks.

Sitting at the vanity in her bedroom, Nikki deftly applied the strokes of makeup that would transform her into "Nikki the model." She loved being a model, even if she posed only for lingerie catalogues or the occasional Macy's or Bloomingdale's ads. At thirty-four, she knew her dreams of strutting catwalks in New York, Milan, and Paris were but dim memories. Still, she was convinced that her biggest break was just ahead of her. It was only a matter of time before her white knight, in the form of the right designer, agent, or lover with big bucks, would come to take her away on a white horse. So far the hot designer and top agent were missing in action, but DJ, her latest lover, was the best prospect yet. In fact, they would see each other that night at the cocktail party she was attending.

Since her first time with DJ, Nikki was convinced that sex had never been better. Every orgasm was a toe-curling, body-shuddering ride to ecstasy. Each release was like an addictive drug that she couldn't get enough of. Nikki had vivid memories, complete with sound track, of her very first orgasm at the age of thirteen while listening to Earth, Wind and Fire in the backseat of John Dailey's dad's Ford. Of course, she'd heard about sex before then from many of the older kids in the neighborhood, but she'd figured if it was something that adults did on the regular, it had to be pretty damn boring. She was shocked and surprised to discover her misjudgment while her dress rode above her head as John clumsily humped her to the brink of unconsciousness. In retrospect, she marveled that she'd even had an orgasm, considering that his technique had left much to be desired. But somehow—surely by accident—he'd stumbled upon her clitoris in the process of putting "it" into "the hole," and soon enough they were both off to the races. Fortunately for her, she had gotten there just ahead of him.

Since those early years she had been on a quest for the perfect orgasm. Sex—specifically orgasmic sex—to her was an end in itself, while most women considered it a conduit to reaching the end of the wedding aisle. Nikki wasn't the least bit confused—she never had a problem confusing love and sex. At least not up until now.

The cocktail party Nikki was attending that night was in honor of a new couture designer who'd become all the rage in New York, Milan, and London. It was a swanky affair held at Pangea, one of the hot party spots along SoHo's border. Models and guests alike wore the kind of high-fashion garbs that usually never left the runway. Not to be outdone, Nikki worked the room wearing a foxtail jacket that stopped midthigh, just above a pair of cream thigh-high boots, and dramatic layers of makeup, complete with rhinestones to decorate her eyebrows. As she steadily hobnobbed with clothing designers, fashion editors, and anyone else who might be able to jump-start her stalled career, Nikki pretended not to notice DJ, until the signal was given and they both sneaked out of the cocktail party unnoticed. They headed to the Benjamin Hotel for a midnight interlude.

Once they were behind closed doors, the two quickly locked themselves in a steamy embrace, with tongues tangled and hands busily removing garments. They were both on a mission to release the sexual tension that they'd each enjoyed building throughout the night. For Nikki it was a thrill to see DJ out, but later she would enjoy the heat of their illicit affair. Why was it that forbidden fruit always seemed the tastiest? she thought as she used her mouth, teeth, and tongue to bring her lover to the first in a series of orgasms. After an hour of mind-blowing sex they lay happily intertwined, their sweat-slicked bodies still savoring the heat.

"Uuhhmmmm," Nikki purred as her talented lover continued stroking her still-throbbing sex. "I could let you do that all night long," she panted. Her eyes were partly closed. She wanted no distractions from the pure physical pleasure that flowed from those highly sensitive nerve endings.

"Someone never seems to get enough." This teasing statement was followed by a wet lick over Nikki's small, sensitive nipples.

"Of you? Never." She ran her fingers through her lover's hair. She never wanted it to stop. She could spend the rest of her life making love to DJ. For the first time ever she feared that she might be in love. What else would explain the physical and emotional yearning that consumed her? It was like nothing else that she'd ever known. Besides, DJ was everything that she could ever want in a partner: sexy as hell, truly powerful, and nine-digit rich. Not to mention those unassailable sexual talents.

"Tell me what you want, baby." The husky tone made it clear that her wish would definitely be granted.

"Lick me there." If sex in the backseat of John's dad's car was a primer, the joys of oral sex were like earning an advanced degree. To Nikki, it was the ultimate physical pleasure—particularly when done right. DJ was a master, and Nikki was the slave.

"Where? You have to tell me where."

"Lick my pussy, baby. Kiss it for me good."

The hot kisses trailed southward, from her pert nipples down a flat stomach to the hot, steamy place that ached between Nikki's legs. She opened them wide to provide unencumbered access to DJ's wet, probing tongue. Long slow licks turned into a gentle sucking. Her legs tightened around her lover's head like a churning vice.

"Hhhhmmmmmm . . ." DJ hummed rhythmically into Nikki's slick sex, sending her on a blissful journey.

"Yes, baby. Yesss!" She grabbed fistfuls of her lover's hair. "Don't stop, baby. Right there." Oh, what talent . . .

Later, Nikki lay coated in another sheen of perspiration, which DJ blew lightly to cool the wet beads. "Is that what you wanted?"

Nikki licked her lips. "You are the best."

"I'm sure that's what you say to all of your lovers." DJ stood to gather pants, sweater, and other assorted articles strewn about the room. *Collecting the evidence,* Nikki thought bitterly.

Feeling sullen, Nikki turned to her side, resting on one elbow to face her lover's retreating back. In a moment of weakness she confessed, "There are no others."

She desperately wished she hadn't said those four pitiful words. She was sounding like one of the whining postcoital women she despised. But it was too late to retract the betraying statement.

"Dry spell?" A note of sarcasm rang out.

Nikki tried to make light of the perilous turn the conversation had taken. "I wouldn't call what just happened here dry by any stretch of the imagination." The last thing she wanted was to been seen as a clinging female.

"Don't forget what we discussed," DJ warned. The main problem with DJ was the platinum ring worn on the telltale left finger.

Nikki got up, reaching for her clothes as well. "What are you talking about?"

"About not getting serious." DJ fixed her with a stern don't-get-mushy-on-me look for added emphasis.

"Who said I was getting serious?"

"Just checking." With that said, DJ headed into the bathroom to take a quick shower before heading home.

Nikki stood on the other side of the bathroom door, quietly seething. Yes, they had discussed "not getting serious," but a discussion hardly changed the way she felt. She flopped down into an overstuffed chair set in front of a fake fireplace. She was tired of being an afterthought.

But that would all change soon. And so would DJ's feelings for her. It would take just a little planning and a little time, and Nikki was nothing if not calculating and patient.

5

THE TEMPERATURE RISES AT *HEAT*

Mallory walked out of the apartment and headed down Park Avenue South inhaling the air of expectancy that a crisp autumn morning in New York offers. Though her mother could not begin to understand the appeal of the city, and her older sister, Judith, was too suburban to ever consider anything beyond a white picket fence, Mallory loved the Big Apple. She had a great social life and a job that put her in the mix. Best of all, she would be getting a big promotion by the end of the day.

Since Mallory's feature story on Saxton ran in the latest issue of the magazine, she had gotten calls and e-mails from countless colleagues in the industry, all congratulating her on the brilliantly written story. She had taken what could have been a mundane celebrity piece and transformed it into an insightful look at big business, the media world, and the challenges of an African-American trying to conquer both. After such a big success, she was certain that her meeting with Chad later today would yield the desired results: a promotion to feature writer.

Ordinarily Mallory would not have been so confident, especially because she knew Chad's flaky history. Yet, according to a very reliable offshoot of the office grapevine, Adam would be out on long-term disability for at least seven months, leaving his position open. Given the fact that Mallory had successfully delivered an impressive interview with Saxton, all bets were that she would step in to fill the post. In fact, Chad had already assigned her two more feature stories.

Mallory sauntered into the office with flair, wearing a slate blue Michael Kors pantsuit, a starched white spread-collar shirt, two-toned Prada flamingo pumps, and a pair of Kieselstein-Cord sunglasses. As she passed her assistant's desk, Vickee handed her a message from Beverly confirming dinner later tonight. Beverly, a high-powered entertainment attorney Mallory had known since grade school, was one of the most feared and respected attorneys in the city. Mallory often chuckled at Beverly's reputation, since she knew that underneath her dragon-slayer persona, the lawyer was really a purring pussycat.

Her meeting with Chad wasn't until two o'clock, so she spent the morning setting up appointments for her upcoming interview with the music mogul Russell Simmons, before the eleven o'clock editorial meeting.

"Mallory, you have a call on line one," Vickee blared through the intercom.

"Who is it?"

"Saxton McKensie," she answered, adding, "He says it's his third call."

"Put him through," Mallory said. She knew that he had tried to reach her before, but she had decided not to return his calls. But now, thanks to Vickee, half of the office knew that he was trying to reach her, so she had to pick up the phone or she could have some explaining to do to Chad.

She nervously ran her fingers through her loose curls before answering the phone. "This is Mallory," she said brusquely.

"Hi, Mallory. I thought you'd dropped off the face of the earth."

Before she could stop herself, she retorted, "You mean the way you did." Ouch.

That stopped him short. "I guess I had that one coming," he said finally.

"What can I do for you?" she asked, wanting to get straight to the point.

"How about joining me for dinner?"

Mallory sat up in her chair, taken aback by his forwardness. Thinking quickly, she fumbled for a response. "I-I have plans."

"What about tomorrow night?"

She stared at the phone, exasperated, then decided to use his direct approach. "Saxton, what's this about?"

"It's business."

"I've already finished the article," she informed him. "In case you didn't know, it's already on the newsstands."

"I do know. In fact, I've read it, and thought it was very well done. I'm impressed."

"Glad you liked it," she said, though she could really have cared less. It was only important what Chad thought, since he was the one that she was hitting up for a promotion.

"So will you have dinner with me?"

She could feel herself weakening. "You haven't told me what this is about."

"I can't go into it over the phone, but I do think you'll be interested in what I have to say."

I cannot imagine that, Mallory thought. But he'd piqued her interest. "I can't do it tonight," she said, even though her calendar was wide open,

"How's tomorrow, at seven thirty. Say at Provence?"

"Fine."

"I look forward to it."

"Bye, Saxton." Mallory hung up the phone abruptly. A mixture of feelings washed through her: nervousness at the prospect of seeing him again, anger that he had the gall to ask her out, and a keen sense of curiosity about the purpose of the meeting. What business could he have with her? She began gathering her files for the staff meeting. Still absorbed in thoughts of him, she headed to the conference room.

As usual, the editorial staff meeting was an hour-long egofest, led by the ego-in-chief, Chad. She had long ago pegged him as one of those guys who was a nerd all throughout elementary, high school, and even college. After landing a prestigious job in publishing, he had rewritten his past, editing out the too-short pants, the acne, and the all-around desire to have someone pay the slightest amount of attention to him.

"First of all, I have an announcement to make before we go over the January issue," Chad said, removing his glasses and smudging the lens. "Alan is going to be out on disability for seven to eight months. So, in light of the excellent work that Mallory did on the Saxton article, I'm asking her to handle feature articles." Once again, the grapevine had proven as accurate as a Ouija board.

Mallory glowed as congratulations were murmured by all. To her, being a feature writer was the ultimate publishing position, unless you aspired to be an editor, which she did not.

Now that his announcement had been made, Chad got on with the business of the meeting. "So," he said to the room at large as he reared back in his chair at the head of the table, "who do we put on the January cover?"

"What about Halle Berry?" Debbie said. "Her new film is being released at the beginning of the year, and you can always count on her to sell some covers." Debbie Ward was an editor with years of experience with Condé Nast.

"Yeah, but we just had Angela Bassett on the last cover. It's time for a guy. Besides, the last time we approached Halle's people, they wouldn't give us the time of day."

"That was three years ago, when we were starting out," Mindy, *Heat*'s managing editor, reminded him. "Since then they've been reaching out to us."

"Yeah," Chad said smugly, "now that we're hot."

"It's to be expected." Debbie shrugged. "She is a big star, so they would have to protect her image. And with an upstart magazine, you just never know."

"And I have to protect ours." Chad let his eyes wander across the room before he asked, "What about Tiger Woods?"

"What about him?" Macy, the lifestyle editor, said.

"He'd be great on the cover."

"I'm not feeling Mr. Woods right now," Macy said, folding her arms tightly. "He needs to be on the cover of a magazine run by, and for, Canablasians. Or whatever he calls himself these days." Other women in the room chimed in with a chorus of approval.

Ron, one of Chad's boys, piped up. "Ya'll just trippin' 'cause the boy likes his meat white."

Macy glared at him. "Anybody that's even half-black and invents his own race that starts out with C-A, as in Caucasian, and only dates white women is the one trippin'. I'm just tellin' it like it is."

"But remember, he is still the number-one golfer in the world."

"So was Jack Nicklaus, and I never saw him on the cover of *Jet* or *Ebony*. And by the way, for all practical purposes, he's as black as Tiger Woods."

"Hey, don't player hate the brother," Chad said, enjoying the sore spot that Tiger rubbed on black women.

"It's not about hatin'," Mallory put in. "It's just that we are an urban lifestyle magazine, and Tiger has disavowed his urbanness and does nothing to contribute to our culture or lifestyle."

"Regardless, I think it's a great idea," Chad insisted. He was not about to let a bunch of women outrank him. He then looked to Devon for support.

As usual, she sucked his dick. "Girls," she said, tossing her ratty weave, "let's not be shallow. Everyone is entitled to his or her own reality, and just because Tiger's does not agree with yours doesn't mean that he is not a good cover subject. Plus, he has opened up the world of golf to our community."

The other women in the room only rolled their eyes. Mallory said, "I heard that Tiger won't even return the phone calls of many of the black golfers that are struggling to go pro, yet he's buddybuddy with Phil Mickelson, Veejay Singh, and the whole country club set. He may have encouraged more

African-Americans to play golf and may even help kids, but he's definitely not trying to help the brothers play in his lily-white, upper-crust sandbox. It almost makes you think that he's afraid of some black competition."

"Yeah, especially from a 'real' black man," Debbie said. "These eight- and nine-year-olds in his Tiger Camp are no threat to him. By the time they become old enough to play professionally, he would have retired with his billions anyway."

"Regardless, it's not our place to make cover decisions based on who a person chooses as his friends or who he chooses to help," Chad snapped. "And I am disappointed with all of you for being so narrow-minded on the subject of the greatest golfer who ever lived. What happened to journalistic objectivity? If you think that Tiger Woods hasn't lived up to racial expectations, perhaps that could be an angle for the story."

Debbie wouldn't let it go. "An article is one thing, but a cover story is something else altogether." A cover decision was one of the most critical made in publishing, because of the huge impact it had on newsstand sales. With hundreds of publications competing for the buyer's attention, the cover had to really grab the consumer.

Chad had heard enough. "At the end of the day, I'm the editor-in-chief here, so it's my decision. And I say that Tiger Woods goes on the January cover. Period."

"So much for consensus building," Macy mumbled.

If looks could kill, Chad would have died of multiple punctures, as several of the women in the room glared menacingly in his direction. Mallory wasn't one of them, though. She chose to pick her battles wisely, and decided that this wouldn't be one worth fighting. Not today.

After the meeting she grabbed a quick bite to eat at the salad bar next door before freshening up for her one-on-one with Chad. When Mallory reached his suite, his secretary wasn't at her desk to announce her, so Mallory knocked twice before turning the knob to walk through.

What she found on the other side was a scene that she'd much rather not have witnessed. Rising like a shot from the floor was Devon, who hastily smoothed out the front of her dress while Chad fumbled with his pants, having obviously just zipped them. Too embarrassed for words, Devon slunk past Mallory straight out the door, while Chad cleared his throat to break the uneasy silence that smothered the room.

"Do you always make it a habit to barge into offices?" he asked with an amazing amount of sarcasm. The man was shameless.

"I did knock," Mallory reminded him. She was appalled by what she'd seen.

"But you didn't wait for the answer."

Mallory shifted uneasily from one leg to the other in exasperation. "Listen, Chad, I had no idea that you were . . . indisposed."

"Whatever," he said, dismissing the subject. "What can I do for you?" he asked, sitting on the couch rather than behind his desk.

Mallory was baffled. After all, he knew very well why she was there. "I think it's a good time for us to discuss my new position." He looked at her blankly. "You know, salary, responsibilities . . ." Her voice trailed off.

Chad was looking at her as though she were speaking Greek and his first language was Hindu. "What new position?"

"Feature writer," Mallory answered, her brow beginning to wrinkle.

Chad crossed one leg over the other. "Who said that you were being promoted?"

Indignation began to simmer in the pit of Mallory's stomach. "If I'm not mistaken, you told the entire staff only hours ago that I would be handling feature stories." She crossed her arms. "Did I miss something?"

Chad stretched his arm over the back of the couch. "It certainly sounds that way. I did say that you'd be handling feature stories, but I said nothing about a promotion."

She couldn't believe his gall. "Do you expect for me to do the work without the pay?"

"You should be happy for the opportunity. You can prove yourself, and if it works out, then you'll get the promotion." His arrogance was unfathomable.

"What do you mean, prove myself? I just nailed a feature story."

"That was one story."

"Since when is it necessary to do a job before getting it? No one else has had to."

"That's the plan. Take it or leave it," Chad retorted. "Unless . . ." his eyes traveled like a loose serpent from her face down her body, lingering for a while on her breasts.

Mallory could not believe what was happening. "Unless what?"

He patted the couch next to him. "Unless we can work something out," he said, licking his lips.

The fire that had been building was now at full blaze. Visions of Devon's sordid scene flashed before her as she struggled to maintain some level of composure. "There's a term for that," she spat. "It's called sexual harassment. And if you ever make a suggestion like that to me again, you'll get the full meaning of it from my attorney."

"Girl, you should sue his sorry ass," was Nikki's advice after hearing the details of Mallory's unsavory encounter with Chad.

"It's not that simple," Mallory explained. She, Nikki, and Beverly approached the host at Pastis, a French bistro in the meatpacking district. New York was the only place that Mallory knew of where restaurants also came with velvet ropes and beefy bouncers. For decades the area where Pastis held court had been the final stop of slabs of meat before being butchered and distributed to restaurants and retailers along the

East Coast. But for the occasional storefront with sides of beef hanging overhead, you would hardly know it now. The new product these West Side blocks exported was cool. Really cool clothing stores, supercool lounges, and of course, übercool bars and restaurants. Pastis was yet another establishment where your cool meter was the deciding factor when requesting a table.

Mallory had watched as a dorky-looking Asian dude in ill-fitting khakis and an Omaha-plaid shirt approached the way-cool host inquiring about a table for four. The host's answer was a snotty "We have nothing available." He turned his head in the opposite direction to dismiss the fashion refugee. Moments after the hapless geek shuffled away, two skimpily clad blondes in hip huggers slithered forward purring the same request and were asked to wait a mere ten minutes.

"It sounds simple enough to me," Nikki huffed as she followed behind Mallory to the host's stand. "If you give him the punnany, then he'll give you the promotion. That's about as simple as it gets." Nikki had on a tight miniskirt, four-inch stilettos, and a black lace peekaboo bustier. Beverly, having come straight from the office, wore her business uniform, a slate gray Jil Sander pantsuit, matched with a conservative white blouse and a strand of pearls, along with a pair of black three-inch "sensible shoes." It was in stark contrast to the oversized bunny slippers, complete with extended whiskers, that she wore around the house.

After maneuvering through the crowd, Mallory came face-to-face with the host, who was a bad Lenny Kravitz copy, complete with a supersized afro and dark aviator sunglasses. "Hi, Jaques," Mallory said, flashing him her trademark smile. "We need a table for three, preferably by the window."

He quickly circled the podium to bestow a fake kiss on each of Mallory's cheeks. "For you, darling, anything," he crooned. "Glad you joined us tonight."

They were seated right away. Because of Mallory's style, and the company that she usually kept, she was great decoration for any room, so she never had a problem getting into any-place in the city. And it also did not hurt that she was a writer for *Heat* magazine.

Once they were settled at a prime table near the window, Nikki resumed her tirade. "Besides, doesn't Mirage Inc. own *Heat*? They are a quarter-billion-dollar company. That's who you sue!" Her eyes brightened at the mere mention of large sums of money.

Beverly quickly put a damper on that idea. "Does the name Anita Hill ring a bell?"

"Anita who?" Nikki asked, knitting her brow.

"She once worked for Justice Clarence Thomas of the Supreme Court," Mallory patiently explained.

Nikki rolled her eyes, irritated at always being picked on by the two "know-it-alls," especially Beverly. Just because she was a lawyer, she seemed to consider herself an expert on everything. "What's that got to do with *Heat* magazine?"

Beverly expelled a breath quietly. Nikki was not her favorite person. "While the whole country looked on—except of course for you—she was humiliated after accusing him of sexually harassing her. Even though he was the harasser, she was victimized again and he came out on top. Which," she said dryly to Mallory, "is no doubt his favorite position."

"You really have to have a clear-cut case with evidence and a pattern of behavior," Mallory added glumly.

Chad hadn't said anything that constituted abuse. He simply leered at her and patted the sofa. His exact words were, "That's the plan. Take it or leave it. Unless we can work something out," which could be interpreted any number of ways, especially by a good attorney. Chad was not as stupid as he looked. He clearly knew the rules of harassment.

"So you're just going to take that shit?" Nikki demanded.

"Honestly, I don't know what I'm going to do."

"Just make sure that you document everything from now on," Beverly advised.

Noting Mallory's deflating mood, she decided to change the

subject. She knew that as long as her friend didn't dwell on the negative, she'd dust herself off and keep on going. Like the time in the seventh grade when she was inexplicably cut from the pom-pom squad. She'd been devastated, but in true Mallory fashion, the next week she tried out for junior cheerleader and was the captain of the squad by the end of the season.

"Let's not ruin a good night out discussing that little twerp." She signaled the waiter to begin the first round of cocktails.

After they gave orders to the waiter, Nikki excused herself. "Nature calls." As she stood up, she shimmied the few inches of fabric down over her hips.

As she sashayed away, Beverly shook her head. "She's a piece of work."

"I know, but she's harmless," Mallory said.

Beverly gave Mallory a doubtful eye. "Are you sure about that?"

"She's a little rough around the edges."

They watched as Nikki disappeared into the crowd. "What's with that outfit? Is she a whore or a model?" Beverly asked.

"She's a model," Mallory said, defending her roommate. "Or she was. She hasn't been getting much work lately."

"You wouldn't know it by the way she struts around like a peacock."

"Come on, Beverly. Give her a break."

Her old friend shook her head. "What I'd like to give her is a lesson in style. The one called the Rule of Three."

"The Rule of Three?" Mallory asked, smiling, expecting one of Beverly's jokes.

"Yeah. It goes like this." Beverly leaned forward as though she were sharing the Holy Grail. "When you are in your twenties, you can work it all, from top to bottom. You can do the come-fuck-me stilettos, with ass-accentuating spandex, and then prop the boobs up for display. But when you get to your thirties, you need to cut it back to two of the three. And once you're in your forties, you'd best pick one and try to do it really well." She and Mallory laughed. "Your girl here obviously didn't get that memo. She looks like a tart that's already been popped."

After her visit to the little girls' room, Nikki headed back toward the table. She could feel a trail of eyes transfixed on her, which she loved, not knowing that the expressions were of bewilderment rather than admiration. She'd gone only halfway when someone called out, "Nikki, over here." She paused in midstrut, then spotted a table of women.

While Mallory and Beverly looked on, Nikki joined the women for a few minutes, engaging in a cozy conversation with a woman wearing long dreads. "Is that Yvette Boynton?" Beverly asked.

"I've never met her, so I'm not sure," Mallory answered. Still, like every other New Yorker who could read, Mallory knew of the legendary gossip queen.

"I believe it is," Beverly whispered. "She and your girl look awfully cozy."

When Nikki finally found her way back to the table, Beverly asked, "Was that Yvette Boynton?"

"Who?" Nikki answered as though she had no idea to whom Beverly was referring.

"The woman sporting the dreads."

"I can't remember her name. She's a friend of one of the designers that I work for. I really don't know her very well."

Nikki sat down quickly and reached for her drink, then took a long pull. "Guess what she told me? There's a party at Chaos tonight for Hubris, the new couture line," she said conspiratorially. "Let's check it out."

"I'll pass," Beverly said. "I've got an early morning tomorrow."

"I will, too," Mallory yawned. "I'm not in the mood tonight for the fashion crowd. Plus, I need to work on a rewrite for Chad. It's due tomorrow."

"Suit yourselves." Nikki shrugged. She'd accomplished what she wanted, getting them off the dangerous subject of

Yvette Boynton. If her roommate became suspicious, that would ruin the plan.

After they'd finished their meal and were headed toward the door, Nikki exchanged a fleeting look with the woman she'd been talking to. While Mallory missed the surreptitious glance, she did catch Yvette giving her the once-over. *What was that all about?* she wondered. With a questioning expression, she looked toward Nikki, but her strutting friend was already pushing her way out the door.

6

STORMY WEATHER

An air of expectancy swirled through the suite of offices and cubicles at Ingram Enterprises. It was fueled by the aura of important deals being done and power moves being made and by the whiff of freshly minted money—all emanating from Saxton McKenzie's elegant corner office. His was a comfortable living room, cozy lounge, and masculine study, all combined into one large space. In the center of the far wall was an intricately carved fireplace. Anytime between the early chill of October and the late frost of spring, a fire was likely to be roaring within the confines of Saxton's sanctuary. He loved the smell of burning wood, its crackling sounds, as well as the ambience of the dancing flames as they licked the timber, moving to their own rhythm.

This passion was a throwback to Saxton's youth. Though his exterior projected the manner of a pretty-boy cloaked in an Ivy League degree, Saxton was a country boy at heart, having grown up outside Raleigh, North Carolina, as the only son, and the youngest in a family of four children. After his father was killed in an accident while operating heavy equipment at one of the local tobacco plants, Saxton was "unofficially" designated the man of the house. Though he was only nine years old at the time, one of his responsibilities was to tend the fire and to keep the wood supply stacked close to the small frame house.

Not only was a crackling fire soothing to him, but it also helped to fuel his thinking. And right now he needed every brain cell he had firing to figure out the best way to structure and negotiate the new syndication deal for *The Ingram Hour*, Deena's highly rated television show. While it was currently shown in fifteen markets, making Deena an immensely popular TV personality, Saxton was in talks with FBC, their television network, to broadcast it into every market in the United States and Canada. The deal would be a major coup for Saxton personally and for Deena professionally, and it would put Ingram Enterprises on the map as a major media player—not to mention heaping close to a hundred million dollars annually onto the bottom line, while placing Saxton squarely in the big leagues, right next to Ogdin Finch, FBC's owner and the Donald Trump of the media world.

Mr. Finch was an icon who was regularly dusted off for closer examination by all of the major business periodicals. Since he attended business school, Saxton had followed his career and from afar had admired his tenacity, business savvy, and finely honed instincts. Saxton was thrilled, if not a little ego-inflated, to be in the midst of a business deal important enough to attract the attention of the highly revered businessman. Though at this stage of the negotiations only Ogdin's senior executives had done the wining and dining, Saxton had been assured that once the deal was further along, he would be communicating directly with Mr. Finch himself.

Lost in the trance of the dancing fire, he reclined in the leather swivel chair with his Testonis propped on his desk and a mug of coffee in his hand. He was immersed in deal points, advertising revenue, Nielson ratings, and other business stats that could give him leverage in the negotiations. Sprays of red-hot splinters punctuated the quiet of the early-evening office hours.

His reflections were cut short by a rap at the door. "Come in."

It was Cindy. "I just wanted to be sure that everything was in order for tomorrow's meeting." Sitting in the chair opposite his desk, she checked off her to-do list. "I've verified diet restrictions and ordered a wait staff to serve coffee, snacks, and lunch. The china and silverware are being delivered. There'll even be chilled champagne on hand just in case there's something to celebrate." Cindy was in her late thirties, unquestionably efficient, and loyal to a fault.

"Let's hope there'll be lots to celebrate," Saxton mused, though he didn't expect the deal to be anywhere near complete. Maybe they would make notable progress on a couple of key points, like per-show compensation or syndication revenue, but that was the best that he could hope for at this stage.

"I've also double-checked the audio/visual equipment and made sure that the slide presentations are in order. Is there anything else?"

"I think that about covers it."

Before she headed out the door, she turned again to face him. "One more thing. Deena called to remind you about the dinner scheduled with her parents tonight."

"Oh, yeah." It had completely slipped his mind. "What time is it?"

"Nine o'clock at Town."

He groaned inwardly. He was not looking forward to a long evening, which it would undoubtedly be. While Deena and her mother prattled on about everything and nothing, there wasn't much beyond surface conversation that he could share with her father, the Honorable Judge Paul Ingram.

All too soon, he was retrieving his suit jacket and heading down to meet his hired car. As it cruised uptown, Saxton sat impatiently in the leather confines of the backseat as though he were being led to the gallows.

As he predicted, the night plodded along without a merciful

conclusion in sight. All through cocktails and dinner he valiantly maintained an interested expression on his face while Judge Ingram droned on about his bourgeois country club and why the Republican party was the best hope to save the masses of poor and ignorant blacks who populated the nation's ghettos. He said this as though the unfortunate were a race straight out of *National Geographic*, people that he'd read about but thankfully had never had the displeasure of meeting face-to-face. In Saxton's other ear a stream of gossip spewed forth between Deena and her mother, Ingrid. He fought the urge to get up from the table and simply walk out of the restaurant. These were his future in-laws.

Though he and Deena had been dating over five years, Saxton hadn't, until recently, spent much time with them. The more he did, the less he liked them. Thank God, he thought, that they at least lived an hour's plane ride away, which unfortunately did nothing to help his plight tonight. Sitting through the five-course dinner with the holier-than-thou twosome was like watching flat paint dry, and Deena, who was immensely proud of her family's accomplishments, did nothing to bring about a merciful ending to his torture. So when she ordered an after-dinner drink to follow a round of dessert, he wasn't certain if his tested patience would make it to her last drop.

"I'd like to propose a toast," Deena said, smiling radiantly. "To my father and his pending nomination to the Supreme Court."

They all clinked glasses, and Deena leaned over to kiss her father on his cheek. He had recently been put on the short list as a possible nominee, following the sudden death of Supreme Court Justice McCall.

"Let's not celebrate too prematurely," Judge Ingram counseled, though he blushed modestly while his wife and daughter beamed proudly. Paul Ingram was one of those high-yellow black men with "good hair" who reigned supreme during his generation. Fortunately, Saxton thought, today's black youth were more appreciative of deeper pigmentation and kinky hair.

"Congratulations," Saxton managed to say through clenched teeth. He knew that people like Judge Ingram—token black Republicans who were trotted out by the president on an as-needed basis—were the worst thing to happen to African-Americans since crack cocaine and cargo ships.

To help himself through the tedium, he mounted a fake smile, which he wore on his face like a plaster cast, and nodded in varying intervals, while happily letting his mind wander free. His imagination roamed away from the table and out the restaurant doors; it ended its journey back in Atlanta during those months he spent with Mallory. His smile became genuine at the prospect of seeing her again tomorrow night.

In many ways, his affair with her had been the most memorable time of his life. For once, he hadn't felt the pressure to meet anyone's expectations: not those of his family, his coaches, his football fans, or his boss. It was like a four-month-long hiatus from the real world—but better, because of Mallory. Every day spent with her, he felt the rush and excitement of a first date, a first kiss, the first time he had made love.

They had met by accident, literally, his first week in the Chocolate City. He had been sitting in the parking lot known as Interstate 85 in the middle of a downpour. Though the impact was only slightly jarring, the asphalt was so slick that his Mercedes Benz had been sent careening into the back of the black Saab ahead of him. Her driver's-side window opened to reveal a pair of the sultriest eyes he'd ever seen. Though it clearly wasn't his fault, he apologized profusely. After saying, "I'm sorry," for the tenth time, he finally came up with a better idea. He asked her if she'd take the next exit to have a drink at the Ritz-Carlton while they exchanged insurance information. By the time they left the cozy bar three hours later, they were both smitten.

They arranged to meet for dinner the next night at Blue Point in Buckhead. When Mallory descended the staircase into the chic, trendy restaurant, wearing a black Narciso Rodriquez cocktail dress, she took his breath away. For someone who was never at a loss for words, Saxton felt like a teenage boy on prom night. He couldn't remember the last time any woman had put a lump in his throat, not to mention caused a major stirring beneath his belt. Mallory had an easy seductiveness and elegance about her. She was beautiful and stylish without effort and intelligent in a way that wasn't overbearing. During dinner, they discussed childhood memories, adolescent dreams, and hopes for their current careers. All things that Saxton could not remember ever having shared with a woman, not in such a frank manner. For some reason he was open with Mallory. He didn't experience the need to guard his feelings.

After dinner they stopped at Tarrazu, a chic coffee shop off Ponce de Leon, for cappuccinos. Later, as they walked to their cars, they were caught in a sudden downpour. Saxton took off his jacket to shield them from the rain. When they neared his car, he fumbled for his keys. Suddenly the jacket slipped from his grip and was carried off by the twirling wind up into a nearby copse of trees. Exasperated, he turned to face Mallory, who could barely contain her laughter. In seconds the rain plastered the dress to the curves of her body and drenched her hair flat. Any other black woman he knew would have had an attitude about her hair getting wet, her makeup being ruined, or her clothes becoming soaked. Instead Mallory fully enjoyed the spontaneity of the moment. The rain only made her look even more sexy than she already was. He reached for her, pulling her close as they both stood there in the parking lot under buckets of falling rain. When their lips met, time stood still as he tasted the sweetness of cappuccino, the tenderness of her tongue, and the dewy freshness of the summer rain. The combination was more intoxicating than the vintage champagne they'd shared with dinner. It was like his first kiss ever, but much, much better.

A horn blared, reminding him that they were blocking the exit of the parking lot. After scrambling into his car, they drove through the pouring rain to his suite at the Ritz-Carlton, leaving his suit jacket hanging in the branches of the tree. Once inside the suite, they peeled off each other's wet clothing. The fitted dress she'd worn earlier only hinted at the beauty and perfection of her tautly chiseled body. And its fabric and cut did little to prepare him for the fullness of her breasts or the round firmness of her hips, all dramatically illuminated by a brilliant flash of lightning, courtesy of the unrelenting storm that raged outside the hotel window.

They made passionate love to the steady beat of the raindrops. It felt like the most natural thing in the world: no coyness, no shyness, and no apprehension, only a deep yearning that washed over them in wave after wave of bliss. Afterward, they lay in each other's arms, whispering under the covers, as if not to disturb Mother Nature.

Reflecting on that night, he again wondered, *Why did I ever end the relationship with Mallory?* Yet he knew why. The answer to his question sat directly across the table from him.

On cue, Deena's voice floated into his consciousness. "What do you think about *InStyle* magazine?"

He reined himself back into the restaurant. "What was that, baby?"

"Mom and I were just discussing having *InStyle* cover the wedding."

Saxton was dumbfounded. "What do you mean by 'cover the wedding?'"

"If we promise them an exclusive, I'm sure they'd do a five-page spread on it," Deena patiently explained. "It'd be great publicity."

Saxton was taken aback. Since when had their wedding become a publicity opportunity? "Honestly, I'd rather it were a more private event."

The famous Deena Ingram charm kicked into high gear. "But, honey, this would be great for the ratings, and with us in negotiations for syndication, every little bit helps," she purred. "Plus, I want the whole world to see my handsome hubby." Deena's long silky hair was by far her best asset, and right now she was working it like a stripper would a pole. She ran her fingers through it lazily and tossed it over her shoulders, before sweeping the thick sheet of hair all to one side.

Ingrid put in, "Besides, if you're spending half a million dollars on a wedding, you may as well make sure that you're getting your money's worth." She took a lingering sip of her after-dinner port.

"A half a million dollars?" A bewildered expression descended on Saxton's face. As far as he knew, they were having a small ceremony, followed by a quaint reception.

"Colin Cowie doesn't do weddings for less than that," Deena said as though this explained away every penny needed.

"Who is Colin Cowie?"

"He is *the* wedding planner. He's done the most important weddings in the world, and he only does six a year. So we're lucky to get him."

Then Ingrid chimed in again. "You must understand, Saxton dear, you're marrying a Boston Ingram, and guests will expect nothing less than the very best, especially considering Deena's position and all."

"Not to mention mine," Paul weighed in.

"Don't worry. It'll be worth every penny," Deena insisted.

At that moment a black-clad waiter floated toward their table. Unable to bear the excruciating night a moment longer, Saxton raised his hand. "Check, please."

7

AN INDECENT PROPOSAL

The next day Mallory dressed with extra attention to every detail, wearing a smartly cut Dolce & Gabbana pinstripe pantsuit with a knit V-neck top and a pair of pointy Michel Perry mules. After spending an extra fifteen minutes with her hair, she chastised herself for acting like a schoolgirl getting ready for a first date with the one guy she'd pined for all year long. To prove her indifference to Saxton, instead of wearing her black lightweight cashmere Michael Kors car coat, she settled for an Armani three-quarter knit trench instead. After all, this dinner with him tonight was strictly business.

Regardless of how often Mallory glanced at the clock on the wall or the watch on her wrist, the day passed slowly. At six thirty, when she was finally gathering her things to leave the office, Vickee stuck her head into the doorway. "Chad wants to see you."

"What's it about?" Mallory asked, checking her watch again.

"He didn't say."

"Tell him I'll be right there," Mallory sighed.

That morning he had summoned Mallory into his office to tell her that he was pulling her piece on hip-hop legend Russell Simmons. This was after she'd pulled every label and publicist contact she had to get the interview scheduled. When she asked him why, he simply said, "I don't recall having to justify my decisions to you."

When she walked into his office, for several seconds Chad didn't look up from the paper that he was reading, leaving her standing there, fuming. "Have a seat," he finally said. After she sat on his sofa and crossed her legs, he finally put the document aside and rose from his chair to join her on the sofa. "I read your rewrite on the state of the music industry. I think it still needs a lot of work."

"What exactly do you mean, a lot of work?" Mallory asked. The story was complete with quotes from industry leaders and historical references. She had no doubt that it was a strong piece.

"I thought it was weak and totally unsubstantiated. In fact, I want you to work with Cissy on fleshing it out." Cissy was a junior staff writer whose skills and tenure were well below Mallory's.

"You've got to be kidding." Mallory popped off the sofa like a piece of toast that was close to burning.

"No, I'm very serious," Chad answered, not wavering. "Unless you've changed your mind," he added, patting the seat next to him.

Disgusted, Mallory said, "The only thing that I may have changed my mind about is the decision to file a sexual harassment lawsuit against you and this company. Or even better, maybe I should go straight to the media and let the world know what a slime ball you are."

"Be my guest," he said, rising from the sofa. "It's your word against mine, and remember, I'm the editor-in-chief."

Mallory stormed from his office, grabbed her bag, and left the building as fast as she could. By the time she arrived at Provence, she was in need of a serious cocktail. She had all but cast aside the jitters that dinner with Saxton had caused her earlier.

When she walked through the door of the quaint East Village restaurant, the maitre d' greeted her warmly even though she had never met him before in her life. "*Bon soir*, Mademoiselle Baylor. Come, follow me," he said in a pleasing French accent. As she passed through the interior dining room to an enclosed tree-lined patio, she could feel the stress of the office falling away. When they reached a cozy table for two in an intimate corner, Saxton rose from his chair to embrace her. Though a hug was customary between male and female colleagues, this one conveyed much more than a casual greeting. Without words it said, *It's* really *good to see you. I've missed you so much, and I'm sorry for everything,* all in the space of scant seconds. Careful not to respond, Mallory pulled away and took her seat, which the maitre d' held out for her. Even before she could settle in, a waiter appeared at her side with a frothy glass of Veuve Clicquot champagne, her favorite. As quickly as he had appeared, the waiter vanished, leaving Saxton and Mallory alone.

"You look incredible." Saxton's eyes feasted on her as though no other woman inhabited the earth.

Groping for her usual cool, Mallory simply said, "Thank you."

The night, the restaurant, the patio, and the champagne—it all felt surreal to her. As though she'd mistakenly walked onto the wrong movie set. Instead of *Nine to Five* she had shown up for *Last Tango in Paris*. Chills that had nothing to do with the crisp autumn air ran up her spine. She valiantly shook off their prickling effect.

"How was your day?" he asked, taking a sip of his vodka gimlet.

"You don't want to know," she said, glad to follow suit. She sipped the effervescent champagne, enjoying its dance across her palate and down her throat. When she returned the flute to the table, she focused on the river of fine bubbles that floated to the top. It was either that or become lost in the sparkle in his eyes.

"Oh, but I do," Saxton said, smiling broadly. She noticed the deep dimple in his left cheek. The same one she had admired in pictures of her son.

Snapping out of her daze, she said, "It was fine, really. Just another day at the office."

He didn't seem convinced. "Do you enjoy your job?" he inquired.

"It's fine," she lied. "Why do you ask?"

"Actually, that's why I wanted to have dinner."

"To discuss my job?"

"To discuss my company." He leaned forward. "Ingram Enterprises is about to launch a new urban celebrity magazine called *Spotlight*. I'd like to talk to you about a position as executive editor."

Mallory was speechless. Though she'd had no idea what the dinner was about, a job offer would have been her last guess. "A job?"

"I've seen your work firsthand, remember. Plus, I've done my homework on your career. I know that you'd be the perfect person for the position." Saxton leaned back and took a sip of his drink. "Would you consider the offer?"

Her left brain was screaming, *No! Absolutely not! It will never work!* But her right brain was jumping for joy, happy at the thought of escaping from Chad and *Heat* magazine. As for the lofty title, that made her nothing short of ecstatic.

Saxton misread her lack of response. "Don't worry. We're not going to fold after the first issue. We have the backing of major investors, an advertising base already built in by the television show, and a budget that will afford you a very comfortable salary."

"Saxton, I don't know . . ." she said, shaking her head.

"I know this is unexpected, but at least think about it."

Her right brain prevailed. "I'll think about it," she finally answered, lightly biting her lip. "But no promises."

"That's all I ask," he said, holding his palms up.

After they placed their dinner orders, Saxton changed the subject. "The last time we met I didn't find out anything about what you've been up to in your personal life."

"That's why they call it an interview, Saxton. And remember, you were the subject," she said, picking up her flute. "Not me."

"Well, that was then, but this is now. So tell me, what have you been up to?"

"Nothing special, really." When she saw that he wasn't taking that for an answer, she continued. "After you left Atlanta, I spent six months in Philadelphia looking at journalism opportunities and eventually found my way to New York." She took a sip of her champagne to help swallow the bitter taste of that time.

"How do you like the Big City?"

For the first time Mallory relaxed. After all, this was a safe subject, and one that she felt passionate about. "I really love it! I love the energy, the fast pace, and even the people." She let her eyes linger on Saxton, remembering the man she had fallen in love with in Atlanta. The one who sat across from her tonight was just as charming, handsome, and engaging, but there was an invisible shield around him that city living tended to produce. In Atlanta he'd been much more carefree and open.

"How long have you been with *Heat*?"

"About three years," she answered. She wondered if her resentment of Chad showed on her face.

"Where is your apartment?" he asked, enjoying the seductive way she toyed with the rim of the flute with her ring finger.

Nowhere near yours, she thought. With Ingram Enterprises money, she was sure that he was on the Upper East Side in some fabulous building with views of Central Park. "I'm in Murray Hill."

"That's a nice neighborhood."

"It'll do, but I'm sure for you that's slumming."

"You forget who you're talking to." He smiled, putting his

dimples on full display. "Remember, I'm a country boy from North Carolina." He even let a hint of his long-lost Southern accent find its way into his voice.

"No, I do remember that, although I must confess—"

"Please do," he interrupted, leaning in closer, reaching for her hand.

She laughed at the corny gesture. "What I was about to say was that I did learn quite a bit about you researching for the interview."

"Oh, really, now?" He straightened in his chair.

She leaned back into hers, too, subtly retracting her hand from his hold. "Well, for one thing, I had no idea that you were a big-time football hero at Notre Dame."

He laughed. "You mean, you couldn't tell by this aging excuse for an athlete's body?"

From what she could tell, even through the two-thousand-dollar suit, his body looked just as good as it had in Atlanta, and then it was a finely tuned specimen of the male anatomy. The thought made her blush.

He smiled knowingly. "I did have a few shining moments."

She shook herself free from his spell. "I'm sure on and off the field."

He was thown off guard by her remark. "What exactly does that mean?"

She didn't answer him right away. The waiter appeared with an assortment of appetizers and proceeded to refill their glasses of champagne from the silver ice bucket beside the table.

As the bubbles rose effervescently to the top of the long-stemmed flutes, Mallory weighed her response. She wanted to steer away from his personal life and leave the past where it belonged. Still, a part of her wanted an explanation for his sudden disappearance, since what they had shared seemed so magical.

She decided to make light of her comment. "I'm simply pointing out that, as smooth as you are, I'm sure that you had things under control, not only on the football field." She speared a forkful of smoked salmon and brought it to her mouth.

He shook his head. "No, I think you've got me all wrong. My first year of college I was a total wreck. In fact, I warmed the bench better than a thermal blanket. I was third-string and pissed off about it." He shrugged as he laughed at the memory.

"Saxton McKensie, third-string? Never!" she teased. "Second-string maybe, just so that you could give your evil Gemini twin a chance to come out and play." Maybe that dual personality explained how he could be in love with her in Atlanta and disappear without a trace once he was in New York. "Besides, I'm sure that competitive streak of yours wouldn't allow you to stay there long."

One thing that she had learned during her research about him was that Saxton was very competitive, and perhaps that too explained their short-lived relationship. Maybe she was merely a deal to be closed, and once he had done so, he simply moved on to the next challenge, which happened to be Deena Ingram. Only she might have turned out to be more than he'd bargained for. Or maybe not. *But if that's the case,* she thought, *why is he sitting across the table from me in a romantic French restaurant flirting shamelessly?*

8

COURTING LADY LUCK

Every so often Saxton and his friend Greg, the self-proclaimed "Love Doctor," would take the Jag out for the two-hour drive from New York to Atlantic City. It was not Monte Carlo, but for a quick diversion it would do. Saxton was fast with numbers, and he had good instincts. More important, he knew when to walk away from the table. So generally speaking, his pockets were fuller on departure than they were on his arrival. While Greg wasn't as lucky at the tables as he was with the ladies, he did enjoy a respite from his Park Avenue OB-GYN practice.

Greg was five feet eleven with a dark chocolate complexion and neatly cropped hair that formed a distinct widow's peak. He was the shade of dark that had replaced high yellow as the pigment of choice for today's black woman. Saxton found it ironic, if not fitting, that Greg, the biggest playboy he knew, peered between women's widely spread legs on a daily basis for a living. Though Greg was reputed to be a first-rate doctor, Saxton could only guess at his initial motivation for the career choice.

The many casinos of Atlantic City, places where a sea of money floated through on an hourly basis, rose on the fringe of the dried-out carcass of the city. By most standards, it could be called a ghetto. The contradiction was as stark as

Saxton's impressive black Jaguar purring past rusted-out cars parked on cinder bricks and dilapidated houses spilling over with destitute occupants. It was not supposed to be that way, Saxton thought. When the new and improved Atlantic City was initially conceived, packaged, and sold to the neglected community, the deal came with a guaranteed promise to deliver economic development to the desolate residents. Of course, nothing ever came close to materializing. It had even made matters worse, since it offered yet another vice for those who had quite enough of them already, thank you very much.

"We should have brought some babes with us and stayed the weekend," Greg said as they pulled into the heart of the city.

"Babes. What babes?" Saxton asked. Greg knew full well that he was engaged to Deena, but he used every opportunity to discount the relationship.

"For starters, I know this set of twins that would make you lose your mind," Greg said emphatically. "Those girls are fiiiiine!"

"Man, I can't say that I'm interested in spending time with any of your bimbos, but two?" Saxton shook his head. "That's out of the question."

Greg looked insulted. "Bimbos? Who said they were bimbos? You don't even know them."

"But I do know you," Saxton responded. "And every girl I've ever seen you with could be classified as a bimbo."

"That's wrong, man. Just because they aren't clawing their way to the top like some women we know," Greg said, eyeing Saxton suggestively, "doesn't mean that they are bimbos."

"Whatever you say," Saxton answered, dismissing the subject. He'd never figured out exactly why Greg disliked Deena so much.

When they walked into the Pacific, Saxton's favorite casino along the boardwalk, they were greeted by one of the hosts. As always, he quickly squired them away from the common trade, who were rounded up and herded along the Garden

State Parkway in chartered buses from points near and far. Old women with blue rinse in their gray hair dropped buckets full of quarters into slot machines with shaky arthritic fingers. Middle-aged men wearing plaid flannel shirts toted in crumbs scraped from the tables of their families as offerings to the craps gods, reverently hoping to turn them into heaps of manna.

Meanwhile, Saxton, Greg, and the other privileged patrons were ensconced behind velvet ropes, rubbing elbows only with bejeweled arms or with other Italian-cut suits. Though Saxton was hardly a snob, he welcomed the privacy his status provided. The few times that he'd pulled out a thick stack of chips at the regular tables, all eyes had turned to him as though he'd descended from the planet Pluto. Then the questions came. "What team do you play for?" was usually the first in the "So How Did *You* Get Rich?" series. Why did white people always assume that a black man with any money had to be an athlete? Or an entertainer? When the first three guesses proved wrong, entitlement got the better of them (even the poorest white trash felt justified in questioning a black man). They'd just outright ask, "So what do you do?" And of course, whenever Saxton answered, "Why do you ask?" he was immediately labeled an NWA—nigger with an attitude.

After he and Greg had each traded five grand for a mixed stack of one-hundred- and five-hundred-dollar chips, they settled in for a few hours of battle with the dealer, whose appearance was quite deceptive. Though he looked ancient, with wispy remnants of hair and liver spots on his hand, he was lightning-quick and had calculators for eyeballs. The minimum bet at his table was a hundred dollars. Since Saxton had played at tables in Vegas and Monte Carlo, where the minimum bet was a thousand a shot, tonight would be casual, not too much pressure.

A rich Texan beneath a two-ton Stetson sat to the left of the dealer, nursing a watery Jack Daniel's and nervously fiddling with his few remaining chips, as though deciding whether to try his waning luck again or to cash out. Two empty chairs away was an old woman who was dipped in diamonds, platinum, and a spray of other precious stones. She was bone-thin but as well preserved as lots of money could afford, with the exception of her thickly veined hands, which held towering stacks of orange chips, worth five hundred dollars each. Greg sat to her left, while Saxton and a quiet elderly Asian man were in the last two chairs.

After the five decks of cards were reshuffled, Saxton placed a blue chip on the table, starting out slow with a simple hundred-dollar bet. Greg laid out two of them, while the woman with the diamond-crusted Rolex tossed out two oranges, and the Texan reluctantly pushed a hundred out in front of him. The Asian sat out the round, suspicious of the two newcomers' ability to play. In a blur, the dealer passed the cards, two faceup for each guest and two for himself, one facedown. He was showing a seven. Sweeping his hand across the table, he took hits. The Texan unwisely added a ten to fifteen, predictably busting his hand, and the diamond diva stood on twenty. Greg held on seventeen and Saxton took a hit on twelve, pulling six for a total of eighteen. The dealer showed his hidden card, which was a ten, so he unburdened the Texan of his bet, paid the amounts wagered to the lady and Saxton, and since Greg pushed with a tie, his chips lived to see another bet.

An hour later, Saxton was up three thousand dollars, and Greg was up a grand. The Texan was relieved of his remaining chips, leaving him free to wander off into the sunset. The Asian guy had jumped in impressively by wagering a six-hundred-dollar bet, only to have the dealer pull five cards for a total of twenty-one. And Ms. Money Bags looked like she might need a Brinks truck upon leaving.

During a reshuffle, Greg pulled a cigar from his breast

pocket. "That was some piece on you in *Heat* magazine. Even I was impressed with you."

Saxton chuckled. "You'll never guess who wrote it."

Greg gave him a puzzled look. "Who?"

"Do you remember Mallory, the girl that I dated in Atlanta?"

Greg frowned, trying to dredge up the memory. He had come down to visit a couple of times during Saxton's stay. At last his face lit up. "Yeah, the cute honey that had your nose wide open when you were doing that merger deal."

Saxton nodded. "That's the one."

"I remember her. She was a hottie!" he said. "So what's up?" Greg gave him a don't-be-holdin'-out-on-me look.

Saxton took several deep puffs of his Davidoff while holding the flame to its tip for an even burn. When he was satisfied that the cigar was well lit, he turned to Greg. "Nothing, really," he said nonchalantly. "She showed up a few weeks ago for the interview. She's a writer with *Heat*."

Greg flashed a comic leer. "That's one way to get favorable press."

"Nothing happened. If anything, it could have been a really bad piece, considering how our relationship ended."

Greg paused, struck by something that had come to him. "I remember. That was around the time that you started dating Deena." He made a face at the thought of her.

Saxton quickly said, "I had to make a choice."

Greg eyed him hopefully. "You're not reconsidering, are you?"

Saxton took a long drag of his cigar, expelling the smoke toward the ceiling. "No, that was the past. I'm engaged to Deena now."

"If you say so." Greg looked at him suspiciously. "But from what I remember, Mallory wasn't a girl who's easy to forget—especially when she's within striking distance."

That was the damned truth, Saxton thought, but he said,

"The only thing she was interested in was the magazine piece."

"Is that the only piece she offered?" Greg smiled snidely.

"Believe me, she's not interested in anything else. And neither am I."

"What do you mean *she's* not interested? That sounds present tense to me. Are you still seeing her?"

"Not really." Saxton coughed uncomfortably. "I did offer her a position with *Spotlight*, though."

"What? Man, you've been holding out on a brotha!" Greg said, raising his palm for a high-five. "I didn't know you had it in you."

Greg was grinning like a man who had just won a long shot. As far as he was concerned, his best friend had talked himself into being shackled to the Bitch from Hell. Deena had become so vain, he could barely stand to say hello to her anymore. But Saxton had blinders on and couldn't see the little horns sprouting from the top of her head.

"It's not what you think. Trust me," Saxton said.

"Hey, I do, man. I do." He smiled slyly. "But do you trust yourself? Working with her every day isn't quite the same as having her a thousand miles away in Atlanta."

"It ain't like that," Saxton said uneasily. Seeing that the dealer was about to resume play, he quickly shoved a stack of chips worth five thousand dollars out in front of him. Greg merely smiled and decided to sit the hand out.

After pondering Saxton's situation over a puff of his cigar, Greg observed, "Just watch yourself, man. You know what they say. You should never shit where you eat."

"Don't worry, man. It's all good."

Even as the words left his mouth, Saxton couldn't help but question his own motives for wanting to hire Mallory. Sure, she was an excellent journalist, but she was also a woman to whom he had an unquestionable attraction. But he could suppress it, couldn't he? He'd done it before, and he'd do it again.

After all, he had a lot at stake here, since he was now engaged to Deena Ingram.

Mallory was pondering the same question.

"A fling five years ago shouldn't have any bearing on a career choice today," Beverly reasoned. Mallory had confided in her since she was, by far, the most pragmatic of all of her friends.

"True," Mallory said. She couldn't help but wonder whether Beverly would feel the same way about her working for Saxton if she knew the whole story. Or if Beverly would feel the same about *her* if she knew the sordid details of their past. She shuddered to think what anyone would say of her if they knew she'd secretly had a child and given him away.

Beverly peered at Mallory, showing a large dose of motherly concern. "Unless you're still attracted to him." They were hanging out in Beverly's Upper West Side apartment, enjoying each other's company and a nice bottle of Chateau Haut-Brion. Though Beverly wasn't wearing the smartly cut business suits that she wore every day to intimidate adversaries, at the moment she was no less serious.

Mallory gave her friend a get-real look. "Have you seen the man? He's gorgeous, he's smart, and he's sexy as hell."

Beverly blinked, her composure shaken for a moment. Mallory knew that she would love for a man like Saxton to enter her own life, unlike the boring corporate types she usually dated. What woman wouldn't? "I'm not blind. But there is a difference between appreciating his charms and being affected by them. As long as you can work there and keep a professional distance, what's the harm?"

"Seeing as how he's also engaged to one of the most popular women on TV, I think I'll be able to contain myself. Besides, all I have to do is remember the outcome five years ago, and if that doesn't throw cold water on my libido, then I should be spayed."

Beverly agreed. "I'm sure that you'll be fine. Remember

what Nancy Reagan used to say: 'Just say no.'" Beverly was like that, Mallory thought. For her most things were black and white, up or down, in or out. She had very little patience with ambiguity in life. If a man stood in the way of her career, she'd just as soon run him over.

"Yeah, but I don't know what's more intoxicating, drugs or Saxton McKensie," Mallory teased.

For the first time a smile touched Beverly's lips. "From the looks of him, I'd say it would be a pretty close call."

Mallory blushed at the memories of the night before, the subtle touches she should have brushed away, before recovering herself. "No, seriously, I'm sure that our relationship would be purely professional."

"Listen, Mallory, even if you decide to take the job, you can always quit if it gets to be too uncomfortable. And with the way things are going at *Heat*, you'd have nothing to lose either way."

"That's true," Mallory said, slowly sipping the dark red wine.

"But remember, you don't have to make a decision this very moment. Take some time to think about it. Don't rush it."

It figured, Mallory thought, that Beverly would advise caution where relationships were concerned. Speaking of which, Mallory had a question of her own.

"What's going on with you and Bill?" Bill was her most recent boyfriend, whom she decided to dump abruptly.

"There is no 'me and Bill.'"

"You didn't even give the man a chance," Mallory chided.

"A chance to what?" she asked, raising her brows. "To prove to me what a player he is? I don't have the time to waste. My motto is, if it barks like a dog, I don't need a veterinarian to tell me what type of dog." Beverly had been notoriously no-nonsense since her senior year in college, when she discovered that her first serious boyfriend, Mike, had not just one other girlfriend, but enough to start a small sorority chapter. He even had a baby by another woman.

Mallory wondered if she were just the opposite of her friend. Maybe she'd given Saxton too much leeway to begin with. She would be wise, she thought, to heed her friend's advice and stay clear of the danger signs. Right now she wasn't sure which was more lethal, Saxton's attraction to her or her attraction to him.

9

BAIT THEN SWITCH

When Mallory was alone with her restless demons, working for Saxton did not seem like such a good idea, but during work hours she felt completely poised to take the leap. The following day he sent a hand-delivered package with a mock layout of the magazine. It showed everything that he had promised over dinner. It was hot and sexy, and it showed graphically all of the exciting, cutting-edge direction that they had discussed while sipping champagne. The next day she received a written offer from Ingram Enterprises with a six-figure salary, a generous expense account, and a number of other fringe benefits.

Intent on not being easily swayed, she continued to debate the pros and cons as she headed into the office Friday morning. When she reached her desk, she found a bouquet of exotic flowers with a note attached:

> *The only thing missing here is you.*
> *From* Spotlight *magazine*

He was really laying it on thick, she thought, smiling to herself. As she lifted the vase to place it on the side of her desk, she saw a note in Chad's angry scrawl:

Come see me NOW!

She took a deep breath and headed down the hall toward his office.

When she walked in, he sat fuming, an all-too-familiar sight these days.

"What's going on?" she asked, tired of the little intimidation games that he had been playing recently.

In answer, he bolted from his chair and charged toward her. The only thing missing was a blast of smoke from his flared nostrils. "Explain this!" he demanded, thrusting a newspaper at her. He was so angry that the whites of his eyes were pink.

Confused, Mallory began to read the blurb that had been circled in red. It was a blind item in the *New York Gazette*'s scandal sheet. It read:

Talk of the Town

What blustery tyrant of an editor-in-chief of a hot urban magazine is boosting himself up by stepping (and lying) on his female staffers? We're told that his couch is busier than the Long Island Expressway at rush hour.

Mallory was baffled. Clearly the writer was referring to Chad, since there were only a few urban magazines in the city and the other two were run by women.

When she did not respond, Chad snatched the piece from her hand. "I will sue you for slander, you lying little bitch," he exploded.

"What are talking about? I had nothing to do with this," Mallory said, now pissed off herself.

"Don't you stand here and lie to my face. In case you've

forgotten, earlier this week you threatened to go to the press. Am I supposed to believe that this is just some crazy coincidence?"

Mallory stepped closer until she towered above him, forcing him to look up to her. "As much as I'd like to take credit for this, you sorry, pathetic piece of shit, I can't, since I didn't have the nerve to put you in your place, which, by the way, is way beneath me."

"Who the fuck do you think you are, talking to me like that?"

"Let's just say that I'm a better person than you are. I don't have to threaten people to get them to sleep with me."

His mouth opened in disbelief. Then he huffed indignantly, "You are—"

Before he could say *fired*, Mallory stepped even closer to him and said, "Don't bother saying it. I quit!"

So Mallory did not have to make the tough decision that had been haunting her all week, after all. Instead, fate made it for her. That afternoon she called Saxton from home to tell him that she was accepting his job offer.

"That is great news. We have to celebrate!" he exclaimed happily.

"I'm really looking forward to getting started."

"How about we meet at Man Ray for a toast to your new job?"

Mallory paused, then demurred. "No, I don't think so. I have dinner plans tonight."

He assumed that she had a date. "If you'd like, you can bring him along," Saxton challenged.

"It's not a date, Saxton. It's with my girlfriend Beverly."

Saxton sounded relieved. "Perfect. I'm having drinks with a friend, too. Why don't the four of us meet for a quick toast after work, and then you guys can go on with your dinner plans?"

Mallory was still hesitant. Drinks with him was a part of the job she needed to avoid. "I don't know."

"Oh, come on, Mallory. I won't bite you. Besides, it'll give me a chance to give you the lay of the land before your first day."

"Okay, Saxton, but just one drink."

Later, when she and Beverly walked into Man Ray's, heads turned throughout the restaurant. Mallory, as usual, was immaculately groomed and dressed, wearing a pair of black leather hip huggers, with a black fitted sweater and black suede boots. Beverly had on her standard uniform, a smartly tailored navy blue pinstripe suit, a cream silk blouse, and Prada pumps. She looked fashionable but more quietly stylish.

Mallory caught sight of Saxton and his friend Greg, whom she remembered from Atlanta, as she and Beverly walked past the other patrons. She was pleasantly surprised to see Greg, but "pleasant" was hardly a word that described how she felt as she saw Saxton. It took an effort for her to keep her composure. He looked gorgeous in a dark navy suit with an Hermes tie loosened at the neck. He and Greg were engrossed in conversation as they each nursed a cocktail.

"Congratulations!" Saxton said to Mallory as he locked her in a lingering hug.

"Move out of the way, man. You're spoiling the view." Greg pretended to push Saxton aside.

"Greg! I didn't know that you'd be here. It's so good to see you." And she meant it. The few times that Greg had come to Atlanta to hang, the three of them had had a great time. She found him to be quite the charmer, a real ladies' man.

"It's even better to see you," he said, whistling appreciatively.

To quell the blush that was heating up her cheeks, she said, "Saxton, Greg, this is my best friend, Beverly. Beverly, this is my new boss, Saxton, and his friend Greg."

Beverly extended her hand for a firm formal shake. She could do without all the kissy-kissy stuff.

"It must be my lucky day," Greg said, giving her his mack-daddy smile.

"It *was* your lucky day," Beverly replied. She gave him the once-over, not liking that easy smile.

After she shook his hand, he took his back and flexed it rapidly. "That's some grip you've got. Remind me not to do anything to piss you off."

"I don't think you're likely to forget," she said, eyeing him warily.

Her tone made Greg straighten up. "Since you put it that way, I'm sure that I won't."

They took seats in the booths that faced the bar. Saxton and Mallory sat on one side, and Greg and Beverly on the other.

Saxton leaned across the table as if to speak to Beverly confidentially, but whispered for all to hear, "Beverly, you have to excuse my friend Greg here. It's the lobotomy. He really hasn't been the same since."

They all cracked up as Greg stood by taking the butt of the joke. "If it makes you guys feel better to pick on me, be my guest."

Knowing Beverly's dislike of players, Mallory could only imagine what she thought of Greg. She patted his hand affectionately. "Now you two leave Greg alone. As I remember, he can be a lot of fun."

"You got that part right."

The waiter appeared shortly with a bottle of champagne. Of course it was Mallory's favorite, Vueve Clicquot. While the waiter was busy uncorking the bottle, Greg turned to Beverly. "Besides reducing me to tears with your grip, what else do you do?"

"I reduce opponents to tears in court."

"Ohhhh, I see. She's an attorney. I should have known," he said to the table at large.

"Besides whining about a little handshake, what else do you do?" she asked.

"Do you really want to know?" he smiled slyly.

"No, not really," she wisecracked. "I was just making polite conversation." Their laughter was punctuated by the pop of the cork.

Greg sat back in the booth, put off that his charm clearly wasn't working with this one. She wasn't taking him seriously at all. He needed to change his tack. "Actually, I'm a doctor," he offered.

"Oh really?" Beverly was surprised. She was certain that he was one of those boisterous Wall Streeters.

Pleased at the change in her tone, Greg pushed on, using a line that had worked for him hundreds of times since med school. "They call me the Love Doctor." The mack-daddy smile found its way back onto his face.

Beverly rolled her eyes and Mallory cringed. Greg was saying all the wrong things.

"Greg is a gynecologist," Saxton offered, hoping to salvage the conversation.

Beverly shook her head. "You know, that should be against the law."

Greg asked, confused, "What? Me practicing medicine?"

"No, you using that lame-ass line," Beverly said, leaning forward. "What kind of women do you go out with? Because obviously you've used it before and it must have worked, or you wouldn't pull it out for me on 'your lucky day.'"

Ouch, Saxton thought. But Greg had it coming. That was the price he had to pay for always dating airheads. Likewise, Mallory sneaked a peek at Saxton. Beverly was being awfully hard on his boy.

Being speechless was new territory for Greg. He stammered, "Hey, I was just trying to be nice."

"That's funny," Beverly said, "so was I."

To stop the avalanche before it careened all the way downhill, Saxton raised his glass. "I'd like to propose a toast to Mallory." He waited for the others to raise theirs. "Here's to her new position as executive editor of *Spotlight* magazine, and most of all to new beginnings."

"To new beginnings," they all said as they clinked crystal.

Saxton placed his flute to his lips, never removing his eyes from Mallory's. Nor did hers stray from his as they shared the stolen moment. *Yes,* he thought, *to new beginnings* . . .

10

GIRL TALK

Nikki was excited. In fact, she could barely sleep all night. She and DJ were having lunch together at the hip SoHo restaurant Barolo. It wasn't often that they had "dates" outside of a hotel room, so this was a red-letter day for her. Though the reservation was for one o'clock, she'd been dressing and undressing, since nine fifteen that morning. After which she sat at her vanity for over forty-five minutes artfully applying makeup, which gave her lots of time to think, plot, and plan. By the time she turned off the light of the three-times magnifying makeup mirror, not only did she look fabulous, but she also had the makings of a great idea to cause some friction in her lover's relationship.

She sashayed out of her Murray Hill apartment full of optimism. That was what she loved most about New York City: it was always brimming with promise. One day you could be walking down the street a complete nobody, and by happening to be in the right place at the right time, the next thing you know . . . the sky was the limit. She wasn't soaring yet, but her prospects were definitely looking up.

Arriving ahead of DJ, she was quickly shown to a prime table in the hip must-be-seen-in restaurant. After ordering a glass of crisp chardonnay, she quickly adopted the pose of the bored supermodel: blank expression, pouty lips, and casually crossed legs. The facade worked well—until DJ entered the room, causing a stir throughout the restaurant—and as usual between Nikki's now not so casually crossed legs. Heads turned, people whispered, and reverence was granted to the famous Deena Jean Ingram.

"Hi, honey," she said, grazing Nikki's cheek, leaving a trail of Chanel Mademoiselle in her wake. She tossed her Gucci bag into one of the empty chairs.

"You look fabulous," Nikki said, licking her lips.

"You don't look too bad yourself," Deena answered, shedding her wheat cashmere coat.

She and Nikki had met through mutual friends over a year ago at the launch of a new fashion line. At the time Deena was still a local TV star, not the national media celebrity she had since become. On the undercover bisexual circuit Nikki had always heard rumors that Deena rolled both ways, but didn't really believe it until her friend Janice, who was the tube through which lipstick lesbians funneled information, told her in no uncertain terms that Deena loved a good licking, and everyone in her circle knew that that was ultimately another woman's job. After Janice made introductions during the party, Nikki shook Deena's hand warmly, and before letting it go, she leaned in closer and whispered into her ear, "You are so hot." Which was lesbian code for: *I'm definitely interested in the tasting menu.*

Deena gave her a thorough once-over, sizing up the situation. It was critical that no one, outside a small clique of likeminded women—many of whom had as much to lose as she did—know of her bisexuality. She could not risk her family's ever finding out. This was why she trusted Janice, with whom she had attended Wesleyan, to screen her female lovers.

In fact, it was with Janice she had shared her first bisexual experience. The two women had been best friends and roommates beginning freshman year. And like all postadolescent girls, boys were a frequent topic of conversation. But Deena's parents had drilled abstinence from sex so deep into her psyche that she truly believed that if she went all the way with a boy, some alarm would go off and her parents would know right away. Or she would get pregnant, and that would really be the end of the world as she knew it. But these fears did little to suppress her raging hormones. One night she and Janice sneaked out of the dorm to attend a frat party at Northeastern, and while she flirted innocently with a cute prelaw major, Janice disappeared with the star of the basketball team, returning later disheveled, but with a huge grin plastered on her face.

Back in their dorm room, Deena asked her what had happened during her disappearing act.

"Let's just say the boy has other talents . . . besides dribbling a ball." Janice took a deep intake of air through pursed lips, before sliding her filmy nightie over her head.

"Tell me, tell me," Deena insisted. She was already in bed, resting on one elbow, a rapt audience.

Janice walked over to her. "What do you want to know?"

Deena spoke softly. "I want to know what it feels like."

"You mean what *this* feels like?" she asked as she began sensually rubbing her own breasts and squeezing her nipples.

Deena was mesmerized. Sure, she'd had a few masturbation sessions herself, but never had she seen someone else do it. As Deena watched with her lips parted, Janice raised one of her breasts to her lips, licking it lightly through the thin fabric of her nightgown. "Or do you want to know what it *tastes* like?" she asked, never breaking eye contact as she continued to tease her own nipples. Deena was too stunned to answer. Not only was she surprised at the question, but she was equally surprised at its effect between her legs. When she didn't say anything, Janice removed her gown and slid into bed with her. Without another thought, Deena reached out to touch Janice's soft tan skin. Her hands glided over the other woman's body, sending waves of pleasure surging through her own. Janice took Deena's hand in hers and brought them to her full breasts. Deena had never felt anything as amazing in its soft firmness. And the nipple begged to be tasted. When she hesitated, Janice gently pulled Deena's head down to her chest with one hand and lifted her engorged breast toward Deena's open mouth with the other. In no time, Deena was devouring her flesh as she eased one leg between Janice's wet thighs to help stoke the fire that was now burning brightly. When Janice began deftly massaging her throbbing sex, Deena's body was seized by intense pleasure. But this was only the beginning. She then inserted a finger, followed by her tongue into Deena's slick sex, sending her careening into sexual oblivion. This was the beginning of years of nightly sessions. During this time she never felt the need to experiment with boys, so she managed to satisfy her parents and actually graduated a virgin—at least technically.

To this day, she trusted Janice with her secret and always screened potential lovers through her, because it would not do for viewers to know that the picture-perfect TV personality Deena Ingram was really a muff diver. Though Saxton would probably have secretly loved it—what guy wouldn't?—she didn't trust him with her sexual secret either. She would never take the risk of upsetting her image, and he was an important part of it. They were the perfect media couple, she thought: attractive, smart, and educated.

After they had ordered lunch, Nikki said, "You know, we can skip lunch altogether. I can think of something else that I'd much rather munch on than calamari on a bed of greens."

Since their first time together, sex between them had been incredible. Deena tried not to see the same girl too regularly; after all, for her it was only about the sex—she wasn't gay. But something about Nikki always kept her coming back for more. The sexual tension was always a stroke, lick, or erotic conversation away from her pleasure threshold. Plus, she had grown to trust Nikki. If rumors started circulating about her even being out with Nikki, it was a signal that she had a loose tongue, and that was one thing that she could not afford. They had been lovers now for six months without a whisper, and Janice would surely tell her if the word was getting out.

"We'll have to do that another time," she said, reaching across the table to touch Nikki's hand. "I've got to get to the office by three o'clock today. A strategy meeting with Saxton and the boys."

"What's going on?" Nikki asked, hiding her irritation. She nonchalantly sipped her chardonnay as though the intricacies of Deena's business dealings were beyond a snore.

"I've got a national syndication deal on the table."

"Is that a big deal?" she asked innocently.

"Let's just say it's a *really* big deal," Deena answered.

Nikki knew that to gain Deena's full confidence, she must appear uninterested in her business and her money. "So when do we pop the bubbly?"

"Soon, hopefully. Saxton is handling the negotiations."

"I hope he knows what he's doing," Nikki casually remarked.

"He hasn't been wrong yet."

Nikki cocked her head. It was time to implement Phase One. "I know you trust him, and you should, but this is your show and you need to make sure that you're on top of all of the decisions he makes. Not just for the TV show, but for the new magazine as well."

"Why do you say that?"

"You know how testosterone-driven men can be, especially when they're pitted against each other. It becomes a game of who has the bigger dick, and as usual, they end up thinking with the smaller of their two heads. I'd just hate to see you caught short because Saxton has a hard-on for a deal."

Nikki's observation sparked a worry Deena always had about Saxton. "I'm sure he knows exactly what he's doing," she said, but a quick twitch of a facial muscle betrayed her concern.

"It's hard to trust men, you know. Especially where business is concerned. Either they're screwing people for a power trip or trying to screw their coworkers for a little sexual thrill."

"Not Saxton," Deena maintained. "He's one of the good guys."

"Didn't you tell me that he'd hired a new executive editor for the magazine? What does she look like?" Nikki challenged.

"I don't know. She hasn't started yet. I think her first day is Monday."

Nikki flashed a world-weary smile. "If I were you, on G.P., I'd check her out. You know how conniving some women can be. What's her name?"

"Mallory, Mallory Baylor. Apparently she was a hotshot writer for *Heat* magazine."

Nikki's expression turned thoughtful. *"Heat?"* She leaned back and folded her arms across her chest. "Didn't I read something in 'Talk of the Town' last week about the editor-in-chief there having affairs with some of the staff?"

"I don't know." All of a sudden, Deena's expression became very worried.

"It's kind of coincidental that she'd be leaving *Heat* just as this comes out. I'll bet she was getting it on with the editor-in-chief there."

"Let's not jump to any conclusions. Besides, I trust Saxton," Deena said, eager to bury the conversation.

Nikki gave an elaborate shrug. "I'm just saying watch your back—that's all."

After lunch was cleared away, Nikki pulled a festively wrapped gift from a shopping bag under the table. "Here, I brought you something."

"For *moi*?" Deena asked, lightly touching her throat.

"Oui, oui, mademoiselle."

"Très bon." Deena pulled the ends of the gold-and-silver braided bow, a smile spreading across her face. She lifted the top of the box to uncover a bed of lavender tissue paper. Underneath it lay an assortment of edible *panties*, in flavors ranging from chocolate to vanilla and raspberry. "You sure know the way to a girl's heart."

"And sometimes it is through her stomach."

"You got that right."

After Deena settled the check, they walked out onto Broadway, where her driver waited curbside in the Bentley. Electronic running boards slid out for her as he opened the door. "Can I drop you somewhere?"

"No, I think I'll do a little shopping. But call me later." For now at least, Nikki also had reasons not to be seen with Deena too publicly. It certainly wouldn't do for Mallory to find out that she was seeing her new boss's fiancée. Up until the final act, Nikki would have to be careful to direct each scene perfectly.

11

A MEETING OF THE MINDS

As she prepared for her new job the following Monday morning, Mallory felt like the new kid on the first day of school. She'd even done something the night before that she had not done in years. She'd tried on half a dozen outfits to decide which one would set just the right tone for her new position as executive editor at *Spotlight* magazine. Even Nikki, who was at first shocked upon learning of the job offer, was excited for her. When Mallory confided to her that she was thinking about declining it, Nikki, much to her surprise, had almost insisted that Mallory reconsider, saying that she shouldn't let a past relationship stand in the way of her career.

"How does this look?" Mallory had asked Nikki as she admired herself in the full-length mirror in the corner of her room.

"It's a little conservative for me," Nikki said. Mallory was wearing a black knee-length fitted skirt, a bolero-styled matching jacket, and black-and-tan Prada spectator pumps.

"Then it's probably just right." Mallory laughed.

Nikki was lying on Mallory's bed on her stomach, resting her chin in the palm of her hand. "So will you be working closely with Deena?"

"Probably not. I get the feeling that she concentrates on TV production and Saxton handles the other aspects of the business."

"So that means that you'll be working closely with Saxton?" Nikki asked, eyeing her closely.

"I'll actually be reporting to the editor-in-chief, a guy by the name of Eric Handley. He was an editor at *People* and at *Vogue*."

"But you will be working with Saxton."

"I get the feeling that *Spotlight* is his baby, so I'm sure that he'll be somewhat hands-on."

"It's the 'hands-on' part that you'll have to worry about."

Mallory came close to a blush when she remembered one point during their evening at Man Ray's. Saxton had leaned back into the booth, spreading his legs. When his thigh met hers, for a moment she let them linger together, enjoying the intimate contact, and remembering the hot passion that they'd shared. As she became warm under the snugness of her sweater, she snapped herself back into reality and abruptly pulled her leg away. "I don't think so. This relationship will be nothing but professional."

"Are you saying that you no longer have feelings for him?" Nikki gave her a penetrating stare.

Mallory returned it without wavering. "That's exactly what I'm saying."

"Well, let's just hope he's on the same page."

"I'm sure there'll be nothing to worry about," Mallory said. Unable to meet Nikki's eyes any longer, she began undressing to hang up her outfit for the next day. She only wished that she were as certain of her feelings about Saxton as she sounded.

The next morning, when she walked into the office, she was greeted by Cindy, who gave her a tour of Ingram Enterprises. The space was divided into two sections: one side was all television-related, while business affairs, administration, and other interests, which were Saxton's domain, formed the other side. After the tour, Mallory was shown to her own office, which was a few doors down from Saxton's. Eric's was between them. The proximity to Saxton was a little too close for comfort, she thought distractedly. She only hoped that the bricks, mortar, and people in between them would be enough of a buffer.

Mallory's office was more splendid than any of the offices at *Heat* had been, even Chad's. It had hardwood floors with a Persian rug and walls that were covered in a rich grass cloth. There was also a small powder room with a mini wet bar and closet. Her spacious mahogany desk and credenza had already been carefully stocked with supplies. She even had a view of the Empire State Building.

Once she was settled in, there was a knock at her door. "Come in."

"Just checking to see if you needed anything." Saxton stood in the doorway looking as if he'd stepped off the pages of *GQ* magazine.

Mallory gave him a broad smile. "No, this is great."

"Glad you like it. This used to be Deena's office, before we expanded and took over the other side of the floor for the TV department."

Talk about too close for comfort, she thought. "It's really very nice."

He was about to turn to leave when he stopped. "Eric will be in the office later. I'm sure that he'll want to begin discussing the editorial calendar."

"Good. I've got some ideas that I'm anxious to share with him."

"Cool. I'm sure that you two will work well together." Before he turned to leave again, he said, "Welcome aboard."

"Thanks," Mallory said, watching him disappear. *Well, that was professional enough*, she thought, not without a tinge of disappointment. *Maybe we can make this work, after all.*

A few minutes later there was another knock at her door. This time when she said, "Come in," she was greeted with the presence of her new editor-in-chief, Eric Handley.

"Don't you look chic," he said, crossing the room in quick, long strides. "I'm Eric. Eric Handley." Not bothering with a handshake, he air-kissed both sides of her face. He was six feet two inches, with a graceful carriage and slender, elegant features. He wore a tangerine orange cotton shirt with navy pin-stripes under a four-button jacket and tight flat-front pants. Only a few men could ever think of pulling off that kind of outfit, and Eric wore it well.

"I'm Mallory Baylor. It's so good to finally meet you," she said, smiling.

"My darling," Eric drawled, "we are going to have a great time working together. We'll produce a first-rate magazine and we'll have a ball doing it." He had a way of speaking as if his complete thought had to be expelled in one long ex-haled breath. This brought a sense of drama to everything that he said.

"I'm looking forward to it."

"Why don't we head to the conference room? We can start developing an editorial strategy and begin discussing personnel."

"That sounds great," Mallory answered as she turned to pick up a portfolio, her planner, and a pen.

They were heading out of her office door when Saxton walked in with his hands in his pockets. "I see you two have met."

"Yes, we have," Eric answered. "And I have to tell you, you have great taste in personnel."

"Just wanted to make sure you two had gotten together," Saxton said smoothly. "Let me know if you need anything."

For the next three hours, Eric and Mallory hashed out a preliminary editorial calendar that would be interesting, provocative, and entertaining. Finding the right balance was one of the toughest jobs an editor did. They both agreed that, because they were producing an upscale urban lifestyle publi-cation, they had to provide insightful analysis of popular cul-ture and current events, as well as to be on the cutting edge of fashion and trends. And of course, celebrity coverage was an important component of any lifestyle publication.

"It could be interesting if we chose a celebrity for each

issue and had Deena conduct the interview," Mallory said. "She could tape it, and we could write and edit the piece. We could also have the subject shot both alone, and with Deena."

"I love that idea. We could call it Deena's Dish, or something like that. It could really be a draw to boost circulation, especially for those millions that already watch her show." Eric's brow knitted in thought, as he ran the format through the creative circuits of his mind.

"The key will be to make sure that each interview uncovers some juicy piece of information that was previously unknown to the public," Mallory added, nibbling on the end of a pencil, an unconscious habit that she'd had since grade school. "People are sick of reading the same overexposed, rehashed facts about celebrities."

"I like that," Eric said, quickly nodding his head. "We'll make it edgy, give them something to talk about."

Mallory was in heaven. This was how editorial discussions were supposed to go. With Chad, if it wasn't his idea, there was no way that he would ever go along with it.

After ordering out for lunch, they worked through the afternoon. Later, as they packed up their materials, they were enthusiastic about the direction in which they were going. "Mallory, I can tell already that it's going to be a pleasure working with you."

After only a day, she felt as if she had known Eric for years. "Thanks, Eric. I'm really looking forward to it." She gathered her things to head back to her office. "See you tomorrow."

She was grabbing her coat and purse a few minutes later when Saxton suddenly appeared in her office doorway. "How did things go today?" he asked, resting his forearm on the doorframe. He had rolled up his sleeves, and she could see the dark hair lightly sprinkled on his thickly veined arms. A sexy five o'clock shadow was covering his jawline, giving him a rugged look that would have been hard for any girl to resist.

"It was great," she said, still glowing from the high of a great creative session. "Eric is awesome."

"So are you," Saxton said with a quiet sincerity.

Embarrassed, though she was not quite sure why, Mallory shifted her weight from one foot to the other. "I'd better get going," she said, glancing nervously at her wristwatch. She was silently deriding herself for feeling, if not acting, like a silly schoolgirl who was standing at her locker next to the one guy that she had a crush on.

Saxton made way for her to pass through the door, never taking his eyes from her. As she headed down the hall he called, "Good night, Mallory. I'll see you tomorrow."

"Good night," she said.

As she walked away, the snug pencil skirt and her long legs gave Saxton even more to think about. Then he shook himself free of where his mind was heading. Given all that he had at stake, both professionally and personally, he vowed to view her as just another employee, nothing more and nothing less.

12

THE QUEEN BEE STINGS

Deena lay in bed going over a stack of reports and memos that had piled high in her in box during the last week. Fortunately, she never had to pay too much attention to business affairs—that was Saxton's territory—but on rare occasions she would delve into the inner workings of the company. And now seemed like a good time, since they were in the middle of launching a magazine and negotiating a syndication deal. While she was looking over the circulation projections for *Spotlight*, her mind wandered to its new executive editor, Mallory Baylor.

Nikki's comments about her promiscuous behavior with her editor-in-chief at *Heat* had definitely stuck in Deena's craw, contrary to her cool and collected response. She was no fool. She realized that women fawned over Saxton all the time. So it was not beyond the realm of her imagination that this Mallory chick might try to put in some overtime. She was probably the type who'd expect to have any man at her beck and call. The best offense was a good defense, so Deena decided she would make her position clear with Ms. Mallory right away. For now, though, she figured she'd best make it clear in her own bedroom.

She listened as the shower stopped and put the stack of papers aside, then removed her reading glasses. When Saxton walked out of the bathroom with only a towel wrapped around his neck, still moist from the shower, she tossed the covers back, revealing a new French lace teddy she'd purchased earlier from La Petite Coquette.

"Let me get a closer look at that," she purred, reaching up to grab the towel to pull him closer.

A coy smile played on his lips. "How close of a look do you want?" he asked. Aroused, he edged closer to the bed and to her face, which was now hovering at crotch level. He was surprised by the fact that she was, for once, initiating sex.

She answered by taking him into her mouth, sucking as deeply as her throat would allow, before beginning a massaging action with her throat and cheeks, stopping occasionally to tease the underside of him with the tip of her tongue. Initially Saxton stood still, with his hips pushed forward to allow her fuller access, but before long he began thrusting back and forth, joining the rhythm that she had started. When she began to hum against him, the vibrations drove him in even deeper, thrusting harder. He grabbed her hair and took control of the pace, before throwing his head back and releasing himself into her accommodating throat.

Deena swallowed every drop. Though she definitely had a thing for women, there was nothing quite like the power of a man, especially one as well put together as Saxton, to really turn her out. One of the things that she really loved about him was his remarkable recovery after an orgasm. So she nuzzled his weighty balls until she felt a renewed stirring above them. When he was again at full mast, she turned over to accept her prize. With her face buried in the crumpled sheets, she moaned deeply as he inserted his rock-hard cock between her legs. The feeling was rapturous as he massaged her on that special spot, holding on to her hips to make sure that his placement was right on the mark. Before long, she was bucking back and forth to meet his firm strokes, her sex quivering as she orgasmed over and over again. It was exquisite. If she could combine Saxton's prowess with Nikki's tongue, she thought dreamily, she'd have a patentable solution for the best sex ever.

After recovering, she reached for her bathrobe. "I heard your new executive editor started today," she said casually.

"Yep, I think she and Eric will be an awesome team." He was stretched out on the bed with his arm behind his head, catching his breath.

"Maybe, but I do think you should have let me interview her before you hired her." Deena was passing her fingers through her hair, fluffing out the sweaty mats that followed a good lay.

Saxton was taken by surprise. Deena never got involved in personnel decisions. "What? You've never done that before. Why now?" He turned on his side to face her.

She continued running her fingers through her hair, not making eye contact. "This is a critical time for us. You know, with the syndication deal and all. Every decision that we make could affect the outcome. And of course, the executive editor will help shape the overall tone of my magazine."

The "my magazine" part did not pass unnoticed. "What about the editor-in-chief? Eric's the person who will control the direction of the magazine." He was trying to figure out where this was coming from and, more important, where it was headed.

"I already know Eric," she said, tying the sash of her robe. "He interviewed me once when he was with *Vogue*."

Saxton lay back again. "Trust me, we are lucky to get Mallory. She was a key person at *Heat* magazine."

Deena stood over him, with her hands on her hips. "Was she an editor?"

Saxton kept a poker face. "No, a writer."

"A feature writer?" Now her weight was shifted to one side, arms folded.

"No," Saxton answered, his tone growing impatient, "although she wrote feature articles."

"How did you meet her?"

He paused a beat before answering. "She wrote the piece on me for *Heat* magazine. The one that got so much attention."

She cocked her head to one side. "That's a little strange, don't you think, for an editor-in-chief to allow a staff writer to do feature stories? I wonder how she managed to pull that off."

"What do you mean?" Saxton finally sat up, knowing that Deena was on the scent now.

"Well, there were rumors that Chad, the editor-in-chief there, was sleeping with a few of his female staffers. I'm just wondering if that's how Mallory managed to get ahead." She fixed him with a penetrating gaze.

Saxton reached for his bath towel, avoiding her eyes. Actually, he'd prefer to avoid the entire subject altogether. "I doubt that. She is totally professional."

"I just hope that you will be, too."

That remark stung him. "What do you mean by that?"

"Just that it's virtually unheard of for a person to go from a staff writer's position to executive editor. I just hope that people don't start questioning your motives."

He was close to losing his temper, but decided to play it cool instead. "It's all about ability, and based on what I've seen, Mallory is more than qualified to do the job."

"I guess we'll see," Deena said. She was satisfied. She had made her point very clear. She was about to head into the bathroom, but stopped and said, "By the way, how's the syndication deal coming along?"

Saxton relaxed. This was territory he felt comfortable with. "Fine. In fact, Monday I got the preliminary deal points from FBC."

"How do they look?"

"Not bad. But not as good as I want them to be," he said. He then relayed some of the more pertinent points of the deal to her.

"Saxton, that sounds pretty good to me." The deal they were offering would be worth ninety million dollars annually to Ingram Enterprises. As far as she was concerned, they should sign on the dotted line—quickly.

"We can get a lot more than that," he insisted. For him the deal wasn't all about the money, but about extracting every possible advantage from a negotiation. After reviewing the angles over the past few weeks, Saxton had finally come up with a position that would assure him the best possible outcome. Historically, whenever Deena's show aired in a different market, the ratings always increased for the time slot, which enabled the network to charge higher advertising rates. The increase was because her format consistently drew a middle- to upper-middle-class audience, both black and white. These viewers, particularly the black ones, represented a segment of the population many advertisers were clamoring to reach. Everything that Deena and he had slaved for over the last four years was to set up this opportunity.

Deena eyed him questioningly. "Are you sure we should pass on that?"

"We're not passing. We're simply negotiating for more favorable terms."

"If you can get the per-segment offer up, I think we should take it."

"Deena," he said with a harder edge, "that's not where the long-term revenue stream will be. It's in advertising."

"Let's just get the deal done," she said, before heading into the bathroom and closing the door.

The next day Saxton was reflecting on that conversation when a counteroffer from FBC came across his fax. He had floated the idea of sharing in incremental advertising revenue in the last meeting and fully expected it to be included in any future offers. But it wasn't there. This latest proposal merely sweetened the per-segment revenue. He summoned Cindy into his office. "I just received an amendment to the syndication offer. It came to my personal fax. I need you to get it to Tom ASAP." Tom was his head of legal affairs.

"Does this change your position? Should I arrange a meeting between you two to discuss strategy?"

He was a little annoyed. "No," he answered firmly. "My position's the same. Tell Tom to review the proposal and build an even stronger argument for sharing incremental advertising revenue."

After removing the document from the fax machine, Cindy walked over to the small copier in his office.

"What are you doing?"

"I'm making a quick copy to run over to Hazelle." Important documents were routinely copied to a file for Deena's secretary to keep her informed on business issues. Everyone knew that Deena rarely bothered to read them, even when she made a production of coming into the office, but they were copied and filed nonetheless.

"Wait." His eyes met Cindy's. "No, don't bother copying it." It would be just his luck that Deena would decide to read the file now that a big deal was on the table, and he didn't need another obstacle—especially an unnecessary one, since Deena knew nothing about business or negotiating. She would be quick to jump at the extra per-segment money they were tossing around, but he knew where the real money was. By taking this approach, it would mean an additional revenue stream worth approximately twenty million dollars annually, while the increase they offered per segment was only an additional five million.

Cindy was surprised by Saxton's decision. She thought for sure that he would want Deena to know that the offer had been sweetened.

"I know what you're thinking, but I know what I'm doing. Deena can be very emotional where business is concerned. This is good for TV ratings, but can hamper a deal. So I'd rather Deena—"

Before he could finish his sentence, the devil herself breezed into his office. With a long honey sable flowing in her wake, she sailed past Cindy as if she didn't exist. She headed straight to her fiancé, whom she gave a too-sexy-for-the-office kiss. "So what was it that you'd rather I do?"

For a split second time stood still, as Cindy and Saxton each racked their brains for an innocent way out of this dicey situation. To buy time Saxton walked calmly over to his credenza to straighten a file he'd tossed there earlier. "Oh, we were discussing ratings, and I was just saying to Cindy that you are on the right track by concentrating on the proclivities of Middle America, and that I'd rather you continue to do that than to ever try to compete with the rubberneckers some of the other talk shows cater to."

"There's no way that I'll ever stoop to their level," Deena said.

Cindy finally took a breath, relieved that Deena bought the lie. She quietly retreated from the office, but not before a conspiratorial glance passed between Saxton and her.

After Cindy was gone, Deena wrapped her arms around Saxton's neck to pull him closer for another kiss, leaving him, for the second time in two days, surprised at her show of affection. When she felt the familiar stirrings in his pants, she grabbed a fistful and whispered in his ear, "Save that for later, baby," and gave him a final kiss.

Now that she had handled matters on that front, she turned and headed out the door to pay a visit to the new executive editor. She needed to put Mallory on notice.

Mallory was at her desk, reviewing the art direction for the premier issue, when the door opened abruptly, without a knock. She looked up to see Deena stroll in as though she owned the place, which in fact she did.

"You must be Mallory," was Deena's greeting. No hello, welcome aboard, or any other pleasantry.

"Yes, I am. It's a pleasure to meet you." She smiled as she stood to greet Deena with an outstretched hand.

Deena ignored the offer of a handshake and simply took the chair opposite Mallory's desk and crossed her legs. "I'd like to be able to say the same."

Her comment stopped Mallory short, giving Deena the chance to give her the complete once-over from head to toe. It was obvious from the sneer that settled on her features that she did not like what she saw.

"Excuse me?" Mallory said.

"I'll be frank with you," Deena said, leaning forward in her chair. "I heard about your past at *Heat*, and I just want you to know that that sort of thing will not be tolerated here."

Mallory was genuinely perplexed. She had no idea what Deena was referring to. "I'm sorry, but there must be some mistake."

"The only mistake that I'm aware of at the moment is the fact that Saxton hired you to begin with. In this company, there will be no exchange of sexual favors for advancement, so don't even think about it."

Mallory was mortified that Deena would accuse her of sleeping with anyone for advancement. Deena Ingram or not, there was no way she would stand there and take that kind of shit. "Listen, Deena, I don't know where you got your information, but I suggest that you check your facts. I've never slept with anyone to get ahead."

"I'm not going to sit here and debate this with you. Just consider this a warning." She stood up and walked to within six inches of Mallory's face. "And I'm assuming, since you wrote the article on Saxton, that you are aware that we are engaged. So keep your hands off!" she said, raising her voice.

"What's going on in here?" They both turned to the door, where Saxton was frowning.

Deena headed toward him on her way out. "Nothing at all. I was simply welcoming Mallory to the company and making sure that she understood a few of our policies. That's all." She looked back at Mallory, nodding grimly before turning again to Saxton. "I have a two o'clock meeting with the producer, but wanted to go over a few ideas beforehand. Do you have a minute?" She ushered him out of the doorway and down the hall, leaving a bewildered Mallory behind.

Mallory nearly staggered back to her desk chair, stung by the attack from the queen bee. What kind of woman had Saxton decided to marry? she wondered. She was pondering what had just happened when her phone rang, startling her back to reality.

"Mallory, there's a Mr. Morris on line one. He said it was personal."

All thoughts of her job predicament vanished. Mallory quickly snatched the phone up. "Mr. Morris?"

"Hi, Mallory. Got some news for you."

Mallory's heart began to race. "What is it?"

"I just got a lead on the Browns."

13

A CHILLY RECEPTION

Mallory lay immersed in warm sudsy bathwater, a liquid cocoon lightly perfumed with a creamy dose of Annick Goutal's bath gel. Even with the addition of six flickering candles to frame the tub's edge, Mallory still had trouble relaxing her mind, body, and soul. What had started out as an ordinary Friday had somehow flipped to a soap opera before turning into a mystery. Fortunately for her, Mr. Morris's phone call did give her some answers about the Brown family's whereabouts, but unfortunately, the answers he gave were more troubling than the questions.

When she had first met the Browns, her impression was of a respectable African-American couple living the American Dream in South Orange, New Jersey, minus the 2.5 kids, since they were unable to have children. Mr. Brown was a well-mannered, bespectacled accountant, and his wife was a kindergarten teacher who was heavily involved in community service. After Mallory took the connecting train rides from Philly to their elegant four-bedroom Victorian house, they discussed, over tea and biscotti, the reasons why the family was suited to adopt her son.

At the time the choice seemed obvious. They were both well-educated pillars of their community, and they seemed to be genuinely nice people. Mallory left their home certain that her child, whom they later named Dylan, would be safe. Though after the adoption she had missed him sorely, she'd never once worried about his well-being—that is, until the Browns abruptly disappeared. It never made sense to her that two upstanding citizens with roots and family in the community would disappear without a trace, but that was exactly what happened.

Her conversation today with Mr. Morris confirmed her concerns. The detective discovered that the company where Mr. Morris had been employed, Tri-State Trucking, was being investigated for laundering large sums of drug money through the accounting books. To her horror, she also learned it had strong mob ties. Fourteen months ago, he reported, right after the Feds began their investigation, the Browns took off, but not before stashing away a half million dollars of ill-gotten gains. Not only was the federal government searching for them, but worse, so was the mob.

Mr. Morris, a former FBI agent who ran his own surveillance company, told her not to worry, since he had excellent contacts from his days in the Bureau. He also assured her that his informants would keep him posted on any developments and, most important, that he would find Dylan. Mallory closed her eyes and prayed that he was right. She only wished that she could pick up the phone and call her mom to hear her soothing voice tell her that everything would be okay. But this burden was hers to bear alone, since no one else knew of Dylan's existence.

As she sat soaking, her mind drifted to another source of her bubbling anxiety: Deena Ingram. The warning salvo that had been fired across her desk earlier had hit its mark. Mallory was infuriated that Deena assumed that she had slept with Chad and, worse yet, had plans to sleep with Saxton. The woman really had a lot of nerve. Mallory considered telling Saxton exactly what happened. In the end, though, she decided not to. She did not want to look like a helpless female running to him because Deena had thrown a hissy fit. No, she would handle it herself and hope that the whole ordeal would blow over once Deena saw that her only priority was putting out a great magazine. Still troubled, she stepped out of the tub and toweled off. Ironically, she had to get ready for Saxton and Deena's engagement party.

Going to this gala was the last thing on earth that she wanted to do tonight. She had been planning to skip it until Eric convinced her that not showing up would send the wrong signal to Deena. After she confided in him about Deena's outburst, he advised her to grin and bear it, at least for an hour. She should give the happy couple her well wishes and then be on her way.

After reluctantly agreeing with him, she had called Nikki to see if she wanted to come along as her guest. Nikki had declined, giving some excuse about an early shoot the next morning. Mallory was surprised that she had not jumped at the chance, since this was just the sort of kissy-face celebrity soiree Nikki usually clamored to get into. She then called Beverly, who was thankfully in town, and after much cajoling on Mallory's part, she agreed to go with her.

Mallory stepped out of her cab at Cipriani downtown wearing an elegant little cocktail dress by Armani. It was simple, yet on her it was stunning. Her hair was chicly styled and her makeup, light and flawless. She looked fabulous without appearing as though she were trying at all. This was a well-dressed woman's best-kept secret.

Beverly was pacing back and forth outside the entrance, looking impatient. As Mallory walked up, she said, "It's about time."

Mallory smiled and shook her head. Beverly was your classic type-A personality. "Let's get inside and get you a drink," she said, looping her arm through Beverly's.

Beverly, who had her hair straight to the shoulders and flipped at the ends, was wearing a cream wool evening suit and double strands of pearls. Her look was always classy but conservative, so the skirt was two inches past her knee, hiding a set of legs that would have made Tina Turner jealous.

Tonight, Cipriani was home to the Who's Who of East Coast high society. It was swirling with elite African-Americans from Boston, D.C., Maryland, and New York, important politicians, including former president Bill Clinton, and celebrities in media, sports, film, and music. And this was just the engagement party, Mallory thought. She could only imagine what the wedding would be like.

Eric spotted them across the room and worked his way through the throng of guests. "Mallory, as usual you look fabulous," he said as he kissed both cheeks.

"Thank you," she replied, straightening the white silk hankie in his jacket pocket. "Eric, I'd like you to meet my best friend, Beverly. Beverly, this is our editor-in-chief and resident bon vivant, Eric Handley."

As the two exchanged greetings, Mallory took in the scene before her. The dining room was like a large fishbowl, with an impressive collection of exotic specimens swimming elegantly about. Hundreds of hybrid long-stemmed white roses were artfully arranged in magnificent sprays throughout the regal room. Draped overhead was a silk banner that read: CONGRATULATIONS DEENA AND SAXTON!

They glanced over at the bride-to-be holding court with her parents over a coterie of spectators that included the mayor and a senator. A network camera crew battled with *Access Hollywood* and *Extra* to get every shot. "You'd think that her father was the guest of honor," Beverly remarked. They watched as Judge Ingram gestured grandly, entertaining his audience with tales of court battles won single-handedly.

"That's one family that sure knows how to work the press," Mallory said, watching the action unfold.

"I don't get it." Eric shook his head. "Saxton seems like a really nice guy. I just don't see him wrapped up in all this bourgeois bullshit." He removed an elegant silver flask from the breast pocket of his Ferre evening suit and took a discreet sip.

"I didn't know this was BYOB," Beverly said.

"I only drink single-malt scotch, and I don't rely on other

people to have it handy," Eric remarked, turning up his nose, "even if they are the Boston Ingrams."

"I hear ya," Mallory said, smiling.

"Back to my observation," Eric said. "I just don't see him with her."

At that moment Saxton joined the group that included his fiancée and in-laws. The tight circle expanded to welcome him in. After all, Saxton was the perfect addition. He was handsome, brilliant, and accomplished—oh, and he had a degree from Harvard.

"No comment," was all Mallory had to say. Though she knew that staying away from Saxton was in her best interest, a wave of melancholy still came over her. He was the father of her child, and a man she was once very much in love with, and here she was celebrating his engagement to another woman. To make matters worse, it was Deena, the Bitch from Hell.

"You don't have to be coy with me, Mallory. I've noticed since day one how you two look at each other." When Mallory's head turned quickly in alarm, he added, "Don't worry. It's not that obvious. It's just that I can smell an attraction a mile away. Even when it's not aimed at me."

"That was all in the past," Mallory said, feeling panicked.

"Isn't that too bad?"

"Here's my favorite executive editor," a voice boomed from behind her. Mallory turned to see Greg with a bosomy honey-blonde on his arm.

"Hi, Greg," she said, greeting him with a hug. "This is Eric Handley, and of course, you remember Beverly."

"How could I forget?" he answered, rubbing his right hand with his left, as though it still stung from her strong grip.

Beverly rolled her eyes.

"This is Candy," he said, introducing his date to the group. "This is Mallory, Eric, and Attila the Honey, oh, I mean, Beverly."

"Sarcasm doesn't become you," Beverly replied. "The less

gifted among us," she added, looking at his bland-eyed date, "might not even understand it."

"To quote the famous philosopher Rodney King, can't we all just get along?" Mallory teased.

"That's easy for him to say," Greg snarled. "He's not taking the beating that I'm getting from your girl." His date just bobbed her head back and forth, as though she were having a hard time following the verbal volleys.

"Don't fool yourself," Beverly said. "The kid gloves are still on."

She abruptly turned her back to him to talk with Eric. In reply, Greg put his hands on his hips and mouthed an imitation of her sassiness behind her back. Mallory watched it all with a curious smile. Could it be . . . ?

The music paused as Judge Ingram made his way toward the stage that had been erected in the center of the room. All around him parted to make way. All glasses stopped clinking, and conversations drew to a discreet close as the distinguished judge approached the microphone.

"Good evening, ladies and gentlemen," his baritone voice rang out. "Ingrid and I would like to personally thank all of you for joining us tonight in celebration of the engagement of my beautiful daughter, Deena, to a fine young man, Saxton McKensie." On cue, applause rang out as Deena and Saxton approached the stage hand in hand. Deena was beaming with joy. She wore a white silk Isaac Mizrahi tuxedo suit and white silk Blahniks. Her long hair was swept elegantly into a pile on top of her head. Saxton looked regal in a tailored Italian-cut suit with a white hankie in his breast pocket.

When they reached the stage, Deena grabbed the microphone and said, "Saxton and I would also like to thank you all for sharing this wonderful occasion with us." She turned to face him. "When two people love each other as much as we do, it only makes sense to want to share it with the world." She then leaned over for a showy kiss. As she did, Mallory thought that she detected the slightest withdrawal from Saxton. She remembered how much he shied away from public displays of affection. Then Deena continued. "I'd also like to thank my father, the Honorable Judge Paul Ingram, for hosting tonight in our honor." She kissed her father on the cheek, and Saxton shook his hand. As the trio descended the platform with Deena in the middle, the orchestra again began to play. Hordes of admirers swarmed over to greet the power couple.

Eric grabbed Mallory's hand. "We have to be politically correct. Let's go over and pay our respects."

"I suppose you're right."

She took a deep breath and followed Eric into the eye of the storm. At its center stood Deena, smiling expansively for the cameras and her audience, just like on TV. When she saw that the next guest in queue was Mallory, her smile seemed to freeze for a frame, but being the professional that she was, she kept her act together. "Mallory, it's so good of you to come."

"Thanks for inviting me." Before she stepped away, Mallory added, "I wish you and Saxton the very best."

Through gritted teeth, Deena replied, "I'm sure that you do."

14

STOLEN MOMENTS

Over the next couple of weeks, Saxton was able to focus almost entirely on the FBC deal, knowing that Eric and Mallory had things well under control with *Spotlight*. They were close to closing the first issue, which was shaping up to be a big hit with advertisers. They had completed an incredible fashion shoot called "The Producers;" it highlighted some of the hottest music production teams since the eighties, all dressed in couture and shot by the famous photographer Leon Bratsworth on a Broadway stage, in homage to the hit play named *The Producers*. The issue would also run insightful articles covering everything from the current-day robber barons on Wall Street to African-American athletes' impact on historically lily-white sports. The only piece that was missing was Deena's interview with Blondie, which was scheduled for that afternoon.

Blondie, who was a dark-skinned brick house with a waist-length blond weave, had hit the rap scene two years earlier, backed by a less than savory group of music producers and rappers. While her vocal ability was marginal at best, her lyrics, edgy tracks, and sizzling personality struck a chord with the urban audience. Now she was releasing a feature film with Will Smith and had an album at the top of the charts, along with a shelf full of industry awards. Only in America.

On the FBC front, Saxton and his executive team had done a thorough job preparing for the final negotiations by compiling the ratings and subsequent increases in advertising that Deena's show had demonstrated to date, market by market. They even looked at similar data for comparable shows, which didn't come close to matching Deena's increases. The statistics told a compelling story: *The Ingram Hour*'s demographic profile was a sure hit with advertisers, which inevitably led to an increase in rates for the network. Based on this theory, Saxton felt perfectly justified in asking for a piece of the pie. But so far it had been a tough sell to FBC. They had barely budged from their last position, giving up only small concessions regarding future rights. Regardless, Saxton decided, he would hold firm to his bid for advertising revenues.

After months of positioning, posturing, and repositioning, he had to be ready for prime time tomorrow. He and the big brass at FBC were finally meeting to come to terms on the syndication deal. If Saxton had his way, the deal would not only be a milestone, but would probably change the way syndication deals were negotiated altogether. It would certainly be written about in the *Wall Street Journal*, *Business Week*, and perhaps even *Crain's*.

About two o'clock that afternoon, Deena stormed into Saxton's office. "Remind me to never agree to interview a rapper again in my life," she muttered, flinging her mink coat across his sofa.

"What are you talking about?" he asked, not looking up from his work.

"The interview with Blondie was a fiasco. Not only was she a blithering idiot, but her manager was more of a gangster than any so-called professional that I've ever met!"

"What?"

"These rap people are nothing but a bunch of hoodlums. I can't believe that Mallory had me interview one of them." She plopped down on the sofa with her arms folded across her chest.

"Aside from the fact that Blondie isn't your everyday BAP,

how did the interview go?" Saxton asked, trying to keep the impatience out of his voice.

Deena made a face. "Let's just put it this way: the moment her manager left the room, she pulled out a joint and proceeded to get as high as Mount Everest."

Saxton was shocked. He sat up in his chair. "That must have been an interesting interview. What did she talk about?"

"Oh, your usual business issues," Deena said sarcastically. "You know, what assholes her label executives were—she even said that Clyde Donovan, the CEO of Noon Records, wouldn't know a hit if it fell on his head. Then she went on to trash Lil' Kim, Foxy Brown, and Eve."

"Wow," Saxton said. "That should sell some issues."

"It may, but this is the last time that I'll ever interview any of those rap people. Make sure you tell Ms. Mallory that."

Saxton tried to reason with her. "If you're going to interview *Spotlight* cover subjects, let's face it, you're going to have to deal with people who you may not necessarily invite to dinner. This is a lifestyle, celebrity-driven magazine, remember?"

The tight pout on her face didn't change. She wouldn't say a word. Finally, giving up, Saxton focused his attention back on the spreadsheet in front of him.

"What's that?" she asked, getting up to lean across his desk.

"It's the ratings comparisons for *The Ingram Hour* for tomorrow's meeting."

"How's it coming?"

"It looks good. I think we have an excellent argument."

"Let's not lose sight of the main objective," she said imperiously, "which is to get the deal done."

"Don't worry about that. They want the deal as badly as we do," Saxton insisted.

"I hope you're right," Deena said as she grabbed her coat and headed for the door. "I want this done."

Mallory peered through the doorway with a fresh-off-the-press copy of *Spotlight* in her hand. The thick glossy magazine had just been couriered over. Mallory had seen the light burning under the door and decided to take the opportunity to show Saxton the premier issue.

"Are you still here?"

Saxton was so absorbed in his thoughts that he didn't hear the knock on his door. He sat reclined in his office swivel chair relaxing with a glass of wine. It was nine thirty at night, usually his quiet time, a time when no one else was in the office except for him.

Startled, he leaned forward abruptly, spilling the red wine right down the front of his white shirt.

"I'm so sorry," she said, rushing toward him. She grabbed several tissues from the box on his credenza. Without thinking she stooped down to begin dabbing his chest in an effort to absorb some of the red stain.

He was about to say, "Don't worry about it," but her caressing touch caused him to swallow deeply.

When she became conscious of how intimate it was to be rubbing his chest, her breath caught in her throat. She knew instinctively that she should pull away from him, but like a frightened animal she froze. Her mind was telling her to go, but her body was strongly suggesting she stay. Before she could react, Saxton held her hand against his chest, cupping it under his. He searched her eyes to make sure she too felt the electricity coursing between them. He could hardly catch his breath.

She inhaled the citrus in his aftershave, mixed with the natural scent of the man himself, one that she remembered all too well from those hot summer nights in Atlanta. She saw the desire smoldering in his eyes. She felt the strong pulse of his heart as it pounded wildly against the palm of her hand.

A force he was powerless to resist pulled him to her. Saxton lightly stroked her cheek, savoring the soft dewy texture of her skin. Drawing her closer, he tasted her slightly parted lips. Even though he seemed to be moving in slow motion, Mallory could not have stopped him if she'd wanted to. Nor could she stop herself from opening her mouth to taste his. A wave of desire washed through her as his probing tongue teased and taunted her own.

Her hand traveled northward from his chest, around his shoulder to caress the back of his neck, holding on to him, not letting go. For the first time in years, Mallory felt alive all over; she was tingly, light-headed, ethereal. How could something that felt so right to her body be so completely wrong? As that thought flickered through her hazy consciousness, she stiffened and pulled away from him.

"No, no . . ." she said, still breathless from the passionate kiss.

Her sudden movement and barely uttered words snapped Saxton back to the present moment. Still panting lightly, he said, "Mallory, I'm sorry. I don't know what happened."

She rose to her feet, dropping the wine-stained tissue on his desk. "I have to leave," she said more to herself than to him. She'd forgotten why she had come into his office to begin with. Then she spotted the issue of *Spotlight* magazine, which she'd tossed onto his desk in her frantic haste to grab the Kleenex.

He saw the discarded magazine at the same time that she did. "Is this it?" he asked, picking it up. He was happy for a diversion from the heat of the passion that they had just shared.

Mallory, running her fingers through her tousled hair, became conscious that her lipstick must be smeared across her mouth—at least what was not smeared around his. "Um, yeah. It was couriered over tonight. I came in to show it to you."

Saxton begin flipping through the slick, glossy pages. "This is really well done!" he said. He scanned the familiar layouts avidly, trying to distract himself from the lingering feel of her soft lips, the sweetness of her touch.

"I'm glad you like it." Mallory smiled in spite of the uneasiness that still hung in the air. All of their hard work had paid off. The publication was really an exceptional debut.

"We'll have to celebrate," Saxton said, smiling at her. "In fact, I've been thinking about planning a corporate retreat. And now that *Spotlight* has been launched, this might be a good time for the whole company to get together and do some team building. What do you think?"

"That sounds like a great idea." They were both forcing inane conversation, trying to pretend as though the last few minutes had not happened. Seeing how tight his smile had become, she started to back away. "Well, I need to get home."

She picked up another tissue and handed it to him to wipe away the crimson traces of evidence. "Cranberry Crush really isn't your shade," she teased to make light of their stolen moment.

He grabbed her hand. "Mallory?"

"Yes?" she answered.

"Again, I'm sorry," Saxton said. He was torn by conflicting emotions. Though his words were sincere and he was sorry about a lot of things, the kiss they shared was not one of them.

Mallory looked deeply into his eyes, not sure what to make of the glow that she saw there. One thing she was sure of was that this should never have happened. She had nothing to gain from getting close to Saxton McKensie again, and a lot to lose.

"So am I," she replied. She turned clumsily, heading rapidly for the door, anxious to reach safety on the other side.

15

MOONLIGHTING

At one a.m., Nikki, clad in head-to-toe Prada, was ensconced in one of the farthest removed velvet-curtained booths left unoccupied downstairs in Flute, the sexy speakeasy on Fifty-fourth Street in Midtown. It was one of her favorite watering holes, shrouded in darkness and flickering candlelight. It was not a place that would ever be described as festive. No, Flute was a little more wicked than that, which suited Nikki's taste just fine.

"I'll have a glass of Perrier-Jouët, with a shot of chambord," she haughtily relayed to the pale, lithe waitress who made an appearance in her booth. Flute had one of the most impressive selections of champagne in the city, hence the name.

Nikki sat back with her long, lean legs crossed lazily while she observed the comings and goings of the other patrons, speculating about the reasons for their late-night trysts. A chronic schemer, she could easily imagine all forms of covert rendezvous, from hidden romantic affairs and exchanges of the narcotic of the moment to grand plots of corporate espionage. She spotted an attractive couple intertwined in a semiprivate booth to her right. They seemed desperate to get their hands all over each other at once. Surely it was an illicit affair that didn't

warrant the time or logistics for a proper hotel room, she figured. Nikki smiled to herself. Only forbidden fruit ever drew
such a hungry feeding frenzy.

When the waitress returned with her flute of champagne,
she asked, "Would you like to start a tab?"

"No, I'd rather not," Nikki said. "Would you bring the bill
a little later? I'm expecting company." Starting a tab could
only mean that she'd end up buying drinks, and her partner
in crime tonight was in a much better position to do so than
she was.

With checks coming few and far between, she had to fast-
track her plans to secure her financial stability. Modeling
was not what it used to be; nor, for that matter, was she.
Etched lines were starting to scatter around her eyes, and her
muscle tone was fading as fast as last season's fashions. To
make matters worse, her competition was descending on
Gotham at younger and younger ages, and the racially mixed
girls were really causing her problems. Magazines seemed to
only want African-American models who were either pitch-
black and exotic-looking like Alek Wek or half of anything
else. Nikki didn't fit into either category. She didn't know
how to do anything else, though. After modeling for ten
years, she couldn't just walk into a company and get a high-
paying job.

Nikki's mood lightened as she spotted her guest making her
way over to the table wearing a sly smile. "Sorry I'm late," she
said, air-kissing Nikki's cheek. "But I got caught up at P.
Diddy's party at Lotus. Everybody was there."

"Not a problem. It just means that I've got a head start on
you," Nikki said, signaling for the waitress.

"I'll have a twenty-year-old tawny port," she ordered, and
then turned to Nikki. "Tonight was a gold mine with all of the
drama unfolding there. Too much drama, too little time," she
said, shaking her head.

"Speaking of which, why don't we go ahead and settle

up?" Nikki asked, quickly getting down to business with Yvette Boynton. "The last few tips I gave you were worth gold."

Yvette reached into her Fendi baguette and gladly pulled out a white envelope, which she slid over to Nikki's side of the table. "I think you'll find that just compensation."

Nikki smiled as she opened the envelope to discover twenty-five crisp hundred-dollar bills. Her relationship with Yvette was turning out to be a lot more lucrative than Nikki had initially counted on. They had met at a party four months ago. Later, over drinks, Yvette told Nikki how she was always looking for hot tips on designers, supermodels, and celebrities or just general good gossip. At first Nikki was not so crazy about the idea, but as the Mallory/Chad/Saxton story unfolded under her nose, she quickly realized how helping Yvette could also serve to further her own agenda, which was to get Saxton out of Deena's life and herself planted more firmly in it—not to mention lining her pocket in the meantime. "Thank you very much," she said.

"No, thank you," Yvette insisted, raising her glass in a salute. "Anything else that I should know about?"

"Hmmmm," Nikki purred, "I do have some interesting information on Kia. I've heard from some very reliable sources that her marriage to Leonard is a complete farce and that she swings to the left and he swings to the right. If you know what I mean." Nikki raised an eyebrow suggestively. Her reliable source was in fact herself. She and Kia, a sitcom actress, had been together intimately on a couple of occasions.

"You're kidding?" Yvette was totally surprised. Not by Kia's sexuality, but by Leonard's. He was a star baseball player for the Yankees and a poster boy for testosterone.

"Trust me," Nikki said, taking a long sip of her champagne.

"Believe me, in matters such as this, I do." Like a good journalist—if you could call a gossip columnist by that title—

Yvette knew a lot more about Nikki than Nikki would have ever have imagined.

Like a feline who had been fed to satisfaction, Nikki stretched and said, "It's been great, but I've gotta run now," before laying fifty dollars on the table for the bill. She was more than happy to pick up the tab.

16

A FUMBLED PASS

It was finally game day for Saxton, and he was in the office early, going over the last-minute details for the meeting with FBC. He felt the same rush of adrenaline he'd always experienced the day of a big game in college.

Cindy knocked before heading into his office with a notepad in hand. "Good morning, Mr. McKensie."

"Good morning, Cindy. And by the way, thanks for having the fire started for me."

"You're welcome. I know how important today's meeting is and how much you love your fire." She smiled, taking a seat opposite his desk. "I just wanted to check to be sure that you had everything you need."

"I think so. But why don't you check the presentation and handouts to make sure that the most updated figures are included?"

"Will do," she said, reaching over to take a copy from the stack on the corner of his desk.

Before she was out of the door, Eric walked in. "Saxton, I need to talk to you. Is now a good time?"

"Sure," Saxton said, leaning back in his chair. "What's up?"

"It's about the Blondie interview," he said, without the normal effervescence that he usually exuded. In fact, Eric was wringing his hands.

"What's wrong?" Saxton leaned forward.

"Nothing, per se. It's just that I received a very disturbing call from Cedric Hammer, her manager. I thought you should know about it." Eric perched on the edge of the chair that Cindy had just left. "Until the fact checkers called Blondie's people to double-check a few of her quotes, apparently Cedric had no idea that she'd trashed the label, her benefactor, and just about all of her competition in the interview, which, according to him, could have some serious repercussions—not only for the deal that they are in the middle of renegotiating with the label, but it could also cause one of those nasty turf wars that rap is famous for."

"So what is he suggesting?"

"He's asked me to pull the interview."

"You've got to be kidding." The premier issue was being given to the distributor at this very minute, and there was no way that they could afford to reprint an entire issue. Besides, the story was awesome. It would create just the sort of buzz that *Spotlight* needed to get off to a competitive start.

"I wish I was," Eric said, shaking his head.

"What did you tell him?"

"That there was no way that we could do that." Eric stood up now and paced the room. "But the real problem is what he said to me."

"Which was?"

"To use his vernacular, he said, quote-unquote, that if we ran that piece of shit, it'd be our first and last issue and that we'd all better watch our asses." Eric, a man of refined tastes, was clearly not accustomed to mixing it up with the likes of Cedric Hammer, the notorious gangster/manager.

"Okay." Saxton got up from behind his desk. "That's a problem."

"I know," Eric agreed, rubbing his hands together. "But if we let this thug bully us now, then we've set a bad precedent for any future subjects. Plus, this issue is too important for us to butcher the cover story at the eleventh hour."

"You're right."

"So what do you think I should do?"

Saxton thought about it for a moment, then said, "Why don't you go ahead and run the issue? I'll have one of our attorneys threaten him with a restraining order. Meanwhile I'll also look into increasing security around here, which isn't a bad idea anyway, given Deena's increasing profile."

"Cool."

For the rest of the morning, Saxton immersed himself in the negotiations' details. At last it was time to go. He and two of his associates walked out of Ingram Enterprises' office and headed to FBC's worldwide headquarters. After a quick ride uptown, they stepped in triangular formation through the impressive lobby of the second-largest media company in the world. Taking in the impressive combination of imported marble, commercial-sized sculpture, and architectural brilliance without gawking was like trying to sneak a quick peek at the Grand Canyon. Three-story floor-to-ceiling glass surrounded the building's lobby and served as the backdrop for a waterfall cascading along three sides. The water trickled down the glass walls into a stream of multihued koi fish, which provided a touch of living color to the slick presentation. It was as much a physical monument to power as it was an office building.

The three were escorted by one of the building's smartly tailored concierges to the private key-coded elevator, which ascended to the eightieth-floor penthouse suite that was Ogdin Finch's private office. An Armani-clad assistant met them as the elevator door slid open, revealing an awe-inspiring view of New York's skyline, which stretched all the way west across the Hudson River. The other man formally extended his hand to Saxton. "Mr. McKensie, I'm Harold Johnson, Mr. Finch's personal assistant."

After a firm handshake, Saxton made further introductions. "This is Tom Wadley and Ralph Boardman."

"If you'll follow me, please." Gliding across the black polished-slate floor, Harold led the group along a wide thirty-foot blond wood hallway studded with recessed pin lights. The art that hung along the majestic corridor rivaled any private collection, and this was only the hallway. Saxton instantly recognized a Matisse and a Renoir among many other impressive pieces.

Before taking his leave, Harold escorted them through two motion-triggered electronic pocket doors, providing access to the conference room inside. What greeted them was visual decadence. The room was glass on two sides; it provided a hundred-eighty-degree view of the heavenly kingdoms nestled in the sky above New York City. A third wall consisted of a floor-to-ceiling aquarium with an exquisite collection of exotic aquatic plants, ranging from water ferns, Asian bamboo, and hair grass to various varieties of underwater moss. At first glance the wall of water revealed only an exquisite display of colorful foliage and sea sponges, until a shark swam menacingly from behind a large pondweed, lurking among the picturesque paradise like a thief in the night. The carnivore had a red underbelly and a mouthful of razor-sharp teeth, which he displayed as he floated in the center of the tank, as though sensing fresh meat just outside the confines of his liquid domain.

While they surveyed the tank, also spotting a neon bright eight-foot eel, the pocket doors opened amid a muffled swoosh of air, and a five-foot-ten leggy brunette entered the room wearing a smartly cut Dolce & Gabbana suit. While the skirt stopped midthigh, it easily rode the fine line between too short and office-appropriate. She wore her hair in a short, wispy, face-framing cut. She looked like a dressed-down Italian poster girl. *Definitely not your typical corporate attorney*, Saxton thought.

"I see that you've already met Oscar." She smiled, motioning toward the glassy-eyed shark that stood watch like a fat man waiting outside an all-you-can-eat buffet. Something about her smile went beyond friendly; it was downright inviting the way she moved her gloss-covered lips. Saxton could tell that she was fully aware of her potent sex appeal.

Saxton was also aware of the power he held over the opposite sex, so he gave her a dose of his own charm. "Fortunately, not up close and personal," he commented with a light but electric smile. It was a little unnerving that his opponent kept a pet shark in his conference room, but the brunette's presence certainly helped to erase any feelings of menace. "I'm Saxton McKensie," he said, giving her the full benefit of his disarming smile. "This is Tom Wadley and Ralph Boardman."

Offering a perfectly manicured hand, she said, "I'm Kate Chandler." Her accent revealed a touch of Britain. She opened the first button of her jacket before taking a seat to the right of the head chair, revealing a creamy white silk shell over a full chest. Saxton sat opposite her, Tom and Ralph to his left.

"Don't mind Oscar," Kate purred. "He's not a man-eater."

But I'd bet that you are, Saxton thought. A mutually curious glance passed between them, as though they were reading each other's minds.

The pocket doors to the room eased open once again, presenting the legend himself: the spit-polished, Savile Row–wearing, original Connecticut WASP, Ogdin Finch III. He was a white man's version of tall, dark, and handsome, sophisticated in a highly polished Pierce Brosnan kind of way. He oozed money, both old and new. According to the business periodicals, his grandfather, a Russian immigrant, initially made a fortune for the family by selling body bags to the Allies by the hundreds of thousands during World War II. But truth be told—which it wasn't, since his family had help in its rewriting—the Finches actually had been gunrunners. After the war, the entrepreneurial Ogdin Sr. quickly turned the fake body bag business into Finch Investments, a private investment firm, specifically for those like himself who had made questionable money during the war and were now looking for ways to clean it up and grow it quietly.

Ogdin's father further developed the company into one of the most exclusive private investment firms in the world. Later, after young Ogdin was passed through Princeton like a baton and it was his turn to tend to the family fortune, he proved to be as much of a visionary as his grandfather had been. He began purchasing cable companies that eventually served as the backbone for what was now Finch Broadcasting Corporation, or FBC. For Saxton, although he was impressed with Ogdin's vision and business ability, that respect was always tempered by the fact that he had gotten off to a head start at birth.

"Gentlemen," Ogdin said, nodding slightly as he took his place at the head of the highly polished mahogany table. His mere presence seemed to suck air from the room. He fixed his dark, laser-sharp eyes on Saxton as though he were able to see through to his soul. "I'll get right to the point." He leaned forward, braiding his fingers into a steeple that he balanced underneath his cleft chin. "We've been impressed over the last year with the performance of *The Ingram Hour*, and as you know, we feel that the time is right to expand its reach." He spoke with the precision of someone who was accustomed to having people hang on his every word. "Which is why we began exploratory meetings a couple of months ago. My goal today is to finalize those arrangements and move forward with our relationship." Kate smiled slightly as she leaned back in her chair, casually twirling a gold Waterford pen between her long, elegant fingers.

A good opening, Saxton thought. He could tell that, even though Ogdin was playing it cool, they were champing at the bit to get this deal done. He had them just where he wanted them. Feeling very much in control, Saxton leaned forward with his elbows on the table, gesturing with open hands. "We've also been pleased with our relationship with FBC, and like you, we are excited about expanding it." Sitting back into his chair, now that the pleasantries were out of the way, he added, "And given Deena's unique place in the market we realize the importance of partnering with a network that offers a natural fit and synergy, and to date that's been our experience with FBC. So we too are anxious to construct a sound and mutually beneficial arrangement moving forward."

Kate slid a stack of documents from a black Louis Vuitton portfolio and passed them across the table. "I'm glad to know that we're all on the same page," she said, producing a pair of black horn-rimmed glasses, which she then perched on the edge of her nose. "That brings me to this contract, which was sent to you last week. As I'm sure that you know, in it we substantially increased the per-episode rate by fifteen percent, bringing the total value of the deal to just over a hundred million dollars."

Taking his cue, Ralph spoke up. "In fact, we did receive this offer, but as we discussed with your executive team, we are interested in constructing a deal that allows Ingram Enterprises to participate in incremental advertising revenues."

Saxton noticed a twitch in the corner of Ogdin's left eye, confirming to him that this was a touchy subject, but not one that Saxton wished to back down from. He knew that you never got ahold of the brass ring if you didn't grab for it. Besides, he was not intimidated by Ogdin's legend, or the trappings of his success.

"We are aware of that, but it's not something that we are prepared to do." Kate leaned back and folded her arms across her chest.

The simple manner in which she managed to say no to such a complicated issue touched a nerve with Saxton. There was no way that he would allow that to be the final word on the subject. He reached into his portfolio, pulling out *The Ingram Hour* ad statistics, which he then distributed around the table. He leaned forward with his hands meshed together in front of him on the table. "This request isn't arbitrary," he said, looking from Kate to Ogdin. "It's based on demonstrated value. These figures show a consistent ten- to fifteen-percent increase in ad sales in every single market that Deena has ever entered." After pausing to let his point sink in, Saxton continued. "This is not a fluke. As you are undoubtedly aware, all of the major advertisers, from upscale clothing designers to the maker of the latest SUV, have struggled with ways to target and reach the affluent, urban middle-class audience. Not hip-hoppers, and not the B. Smith generation, but the dual-income upwardly mobile young family of four with two cars, a stock portfolio, and all the latest gadgets. Well, that's precisely the audience that *The Ingram Hour* entertains on a daily basis, in addition to a substantial portion of mainstream America. In light of that, we think it's only fair to share in the incremental value that this unique relationship brings to the network." As Saxton glanced from Ogdin to Kate, he sensed an easing up in their position. He even detected a smile creeping along the edges of her mouth.

Tom picked up from there. "Here's a proposed monthly schedule that would tie our percent of revenue share directly to incremental ad sales." He, too, passed out paper.

Ogdin, who hadn't spoken since opening the meeting, leaned forward as though to take the document. Saxton could taste the sweetness of victory. But instead of picking it up, Ogdin braced both elbows on the table. Without even glancing at the growing mound of documents in front of him, he looked directly at Saxton and out of left field asked, "Have you seen Deena's ratings lately?"

"Of course I have," Saxton answered evenly. Where the hell was he going with this?

"Well, I take it, then, that you are aware that they have flattened out over the last few months."

"I wouldn't call them flat." Ogdin was reaching for straws. Deena's ratings were so high that they had reached a natural plateau. No show's ratings increased forever. It was not mathematically possible, and Ogdin, of all people, knew that.

Ogdin pushed a button under his place at the table, and a sixty-inch high-definition screen eased from the ceiling. Simultaneously shades slid down to cover the windows and the lights in the room gradually dimmed. There, across a line chart labeled THE INGRAM HOUR, were Deena's ratings for the last year, week by week. The line zigzagged in a distinctly upward trend for the first through the third quarters and then showed a leveling off in the last quarter.

The pen that Kate had been twirling became a laser pointer, its red beam highlighting the final quarter's results. "The point is," she said, removing her glasses along with the sexy demeanor, "we're concerned that Deena's audience share is not growing."

Ralph, Saxton's programming expert, jumped in. "Sure, it may have leveled off some, but the fact is that she's in either the number-one or the number-two spot each consecutive week and her advertising results are incomparable."

Impatient with further discussion, Ogdin sat back in his chair. Though he did want a syndication deal with *The Ingram Hour*, there was no way he'd let some little black boy from the sticks twist his arm for a share of his hard-won ad revenue. Sure, it was a sound negotiating strategy; in fact, it was something that he could see himself doing. But coming from the likes of Saxton McKensie, it was offensive. The kid had tried to wash off the pine residue from North Carolina along with the country twang while at Notre Dame and Harvard, and he did have a law degree and some impressive success on Wall Street, but bottom line, he was still a nigger—one who had obviously forgotten his place.

"We've offered you a hundred-million-dollar deal, and by *anyone's* standards that's a lot of money." Saxton interpreted: *And to you black people, it's a shitload of it.* "But you're asking for advertising revenue without participating in the structural elements that entitle you to it." Crossing his arms across his chest, Ogdin leaned back in his chair. "My grandfather built the foundation of this company on the principle that you spoke of: demonstrated value. And that's how I continue to make decisions today. But you want to take value in a profit center that you haven't staked a claim in. Over fifteen years I've built a company that puts me in the position to garner advertising revenue. That is the backbone of this company. So pardon me if I don't simply open up my vault," he lectured. "But if you insist on structuring a deal like that, then I must insist on demonstrated performance."

Saxton and Tom exchanged a quick glance. "What exactly are you suggesting?" Tom asked.

Instead of Ogdin answering, his henchwoman, Kate, did it for him. Another line chart appeared on top of the one previously shown on the screen. It was labeled THE GINA DAVIS SHOW. Gina Davis's talk show was a black woman's version of Jerry Springer. Her programming was likely to be "My Baby Daddy's Bi Lover Is Sleeping with My Father" or "Confessions of a Schizophrenic Lesbian Kickboxer." Saxton was appalled that they would stoop to compare *The Ingram Hour* to such filth.

"What we are suggesting is, if we are going to be taken to the bank on a deal, we want to know for sure that we are riding a definite winner. And as you can see, the answer is not as clear-cut as you might like to think. *The Gina Davis Show*, while trailing *The Ingram Hour* for the first three quarters, has gained substantial momentum and is now clearly on the upswing."

"And by the way," Ogdin added, "her people aren't holding me ransom for an unwarranted share of my business."

Saxton could not believe what he was hearing. They were considering giving an expanded syndication deal to that sensational freak show host Gina Davis? There was no way that Gina's show garnered the type of advertising dollars that Deena's did. Searching his memory, he recalled that her advertising take was a good twenty percent below Deena's. This had to be a bluff. Either that or it was somehow personal.

This was the point in the game where he could either hold his ground or walk away with close to a hundred million dollars, which was nothing to sneeze at. Before he could make a decision, Tom, who had taken it personally, huffed, "You can't compare *The Gina Davis Show* to *The Ingram Hour*."

It was a crucial mistake. Saxton saw anger light up immediately in Ogdin's face. He was sure that Ogdin was thinking, *Who does this Negro think he is, telling me, Ogdin Finch, what I can do?* He abruptly stood up. "Gentlemen, not only *do* I compare it, but I will continue to do so. I didn't get where I am in business by giving away a deal or by being held over a barrel. Since you insist on playing hardball, so will I. For the next three months I will monitor Deena's and Gina's stats, and whoever has the highest rating in thirteen weeks is who we'll expand syndication with." He then turned to leave. "Good day, gentlemen."

Kate stood next, a cue for them to pack their gear. The meeting was over. As they followed her from the room, Saxton was stunned. He couldn't believe it. Not only hadn't he won the game, but he had been sidelined for thirteen weeks. This was definitely not the outcome that he had predicted.

Saxton, Tom, and Ralph were like the walking wounded as they exited FBC's offices. None of them could fully comprehend the unforeseen mess that had come of Ingram Enterprises' signature deal. Where had they gone wrong? Never in a gazillion years would Saxton McKensie, the Harvard-educated attorney-cum–deal maker, have predicted that he would walk away from this building today without a done deal. Maybe he might not have gotten *exactly* the deal that he wanted, but it was unfathomable for him not to have one at all—and worse yet, to be pitted against that tawdry freakfest, *The Gina Davis Show*. It was an unpardonable insult. Worse was the fact that he'd have to explain it to Deena. Thankfully, she had a meeting out of the office this afternoon and probably wouldn't be back into the office today.

The three battle-weary men quietly rode back downtown to lick their wounds within the private confines of their offices. No one was in the mood to rehash the devastating defeat. Saxton wanted to blame Tom for his last emotional comment, which he was sure had pushed the egomaniac Ogdin Finch right over the edge, and Tom silently blamed Ralph for not analyzing Gina's ratings closely enough while he researched Deena's—maybe then they would have been more prepared for the detour into left field. And Ralph wanted to blame Saxton for being such a bullheaded negotiator to begin with and not taking the sweetened offer that had been put on the table. So rather than starting World War III in the backseat of the car, they all sat in stony silence as they rode through the maze of Midtown traffic.

With his head hung low, Saxton walked past Cindy's desk, thankful that she wasn't there. He was not ready to face anyone at this moment. All he really wanted to do was lock himself behind the doors of his office and sulk in privacy while trying to figure out how on earth he would explain this mess to Deena. The prospect of that conversation plagued him almost as much as not getting the deal to begin with, especially since it would be peppered with a string of I told you so's. Fortunately, he had the rest of the day to figure it out, he thought as he opened the door to his sanctuary—only to find Deena, Cindy, and a bottle of chilled Dom Perignon poised at the ready.

"Congratulations!" both women squealed in unison as Deena uncorked the bottle of Dom, sending frothy streams of bubbly spraying through the air. She rushed toward him for a big bear hug and a splashy celebratory kiss, while Cindy stood back wearing a proud smile. They were all on their way to the big leagues—or so they thought.

When Saxton failed to roar and pound his chest in victory, Deena calmed down and began to pour the champagne into the two crystal flutes. "Don't keep me in suspense. Give me the details."

This was like a waking nightmare for Saxton, with Deena's unexpected presence, Cindy standing by as an eyewitness, and an uncorked bottle of champagne. "There's not much to tell," he answered vaguely.

Deena cocked her head like an alert puppy that had just heard a particularly high-pitched noise. "Not much to tell? I

wouldn't exactly call a hundred million dollars not much."
Seeing his pained face, she became alarmed. "What happened?" she asked, setting her champagne flute down.

"The deal has been put on hold." There, he'd said it.

"What?" she growled. "What do you mean 'on hold?'"
Saxton saw the deep furrows that always entrenched themselves between Deena's brows whenever Her Highness was
upset. He turned to Cindy. "Would you excuse us, please?"

"Of course." The woman gladly scampered from the room.
She did not want to bear witness to what she knew was about
to be a clash of titans. Besides, judging from the scowl on
Deena's face, she'd be able to follow the shouting match just as
easily from the other side of the door.

Once she had left, Saxton sat down heavily behind his desk.
"He threw us a curve ball," he said, tossing both hands, palms
out, in the air. "They argued that your ratings were leveling off
and that *The Gina Davis Show* was gaining in market share. So
he wants to wait thirteen weeks to see who has the highest ratings before making a syndication decision."

"*The Gina Davis Show?* You've got to be kidding me!"
Deena was furious, setting her hands on her hips.

"I wish I was." Saxton shook his head.

Deena was not buying the poor-poor-pitiful-me act. "How
the hell did this happen?" she demanded. She started pacing
back and forth in front of his desk like an agitated panther. She
was pissed. One minute FBC was offering her nearly a hundred
million dollars, and the next minute there was no deal at all.
She would be the laughingstock of the media world, since
she'd already had her publicist leak the fact that the deal was
all but done. Maybe Nikki was right. Maybe Saxton blew it
because of his huge ego.

"Deena, I don't know. You can't always predict every outcome in tough negotiations."

She marched over and planted both of her palms down on
his desk. Then she leaned in to within inches of his face. "I

guess not," she sneered, "especially when you think you know it all."

Here it comes, Saxton thought, bracing himself. "What are you talking about?"

"You know exactly what I'm talking about. Instead of taking a good offer, you had to be the big man and got greedy."

He'd spent years making more money for Deena than she'd ever dreamed of, and after one setback she was ready to nail him to the cross. Saxton stood up to face her. "This has nothing to do with me being a big man or getting greedy. In negotiations—something you know nothing about—it's expected that you look for every opportunity. Why do you think you can roll up here in your chauffeur-driven Bentley, draped in a ninety-thousand-dollar sable coat? Believe me, it ain't because Ogdin and the boys think you deserve it. It's because of me," he said, finally pounding his chest. "So don't you *ever* accuse me of ineptitude. Otherwise, you'll be looking for another partner." The scathing look that he gave her said clearly that he meant partner in both senses of the word—business and personal.

Though the gauntlet he'd thrown down stunned her—she'd never seen him this angry before—she still didn't back away from his challenge. Their eyes locked for long, cold seconds. "I just might do that," she spat, before turning abruptly to snatch her fur coat from the sofa. She stormed from the room, leaving Saxton fuming and the untouched flutes of champagne going flat.

17

PLAYING WITH FIRE

It was late and Saxton was drowning his sorrows in his second snifter of brandy while reclining on the sofa in his office. His shirt was open at the neck and his tie hung askew. The alcohol helped to blur the rough edges from the devastating events earlier in the day. He wasn't sure what was more shattering to him: FBC snatching the rug out from under him or Deena pouring salt on the resulting wound.

The crackle of the fire was a soothing backdrop as he reflected on his life and the choices that he had made. Looking around the plush office, he was also reminded of how far he'd come from the small house in North Carolina. His mother, who passed away while Saxton was at Harvard, had nearly burst with pride when he was accepted to the prestigious university, but she always told him, "It's not how far you go that matters. It's how you get there that really counts." Remembering her down-home philosophy only heightened his present sense of gloom. While there was no arguing that he was a very successful man, he was realizing firsthand that his success all came with a price. The million-dollar questions were: Just how steep was the price, and was he really willing to pay?

"Saxton?"

He turned toward the door and saw Mallory peeking in, still holding on to the doorknob.

When he didn't answer her right away, she quickly took in the snifter and the forlorn expression on his face. "Mind if I come in?"

"No, be my guest," he answered, motioning her into the room with a fluid wave of the hand that still held the glass.

"Are you okay?" she asked, venturing in until she stood by his side.

"Who, me?" He pointed to his own chest. His words were not quite slurred, but definitely more languid than normal. "Oh, I'm fine," he said unconvincingly.

"I heard what happened. I'm really sorry."

"That makes at least two of us," he said, taking a sip from the glass.

She placed her hand on his. "Do you want to talk about it?"

Saxton lowered his head and after several seconds shook it slowly. "You know, there really isn't a lot to talk about. I did what I thought was the right thing, and unfortunately, it didn't turn out the way I wanted it to." He shrugged his shoulders and met her gaze. "I guess that means that I don't have all of the answers after all." He took another sip.

She felt so bad for him. He looked dejected and hurt. "Hey, don't be so hard on yourself. So what if this deal hasn't closed yet? You've already built an incredible company that you should be proud of."

He snorted. "Tell that to Deena."

Mallory shrank away. Just the mention of Deena's name caused her to tense up. She had yet to tell Saxton about their little conversation in her office.

Saxton saw the change in her mood. "Listen, Mallory, there's something that I've wanted to tell you." He wore a sardonic smirk on his face, though it was directed not at her but at himself. "Even though I have apologized to you for what happened after I left Atlanta, I never really gave you a complete explanation."

Mallory went still, not sure if she really wanted to know where this conversation was going.

"When I first met Deena, I was impressed with her, and I felt like she was a nice person."

With great effort, Mallory kept from rolling her eyes. "Nice person" hardly described the witch who'd ridden into her office on a turbocharged broom.

"After we started going out, she offered me the opportunity to build what we now have. And I took it. The only problem was that the personal relationship was tightly intertwined with the professional relationship. I didn't want to give up one, so I was stuck with the other."

A bad taste suddenly settled in Mallory's mouth. "So are you saying that you got with Deena instead of me in order to help your career?"

He lowered his head. "Don't get me wrong. I was doing well before I met her but . . ."

"But what?"

He looked up in shame. "I got caught up in the business and didn't want to let it go. I never wanted to take the personal relationship as far as its gone, but Deena pressured me, first into the relationship, and then the engagement. I guess I thought that it was okay and that we'd both live happily ever after. Until . . ."

"Until what?"

"Until you came back. Before, I was able to ignore it, but after seeing you again, I realize what I've been missing." He looked into her eyes, pleading with her to understand. "And that's love. I know I've had a bit to drink, and I don't want to sound sappy, but the truth is that I've never loved Deena the way that I loved you."

Mallory's breath caught in her throat. After all these years she was finally hearing the words that she'd prayed for since the day they met. She looked deeply into his eyes and found truth, regret, and love gazing back. She didn't know what to say or how to feel. Confused, she walked over to the fireplace and placed her arm on the mantel, trying to sort out her turbulent emotions. The warmth of the crackling fire enveloped her, easing the tension in her body. She closed her eyes and let her head slowly roll around the axis of her neck, chasing away the tension that had begun to build there. Before she could exhale, she felt a pair of warm, strong hands kneading the knot of muscles at the top of her shoulders.

She reveled in the heat of his touch. All the doubt, anger, and anxiety that she'd been hauling around magically dissipated like ashes caught in a sudden breeze. Saxton's hands felt so good that she couldn't prevent a soft moan from escaping her throat. He gently turned her around to face him. Holding her face in his hands, he tasted her lips. Then he began probing between them for more.

The taste of the brandy, combined with his sensuous lips, mouth, and his teasing tongue wiped away any resistance within her. She wrapped her arms around his neck, pulling him closer, eager to meet his desire. She felt him growing hard and urgent against her thigh. Again, a deep moan escaped her throat. Flashes of the blissful intimacy they'd shared in Atlanta made her skin tingle all over.

He eased her down onto the thick Tibetan rug on the hearth and lay next to her. The burning wood in the fireplace snapped and crackled as he kissed her passionately. His hands sought her breasts and nipples, causing Mallory to melt under his deft touch. Her hands began to roam over his body, while he unfastened her blouse and pulled apart her bra. Finally he tasted her breasts, for the first time in over five years. He licked, sucked, and devoured her flesh like a starving man. The sensations caused a hunger in Mallory that she'd forgotten could exist.

They were both in a sexual frenzy as zippers and buttons came apart. The heat from the fire was nothing compared to what coursed through their blood. Saxton positioned himself on top of Mallory and gave her what she wanted, every inch of his hot, hard, and long penis. As he penetrated her hot sex, Mallory lunged upward, unable to get all of him quickly enough. The flickering flames danced only a foot away from their churning, sweat-slicked bodies. Her fingers held firmly to his chiseled biceps. Her lustful eyes feasted hungrily on the thick patch of hair nestled in the center of his chest, devouring the ripple of muscles over his torso, finally stopping to savor the sight of their bodies moving together in a rolling, pulsing dance of their own.

Saxton searched eagerly and, after finding her panting mouth, kissed her hard while filling her body with his own, time and time again. He squeezed her round cheeks, positioning himself to stroke her even deeper. He then took her long legs by her calves, holding her open wider. When he was sure that he'd touched her core, his body tightened and shuddered. The sensation was like touching a live wire. The ensuing surge of passion flowed through his body unchecked. Afterward, they collapsed in each other's arms, slumbering in front of the dying fire.

As reality eased its way into Mallory's consciousness, Saxton held her tight.

"It feels so good to hold you," he whispered between kisses that he planted along her brow while running his fingers through her hair, soothing her. "I've missed you so much."

"I've missed you, too," she confessed before thinking to censor her words.

He faced her directly now, staring deeply into her eyes. "You are so beautiful. I don't know what I could have been thinking to ever leave you."

Looking into his eyes, Mallory saw intense longing and naked desire. She also saw the eyes of her own child, causing her to abruptly turn away.

Saxton saw the flicker of pain as it flashed across her face. "What's wrong?" he asked, alarmed.

"N-n-nothing," Mallory said, shaking her head. "I've got to go."

She pulled apart, stumbling to her feet. She looked about

the room, surprised by what she saw. Anxious to run away, she quickly gathered her clothes.

Saxton rose to his feet, too. "Mallory, talk to me," he pleaded.

"I've gotta go," was all she said as she ran from the office, knowing it was too late to ever turn back.

18

THE BACHELOR AND THE BARRACUDA

Where business was concerned, Beverly was a tooth-baring, take-no-prisoners female tigress. Nothing came between her and her clients. She was fiercely loyal to them and would go for her opponent's jugular to protect their interests.

TJ Marks leaned back confidently into the leather booth at Tao, an Asian restaurant on Fifty-eighth Street in Midtown. A freshly lit Cuban cigar dangled between his perfectly capped teeth. "Trust me, this is a good deal," he said, flashing his famous two-carat smile. It was his money smile, the one that usually closed deals for him. "It doesn't get any better than this."

TJ was a music industry executive who had boyish charm laced with sugarcoated venom. By the time most people figured out that his good humor was lethal, it was usually too late, but not for Beverly. She not only knew of his double-dealing reputation, but could smell a bad deal under the covers in the dark.

"You are right," she said. TJ caught a whiff of the heady smell of success and leaned back even farther into the leather upholstery. "It is a good deal. For you." She leaned forward, sharpening her claws.

"Wh-what do you mean?" he stammered. He expected this deal to be a slam-dunk for him, all net. He definitely wanted

Giles, the young R & B crooner with the vocal pipes of Luther Vandross, the dance moves of Usher, and the good looks of Lenny Kravitz on his roster, and he was counting on the boy's hunger and ambition to get a favorable contract. In fact, he was hoping that the singer would be as naive as many new artists were and have Uncle Jimmy represent them instead of a top attorney like Beverly. Fortunately for him, Giles's mother had contacted Beverly and asked her to help him out. Though she had a full plate already, she made the time to represent the singer.

"Just so that I'm really clear, let me run it down for you."

Giles, sitting next to her, cringed at her challenging tone. Like most new artists, he was just anxious to do a deal. The fact that the revered TJ Marks was offering him a million-dollar one made it a no-brainer for him. He couldn't wait to sign on the dotted line so he could floss to his friends about his record deal.

Beverly had other ideas. "First of all, your video commitment is not substantial enough."

"Not substantial? We are committing to produce a top-shelf video with Billy Woodruff. He's the best video director out there."

"One video isn't enough," Beverly said. She took a sip from her glass of chardonnay to give him time to think about it.

TJ sat back and crossed his arms across his chest, while Giles held his breath. He had visions of BET, MTV, and his own posse dancing in his head.

"Look at him," she said, gesturing to her client. "He is eye candy for the ladies, he moves better than Michael Jackson in *Thriller*, and by the way, he can really sing. So why wouldn't you want to do as many videos as possible? How else will you be able to adequately promote his assets?"

"Do you know how much videos cost?" Condescension crept into TJ's voice. He didn't like to be countered at all, especially not by a woman.

"Of course I do. But I also know that another label—who

shall remain nameless—has offered us a deal that commits to three."

Giles sat in stony silence, beads of sweat threatening to pierce his brow. Even though she had warned him before the meeting to let her do all the talking, he was still worried. This was the first he'd ever heard of another deal. Beverly nudged him discreetly under the table to make sure that he didn't blow her cover.

TJ frowned and stubbed the already unlit cigar in the ashtray on the table. "There is no way I can commit to three videos."

Beverly didn't blink. "Well, I guess we don't have much else to talk about, now do we?" She raised her hand to signal for the waiter. The sweat beads won the battle across Giles's brow as he looked nervously from Beverly to TJ.

When TJ saw that she wasn't bluffing and was in fact reaching for her portfolio, he said, "I'll tell you what. I will commit to two, but that's as far as I'll go." Agitated, he picked up his cigar and reached for his solid gold lighter.

"Plus, there is another issue," Beverly said flatly. TJ stopped midflick. "Fifty percent recoupment on video costs is unacceptable. Giles would be lucky to end up with the shirt on his back by the time those other production costs eat away at his royalties."

TJ sighed and shook his head. "Come on, Beverly."

"I'm just looking out for my client." She maintained eye contact, waiting for TJ to continue, which he did.

"You're killing me," he lamented.

"You look pretty healthy to me," she said, appraising his thirty-thousand-dollar Audemar Piquet watch and custom hand-tailored suit. "I'll tell you what, sixty-five, thirty-five and we've got a deal." She held out her hand.

"We've already given you guaranteed tour support." He held up his hands as though he were being robbed.

"One thing has nothing to do with the other."

"Let me think about it."

She reached over to grab her portfolio. "While you're thinking, we'll be returning that urgent call from your competition." She looked over to Giles, whose jaw was nearly on the table. He couldn't believe that she would really walk away from a deal with Arouse Records over a fifteen percent differential. It was all he could do to keep from screaming, "I'll take it!"

The silence lingered on and on. Finally, TJ shook his head. "Okay, you win. Sixty-five, thirty-five it is."

"You've got yourself a deal," she said, reaching over to shake his hand. Giles finally exhaled.

Later, after TJ and Giles were gone, best of buds now, Beverly sat at the booth making notes in her T-Mobile for the next day's follow-up. She would redline the agreement in the morning and try to have the deal done by the end of the week. She smiled to herself, pleased with the outcome of the negotiations. She would have taken the fifty.

As she was putting her cell phone, pager, and Palm Pilot away, a familiar face at the bar caught her eye. It was Saxton's friend Greg, sitting with a chick who looked like she was straight out of a music video herself.

Since she was in a good mood, Beverly decided to have a little fun. She walked over to the bar. "Hi, Greg. Long time, no see."

"Oh, Beverly. How are you?" He looked nervously from Hootchie Momma back to Beverly. He remembered what had happened last time. When he saw that Beverly was waiting for an introduction, he said, "Beverly, this is— I'm sorry, what was your name again?"

"Trina, but my friends call me Treen," she said, smiling broadly.

Beverly sized her up, immediately realizing that everything about her was fake, from the thirty-eight-D boobs, the light green eyes, and shoulder-length weave to the long bloodred nails. She was a real-life tart-style Barbie doll. "It's nice to meet you, Trina." Beverly was about to add a comment when she noticed that one of the girl's fake eyelashes was hanging precariously off the end of her eye, and she obviously didn't know it. Beverly leaned in closer to the girl and whispered, "Your eyelash is hanging off."

"Excuse me?" The music and the din of conversation was booming, so Beverly had to repeat herself. Again the girl said, "Excuse me?" but this time with an edge in her squeaky, high-pitched voice.

"I said, your fake eyelash is hanging off!" This time Beverly spoke in a loud voice that matched the girl's surly attitude. Not only did Greg hear the embarrassing comment, but so did the people who stood nearby. The bimbo was mortified. Embarrassed, she grabbed her fake fur coat from the back of her chair and stormed away from the bar, without so much as a good-bye to Greg.

Beverly couldn't help but laugh. She needed a release after the tense round of negotiation she'd just endured with TJ. She shook her head after the peals of laughter subsided. "You sure know how to pick 'em."

Greg was quick to answer. "Hey, I just met her."

"Better luck next time," Beverly quipped, then turned to leave.

Instead, Greg placed a hand on her arm, nice and easy. He smiled at her, not mad about the tacky girl he'd lost. "The least you could do is join me for a drink, now that you've chased my date away."

Beverly was taken aback. Verbal warfare she was ready for, but an invitation to chat was definitely unexpected. She looked at her watch. Less confidently she said, "Okay, but I can't stay very long."

"What are you drinking?"

"I'll have a port."

"I would never have taken you for a port drinker," he said, eyeing her with new interest. "You seem more like a white wine girl to me."

Beverly tossed her head back and laughed. "There's a lot about me that you don't know," she said.

For the first time Greg saw through Beverly's carefully constructed shell of professionalism. He liked what he saw: the beautiful toothy smile, the full sexy mouth, and the dark brown eyes that always seemed to sparkle with mischief. Plus, he liked that booming laugh of hers. It reminded him of his favorite aunt, who was also never known to mince words or a good laugh. "It seems that I have quite a bit to learn," he said, motioning for the bartender. "A port for the lady, and I'll take another dirty martini with Grey Goose."

When their drinks arrived, Greg watched intently as she took a sip of the thick, rich liquid. "Don't think that you can get me drunk and take advantage of me," she teased him.

"Me? Take advantage of you? Somehow I don't see anyone ever taking advantage of you. Least of all me." He shook his head.

She looked at him with mock surprise. "This, coming from the self-appointed Love Doctor?"

Embarrassed, he dropped his head and shook it from side to side, wearing a bashful smile. "All right, all right." He held his palms up in surrender.

She smiled at the nicer side of him that had suddenly emerged. "How did you end up becoming a doctor anyway?" she asked. Beverly propped her elbow on the table and rested her chin in the palm of her hand.

"It's actually a funny story," he said, setting his drink on the table. "When I was in the ninth grade, I broke my arm playing football—that's not the funny part," he added.

Beverly smiled and thought to herself how cute he was. She loved his smooth dark complexion and the widow's peak that gave his even features character.

"Anyway," he continued, "when we got to the hospital, there was this black doctor in the ER who was running the show. Everyone there looked up to him: the nurses, the patients, and even the other white doctors. So I thought to myself, 'That's going to be me.' And the rest is history."

"That's why positive role models are so important for our kids."

"Yeah, and that's why I spend at least two Saturdays out of every month mentoring young boys who don't have fathers."

Beverly suddenly saw him in a different light. She would never have imagined him to be socially conscious. "Wow, that's great."

He winked at her. "You see, there's a lot that you don't know about me, too."

"So tell me everything." She leaned in closer to him.

"Well, I'm from Brooklyn. I am the youngest child in a family of five. I have four sisters."

"You must have been spoiled rotten."

"Spoiled! No, I was the one they always ganged up on. Anytime anything was broken in the house, no matter who did it, they all got together and convinced my mom that it was me. I love 'em dearly, but little girls are more conniving than little boys. And something tells me that you were probably really good at it." He saw the mischievous little smile that quirked her lips and knew that he was dead right.

"Who, me?" she asked innocently.

"Go ahead and fess up." Greg leaned back in the chair waiting on her confession.

"Unfortunately, I didn't have anyone else in the house to blame anything on. I was an only child, so the kids in the neighborhood were my only siblings. In fact, Mallory is like a sister to me. We were thick as thieves, always up to something." She smiled, remembering the old days. "When we were in the fifth grade, we decided to create a fair for the other kids in the neighborhood. So we made games, borrowed a pony from one of our neighbors, and charged for rides and the prizes, which we made by hand. We organized the whole thing and had it in Mallory's backyard. After raising over three hundred dollars—which was a lot of money back then—we donated it all to the Sickle Cell Anemia Foundation."

"That's pretty enterprising for a couple of fifth-graders."

"We didn't know what the words no or can't meant. And still don't."

"I believe that." Greg took a sip of his drink, enjoying the conversation and getting to know a real lady, the first one in a long time.

Beverly took a look at her watch. "I've gotta run. I didn't realize how late it'd gotten. I have an early day tomorrow." She began gathering her things.

Greg reached for her hand. "Can I see you again?"

The touch of his hand surprised her. What surprised her even more was how nice it felt resting on top of hers. "Maybe."

"How can I get in touch with you?"

"I'm sure I'll see you around," she said coyly.

"I'm counting on it."

19

THE PLOT THICKENS

"Tough day at the office?" Nikki asked. She was sprawled out on the sofa in a leopard-print bathrobe, eating a bowl of Ben & Jerry's strawberry ice cream, when Mallory walked in, disheveled and anxious.

"It has been a long day," Mallory answered, tossing her bag on the coffee table, which was littered with an assortment of Nikki's fashion magazines and the latest catalogue from Barneys.

She set her bowl of ice cream on the table, giving Mallory her full attention. Disheveled or not, there was something different about her, a certain glow that, based on Nikki's vast experience, usually followed a good lay. "What time is it?"

Mallory glanced at her watch, surprised and embarrassed at how late it was. "Eleven thirty," she said, lamely adding, "I had a lot of work to catch up on."

I'll bet you did, Nikki thought. She knew it would just be a matter of time before Mallory and Saxton rekindled that flame. The timing couldn't be better, as far as she was concerned. Now she could implement the next step of her plan.

"Besides, there was a lot of drama in the office today," Mallory said. She was anxious to talk about anything else except the reason for her late night in the office.

"What happened?"

Mallory took a deep breath and exhaled. "FBC pulled back from the syndication deal today. And though television operations have nothing to do with *Spotlight*, the whole office was in mourning. Everybody knew how important the deal was to Saxton, Deena, and to the entire company."

"You're kidding!" Nikki was surprised at this development. Based on everything that Deena had told her, the deal seemed to be a sure thing.

"I wish I was," Mallory said, shaking her head. "Apparently FBC wants to wait a few months before making a commitment. They've decided to compare *The Ingram Hour*'s ratings to comparable shows first. If Deena's ratings continue to lead, then they'll do the deal."

Nikki slipped up. "I thought that deal was all but done."

"Why'd you think that?" Mallory asked, puzzled. She had never given her that impression. In fact, she didn't remember discussing the deal with Nikki at all, although it wasn't exactly a secret, since it had been mentioned in more than a few trade publications.

"Oh, I-I just assumed it, since the show, and Deena, are so popular," Nikki stammered.

"I guess popularity isn't always enough."

"Especially when multimillion-dollar negotiations are at stake," Nikki said. "Was Saxton handling this for Deena?" Of course she knew that he was, but as usual, she was fishing for more information.

"Yeah, he handles all of her business affairs."

"She can't be too happy with him right now," Nikki said, picking up her bowl of ice cream.

"It's not really his fault." Mallory genuinely felt sorry for him after hearing from Vickee of the blowup that he and Deena had after he returned to the office empty-handed. The office grapevine was fully functional, reaching to her office at lightning speed.

Nikki paused with her spoon halfway to her mouth. "What do you mean, not really?"

"Well, I heard that he did drive a hard bargain with the network and even declined a larger offer they recently made."

"What did Deena have to say about that?"

"Actually, she didn't know about the latest offer," Mallory confided. Cindy, disturbed by Saxton's instructions not to tell Deena about the new FBC offer, had confided her concerns to her fellow secretary, Vickee, who Mallory had hired away from *Heat*.

Nikki remained cool as she digested this latest piece of inside information. If Saxton's questionable hiring of Mallory wasn't enough to piss Deena off, once she found out about this new development, she should be ready to get rid of that two-timing, egotistical ladies' man once and for all. Especially if everyone else also knew the details of how her precious fiancé had deceived her and, worse, cost her a nine-figure deal. It was time for her to make another phone call to Yvette. Besides, she thought, eyeing the catalogue on the table, she'd been wanting a fur-trimmed cashmere coat that she'd seen at Barneys. Now all she had to do was go dialing for dollars. "Well, I hope it all works out okay," she offered nonchalantly, getting up to head into the kitchen.

Mallory walked into her bedroom, anxious for some time alone to digest all that had happened tonight. The memory of the hot sex in Saxton's office lit a fire in her loins, but also warmed her cheeks in embarrassment. *How did I get myself in this situation?* she wondered. She kicked off her boots and reclined on the bed, staring at the ceiling.

Just then the phone rang, snapping her out of her somber reverie. Mallory reached over to the side table to pick up the call. "Hello," she said, still spread out on the bed.

"Mallory?" a man's voice came through the phone. At first, she did not recognize him.

"This is Mallory," she answered, trying to place the voice.

"It's Bob Morris."

Mallory immediately sat up. "What's happened?" she asked, alarmed.

"Just an update," he said. "I've just heard from my sources that the Browns are hiding out in the Niagara Falls, New York, area. The best guess is that they're biding their time until they can safely make it across the Canadian border. Apparently, they spent the last year in North Carolina using the aliases Jonathan and Emily Ponder."

She jumped up and began pacing nervously around the room. "We've got to get there. We have to find them, now!" If they made it across the border, she might never see Dylan again.

"We will, Mallory. But first we have to track them down. Just sit tight. I'll call you as soon as I get more news. I've gotta run, but I'll be in touch." He hung up the phone.

"Go where, to find who?" Nikki had suddenly appeared in her doorway.

Her unexpected presence startled Mallory. "Nothing," she said, trying to compose herself. "That was Eric, just a problem at the magazine with an interview we're trying to put together," she lied. She got up and walked past Nikki into the bathroom.

When she was safely out of sight, Nikki picked up the phone and dialed star six-nine. She got a recording: *"You've reached the Morris Surveillance Agency. Please leave a message at the tone, or page me at 888-555-1234 if this is an emergency."* Nikki hung up, mystified. Who was Mallory trying to find, and why was she using a private investigator to do it? Apparently, there was a lot more to her sweet, innocent roommate than met the eye.

20

SOUTH OF THE BORDER

Things had not turned out the way they were supposed to, Linda Brown thought as she sat fretting over the mess that had been made of her life. When and where had it all gone so horribly wrong? To say that life had thrown her a curve ball would be a gross understatement.

For so long her life had been as perfectly planned and tightly knit as the hand-sewn quilt that lay draped across the back of the sofa. It was her one possession that had traveled with the small family from one secret hiding place to the next. She and her mother had made the quilt together during the summer of her senior year in high school. During those idyllic days, if anyone had suggested that she would be a fugitive on the lam, she would have accused him of delusional lunacy.

In her black-and-white picture in Clear Brook High School's yearbook, she looked like a deer caught in the glare of headlights. The caption underneath it bore the dubious distinction MOST STUDIOUS, which was also a pseudonym for MOST BORING. Like any *Glamour*-reading, zit-fighting teenage girl she had resented her choir girl, bookworm existence. Only too late she had come to realize that boring was good. How, she wondered, had things spiraled so quickly out of control? One minute her biggest concerns were lesson plans for four-year-olds and whether Dylan was too big for his car seat, and the next thing she knew she was aiding and abetting embezzlement, running from the law, and dragging her young son along for the bumpy ride. And to think, Jonathan was supposed to be what her mother called a "safe choice." He had been a nerdy finance major, complete with a pocket protector.

Years later, when they ran into each other at a dinner party given by mutual friends in South Orange, New Jersey, Linda remembered feeling as though the nerdiness had been replaced by a measure of cockiness, which she had found attractive at the time.

"We should have the papers within the week," her husband said. He was studying the map that lay spread out on the floor. He had found an underworld figure who, for the right amount of money, would give them passports that were good enough to cross the border. Unfortunately, that amount of money proved to be the last of the stash that he had managed to take before their getaway last year. He had since learned that life on the run was not cheap, especially with a wife and kid in tow. The stress had taken its toll on him. He was not cut out for a life on the run, but when he started the money laundering scheme for his bosses, he never thought it would get to this. After all, he was brilliant with accounting and thought himself to be too clever to be caught, with all of the sophisticated offshore accounts and bogus companies he'd set up.

"Where are we going now?" Dylan asked. He was sprawled on the floor alongside his dad, staring at the connection of lines as though he knew exactly what they all stood for.

"On another trip," Jonathan answered.

"Where to?" the curious little boy asked. Dylan had come to look at their frequent travels as real-life adventures. While he waited on his dad to reveal their next destination, he continued to study the map, the tip of his tongue peeking out from his mouth.

"We're going to Canada. Do you know where that is?"

"It's that way," Dylan answered, pointing north of the United States. Though he had been kept out of kindergarten,

Linda, who was a teacher, had given him a home-school education. No matter what else was happening, she always took time out each day to teach him. The only thing that she could not make up for was a lack of playmates. Unfortunately, it was too dangerous for them to allow Dylan to have close friends, since there was no way to control what a five-year-old might say. A slip of the tongue could have devastating consequences for all of them.

She bent down to scoop him up. "Is that your final answer?" This was their favorite game. She would ask him a question, and after he gave an answer, she would mimic Regis until he was sure that it was right. If he did have the correct answer, he would get a treat, and if he didn't, he would have to continue studying.

He gave her a stoic, big-boy look. "That's my final answer."

"Are you sure?" she said.

"I'm positive."

"I thought your name was Dylan," she joked as she began tickling his belly.

Laughter pierced the air as he squirmed in her arms to get away, though not trying too hard.

While mother and son continued to play on the floor of the little house, Jonathan headed into the kitchen with his cell phone. When he came back, Linda could read the concern on his face, a skill that she'd honed all too well.

"Sweetie, go get ready for bed for me," she said to Dylan. She could tell that it was time for one of those dreaded conversations that inevitably led from bad news to worse. As she stood up, she could feel a knot beginning to twist in the pit of her stomach.

"But, Mommeeee." He was just getting wound up. "Let's play some more." A frown pinched his handsome face. Dylan was almond brown with the deepest, largest dark brown eyes she had ever seen on a child. They were framed by thick, dark lashes.

"Later, baby. Go get ready for bed now. I'll be in in a minute to read one of your favorite stories." She nudged him toward the back bedroom.

"Ah, maaan." Dylan trudged off like a prisoner being led to a cell, pouting all the way.

When he was out of earshot, she sat down on the worn sofa. "What is it?"

Jonathan began blinking rapidly. "It's Mallory." He sat down next to her on the secondhand couch. As beat up and tired as that old stained sofa was, it still looked better than the two of them did.

Linda simply looked at him, not comprehending. She was braced for news of federal marshals rounding the bend or a gang of mobsters waiting in the shadows, but not Mallory Baylor, Dylan's birth mom, whom she had all but erased from her mind. As bad as the other calls would have been, this one was harder for her to bear in many ways.

"She's hired a private investigator who's somehow managed to trace us to this cell phone." Jonathan took a deep breath. "He's asking that we let her see Dylan." Here was yet another wrinkle in his plan.

He was proof of the old adage "If you want to make God laugh, make a plan." As far as he could see, God must be hysterical right about now. His journey to becoming a wanted money launderer and embezzler wasn't one that he'd started on intentionally. He still remembered the first time his boss, an Italian from Jersey City, asked him to "hide a few of the profits." When Jonathan balked, he was offered a substantial bonus, which allowed him to buy the newest Mercedes coupe that he'd been wanting ever since his bourgeois neighbor, a cocky Wall Streeter, had shown up with one a few months earlier. As time went on, the sums became larger, as did his bonuses. Though he knew it was illegal, he managed to convince himself that he was only doing what the corporate embezzlers on Wall Street did every day, and besides, he further reasoned, he wasn't hurting anybody. It was really a victimless crime, so he was able to sleep at night.

For a long time it was easy for him to pretend everything was normal and that he was just your everyday accountant. He'd convinced Linda and himself of that until the phone calls started coming. The first one that caused him to break out into a cold sweat was from the IRS; later came another from the Justice Department. By the time he finally confided in Linda, he was a nervous wreck, not sure whether to be more afraid of the Feds or the mob. He convinced Linda that they had to run.

"Maybe we should give him back to her," he said, calculating the factors involved. Having the kid along was a real burden.

She turned to face him with fierce determination. "You are out of your mind!"

"Listen to me, Linda," he pleaded. "It is probably the best option for all of us. He'll be safer and we'll stand a better chance of getting away."

She glared at him. "You may have taken everything else away from me, but you're not taking my son." Tears began to stream down her face. It amazed her that she had any left. She had been crying nonstop for two years now. She'd shed tears for her empty future, for her lost past, for the fading memories of her family, and now she cried for Dylan.

21

WHAT'S LOVE GOT TO DO WITH IT?

Mallory and Eric had grown closer over the weeks they'd spent together hashing out creative editorial concepts and building the working foundation for *Spotlight*, and their hard work was paying off. Given Eric's vast contacts, Saxton's high-powered connections, Mallory's editorial skills and the cachet of Deena Ingram's name, they had an impressive lineup of celebrities for future cover and feature stories.

Things were coming together well for the growing staff at *Spotlight* magazine. They'd hired a brilliant creative director, Kevin Stuart, away from *Details* magazine; a fashion director, Kym Yong, from *Vibe*; a photo editor; a features editor; two feature writers; and three staff writers. Mallory had also hired Vickee away from Chad to work as her personal assistant.

"You have no idea how happy I was when you called me to come work for you. I really don't know if I could've taken another week of Chad the Sleaze Ball," Vickee said, shaking her head. "It had gotten so bad that most of the women in the office, including me, refused to be alone with him."

"How does he continue to keep his job?" Mallory asked, shaking her head. There were so few opportunities for African-Americans in the media industry to begin with that it angered her that Chad would make the going even tougher for the few that did manage to find work.

"Beats me," Vickee answered. "But you know Mirage is a privately held company, and I understand that the principal, Richard Pope, attended Yale graduate school with Chad. So they are thicker than thieves."

"It just pisses me off that he's able to get away with that," Mallory said. "I should have done something about it rather than let him continue to harass other women."

"Don't beat yourself up, Mallory. The way the laws are written, there's not a lot you could have done. Remember, he's always careful not to have any witnesses, and he never leaves a paper trail, or any other evidence, for that matter. So it's always his word against yours, and who do you think Richard is most likely to believe?"

"You're right," Mallory conceded, "but it still sucks."

"Well I, for one, am glad that you decided to leave," Vickee said as she closed the door to Mallory's office behind her.

"So am I," Mallory said, mainly to herself.

Chad wasn't the man foremost in her mind, though. After last night, the difficulty of working with Saxton had increased tenfold. She'd been avoiding him all day, not wanting to confront the aftermath of what they'd done. The steamy bliss of last night had been replaced by the cold, glaring realities of the morning.

Several minutes later, while Mallory was reviewing the contact sheets from the latest photo shoot, Deena stormed into her office. She was enraged, waving a single sheet of newspaper in the air as though it were a smoking gun. "What the hell is this?" she demanded.

Mallory was taken aback. "What are you talking about?" she asked, looking up from the photos.

"Why don't you tell me?" Deena sneered, tossing the page onto Mallory's desk.

When Mallory saw the TALK OF THE TOWN heading, she

dreaded what was coming next. As Deena stood over her, she reached for the article and begin reading the section that had been circled.

> When things got too *Hot* at a certain urban magazine, which attractive female writer fled before taking a huge promotion at one owned by her former lover and his celebrity fiancée?

The blood drained from Mallory's face as images of the night before flashed luridly in her head. This couldn't have happened at a worse possible time.

"What the hell is this about?" Deena demanded, flinging her hair from one side to the other. "Did you or didn't you have an affair with my fiancé?"

Mallory felt like she'd been slapped in the face. Her mouth hung agape in shock. Before a response registered, Saxton walked through the door, straight into the eye of the storm.

"Deena, that was a long time ago, before we even met," he said. While Mallory sat shell-shocked, Vickee had acted quickly and run into Saxton's office to fetch him.

His voice startled Deena, who had intentionally decided to ambush Mallory rather than confront Saxton first. She spun around. "Oh, so you're here to take up for your girlfriend?" she hissed at him.

Mallory lowered her eyes, not wanting to see the guilt written all over Saxton's face. It mirrored her own, though thankfully Deena was staring at him.

"Like I just said," Saxton stumbled, "that happened a long time ago, before we even started dating."

"Whether it was last night or ten years ago, it doesn't matter. You still lied to me. Just a month ago, you told me that you had met Mallory when she came to interview you for *Heat*.

Had you conveniently forgotten that you'd *fucked* her before?" Deena spat. She turned to Mallory. "Well, sweetie, I guess it must not have been that memorable."

The realization that Deena had misread his guilty expression for remorse over lying to her gave Saxton the edge he needed to regain some control over the explosive situation. "That's enough," he said, moving toward Deena, with his poker face firmly back in place.

"I'd say it is!" Deena retorted, her eyes burning brightly with anger.

Saxton lowered his voice. "You're right. I was not completely honest with you. I didn't want to tell you about our past, because I was afraid that you'd do exactly what you're doing now, blaming Mallory, and judging her based on it."

Mallory stood up from behind the desk. "Listen, Deena, I hadn't seen, heard from, or thought about Saxton since he left Atlanta over five years ago," she said weakly, not convincing even herself. "It was only after another writer had an accident at the last minute that I was asked to interview him. So, you see, our relationship is nothing but professional."

"Given your past sexual relationship with Chad at *Heat*, I would have to question which profession," Deena snapped. Her insinuation hung like lead in the air. "It's not every day that a staff writer is promoted to executive editor, now is it?"

"Deena, that's enough," Saxton said. He took her arm gently but firmly, and led her out of Mallory's office.

When the coast was clear, Mallory sank back into her desk chair, with Vickee looking on from the far corner. "So much for being glad to be here," she said, running the back of her hand across her forehead.

"I wouldn't worry about her too much. Saxton runs the show here, and he doesn't seem like the type to let her bully him around."

"I hope you're right," Mallory said, massaging the knotty kink that had formed in the back of her neck.

"Why didn't you tell me about you and Saxton?"

That one Mallory could answer honestly. "Because there was really nothing to tell."

Vickee seemed to accept that. "Don't let her get you down," she said, putting a hand on Mallory's shoulder.

Mallory looked up at her. "Thanks, Vickee, for covering my back. If you hadn't gone to get Saxton when you did, I'm not sure that either one of us would still be here."

"Don't worry about that. I'll always have your back."

Just then Eric appeared in the doorway. "What happened here?" he asked with exaggerated surprise. "I feel like I just walked into a wake."

"You almost did," Mallory said. "Mine." She sat him down and told him the whole story.

"The drama up in here is hotter than on *As the World Turns*," Eric said, fanning himself with the pink handkerchief he had extracted from his jacket pocket.

"At this point I'd settle for a little comedy instead," Mallory said, staring up at the ceiling and taking a deep breath.

"Don't worry about Deena. I know how to handle that diva. It takes one, you know, to handle one," Eric quipped.

"Well, she's all yours."

Now that the fireworks were over, they all dispersed to their own offices, leaving Mallory drained from the theatrics.

The "Talk of the Town" piece was the last thing that Mallory expected to read, since no one in New York, except for Nikki and Beverly, knew about her past relationship with Saxton. The first gossip sheet leak about Chad's sexual harassment seemed random to her, but this was starting to feel very personal. She knew Beverly would never tell anyone. So that left just one person. . . .

Later that afternoon, Saxton walked into Mallory's office and closed the door, looking rather sheepish. "I'm sorry about earlier," he said, his hands stuffed in his pocket.

"Which part?" Mallory asked snidely. "Last night, the fact that your fiancée attacked me, or that you lied to her so easily?"

He looked like the losing fighter after the last round of a long bout. "Mallory, about last night. I did not mean for that to happen. I never planned on it. I-I don't know what else to say, except that I've never wanted to do anything to hurt you," he pleaded.

Mallory saw the pain and confusion in his eyes, but it didn't excuse his behavior. "Is it that easy for you to cheat on Deena and then lie to her face the next day?"

"What would you rather I do?" he asked, his voice an urgent whisper. "Should I have just told her that she was right? That we'd made love last night, and oh, by the way, it was great? Is that what you want?"

She glared at him. "What I really want," she said coldly, "is for you to leave me alone."

He turned and stormed out the door.

Since learning that *The Ingram Hour* had been put on a thirteen-week notice by FBC, Deena had become consumed with her talk show's ratings, as well as her public image, which she felt was inseparably linked to the show's eventual success or failure.

"There is no way that I can let that slut Gina Davis steal a hundred-million-dollar syndication deal from under me," she said to CoAnne, her personal publicist. They were in Deena's sun-drenched corner office going over the details of the *Spotlight* premier party, which was scheduled for the following weekend.

"Certainly *Spotlight*'s premiere will garner some positive press, but we've got to come up with a great All-American story, one that will rivet the imaginations of the masses, *and* more important, make them tune in to *The Ingram Hour*." CoAnne was a snappy Jewish princess who spoke with a nasally twang that was definitely an acquired taste. She was also pragmatic and not embarrassed to say what other people only had the guts to think. She was known, for good reason, throughout the city as the pit bull of the PR world.

"One that hopefully doesn't involve my fiancé and that little twit in the office," Deena said. She exhaled deeply, blowing her wispy bangs up over her head. Mallory was definitely a thorn in her side. It bugged the shit out of her to see Mallory sashaying about the office with that effortless style of hers. She walked into a room, and all eyes, male and female, naturally went to her. It had taken fame, and years of practice, for Deena to achieve that same reaction from people. What really pissed her off was that right now she was powerless to get rid of Mallory. She was savvy enough, even in her furious state, to know that, if she forced the issue, it would only push Saxton closer to Mallory. After all, hadn't he just stuck up for her? The vixen had him wrapped around her little finger.

"That whole thing was quite unfortunate," CoAnne, said, referring to the blind item that was planted in the "Talk of the Town" gossip column.

Deena twisted her mouth in distaste. "I don't know who to hate more, Mallory or that sleazy gossip hag Yvette."

"Listen, honey, I'd start and stop with Mallory," CoAnne said. "Yvette was just doing her job."

Deena stood up from her desk and turned to look out of her window at the expansive view. "There's a little more to it than that. Yvette's swipes at me are definitely personal."

CoAnne leaned forward inquisitively. "Why do you think that?"

"We went to grad school together at Columbia and studied journalism. In fact, she was the valedictorian of our class."

"And?" CoAnne still didn't see the relevance.

Deena turned around to face her. "I'm a nationally known talk show host and *she* writes a gossip column," she said as though it explained everything. "She's just jealous."

CoAnne crossed her legs in the opposite direction as she pondered Deena's theory. "If that's the case, we've got a bigger media problem than I originally thought. Trust me, the last thing you *ever* want is a syndicated gossip columnist with a hard-on for you. I'd sooner pick a fight with Mike Tyson."

"Gee, thanks." Deena rolled her eyes.

"Just remember, you may be the bigger celebrity of the two, but unfortunately she has the bigger gun."

This was not what Deena wanted to hear. "That's why I pay you." She fixed CoAnne with a I-hope-you-get-my-drift stare.

Unfazed, CoAnne said, "I do have one idea that might push you over the ratings edge."

"I'm all ears," Deena said, leaning forward over her imposing conference table–sized desk.

"It's simple really. You need to move your wedding day up."

"What? What's this got to do with my wedding?"

"Duh!" CoAnne said, tilting her head sideways. "Keep up with me here. Can you think of any other event that does a better job of spreading goodwill than a big white wedding? And yours is destined to be a media frenzy anyway, so why not cash in on it early?"

"You really think I should?" She knew that weddings were supposed to be about intimate vows between two people who loved each other, but when you looked at it from a media standpoint, what did love have to do with it—especially when she was fighting to save her career?

"I think you have to do it. The wedding should be just after the first of the year, so that you can catch a ratings tailwind that would last through to the last three weeks of the thirteen-week ratings comparison period."

Deena's thoughts flashed back to the ugly scene earlier in Mallory's office. Even though they both claimed that their affair was in the past, there was something about the tension in that room—between the two of them—that had her even more worried than she had been before. In short, they both looked guilty as sin to her.

After weighing the possibilities, Deena said, "You know what? That is genius!"

This was one way to stop whatever plans Ms. Mallory had up her sleeve. Why hadn't she thought of it herself? After all, there was no need to wait. That would only let Mallory sink her vicious claws further into Saxton.

Now all she had to do was to convince the groom. She and Saxton hadn't spoken since the run-in this morning, so it might be a little difficult for her to convince him now to take a faster run down the aisle. She had some damage control to do. She had to get him to agree. It was the least that he could do, she reasoned. It was because of his mishandling of the deal that she was in this position in the first place.

Ten minutes later, Deena sauntered into Saxton's office and found him on the telephone. When she walked over and sat on his desk facing him, he didn't so much as glance in her direction, so she crossed her legs, posing in front of him. He angled his body away from her line of sight and continued to talk into the receiver. Nettled, she tossed her head back, letting her hair flow over her shoulders. She positioned herself behind his chair and began kneading the tense muscles in his neck. He glanced back over his shoulder, but kept his conversation going.

When he finally hung up, he stood and said, "What's up?" He still wore a sheepish, semiguilty look.

"I just came by to check on you." She wrapped her arms around his neck, pulling him closer. "I love you, sweetheart," she purred softly into his ear.

"I love you, too," he said, though the words caught in his throat.

"Do you?" She looked into his eyes, searching for a sign of his love.

"Of course I do. Why do you ask?"

"It's just that things haven't been the same between us." She lowered her head sadly as though she were on the verge of tears.

He was glad to be able to clear the air, and he hoped to get his life back on track. He really did feel bad for cheating on Deena. It wasn't his MO at all. Now he just had to put it behind him and concentrate on fixing his relationship with his fiancée. "That's behind us now. We both said some things that we didn't mean. It's over now." He hugged her close to him.

"Nothing means as much to me as you do, especially not some syndication deal," she said, forcing sincerity into her voice.

"I know that."

She brightened. "Why don't we go have dinner? Maybe stop by Tse Yang."

Saxton looked at his watch. "Cool. Let's meet in the lobby in twenty minutes."

"Great," she said, smiling, happy to be over the first speed bump. She headed out of his door with a new bounce in her stride toward her end of the building. As she passed Mallory in the hallway, she greeted her with a snappy toss of her long hair.

Soon she and Saxton were cozily ensconced in one of the burgundy leather booths at the restaurant. Two martinis into the evening, she sprang the idea on him as though it were nothing more than a spontaneous thought. "Why don't we get married at the top of the year? Let's not wait until June."

He was taken by surprise. "Why the sudden change?"

"I love you," she said, looking earnestly into his eyes. "I don't want to wait until June to be Mrs. McKensie." She reached for his hand under the table and squeezed it affectionately.

He didn't look enthusiastic about the idea at all. "I thought Colin Cowie needed at least a full year to plan a wedding." He scratched his head as more details of her voluminous planning came back to him. "Before, you and your mother made such a big deal over having enough time to secure the best venues and to plan for every minute detail, but now you're willing to give up five whole months of preparation time?"

Deena was the picture of sincerity. "Not until it looked as though I might lose you did I realize just how important you are to me. I don't care about some fancy wedding. I just want us to be together, sooner rather than later."

This lover's vow was in stark contrast to all of their previous conversations about the wedding. Nor did the thought of moving the wedding date up sit well with him. Indeed, the idea of getting married at all was beginning to cause him indigestion. Saxton felt like a fish caught dangling on an angler's hook. Tearing himself away from its grip would be painful, but ultimately, so would the end result of being hauled aboard.

22

THE WILD AND THE WICKED

The premiere for *Spotlight* magazine was one of those parties that the hip, the young, the fashionable, and the famous all felt obliged to attend in order to continue accruing their cool points. Caché, the hottest event company in New York, was planning the big bash, which was already being billed by the media as one to remember. Invitations were rolled up and slid inside handblown bottles with strings attached. Once removed, they instructed the invited guests to be at Pier 62 no later than eight o'clock, ready to cruise the Hudson River.

By seven thirty on the big night a steady stream of limos was rolling to a stop alongside the pier, bearing some of the hottest trendsetters in Manhattan. As long legs sprang from chauffeur-driven black limousines, followed closely by custom-tailored suits, a sexy procession headed down a long red spotlit carpet to the end of the pier, where a sleek two-hundred-foot yacht sat waiting. Sailors dressed in crisp white uniforms and black bibbed caps stood at alert, ready to assist the passengers up the gangplank. The floating mansion was all rich dark woods, spit-polished brass, and shining chrome. As the swanky guests reached the deck, they were welcomed aboard by a staff of white-suited waiters, who offered snifters of brandy and cognac, hot toddies, or glasses of port to stave off the chill of the late-November air blowing down the wide river.

Once the yacht was full of passengers, the huge motors revved up to set sail underneath the full moon of a New York sky with the *Spotlight* staff and four hundred twenty guests onboard. As the sleek vessel pulled away from the docks, the energy along the deck and throughout the fifteen-room yacht was tangible—an air of great expectation fueled by some of the hottest people in the world on a luxurious yacht.

Regardless of personal conflicts, this was not the kind of party that Nikki would have allowed herself to miss under any circumstance. Besides, she figured, with more than four hundred people in attendance, she would surely be able to keep her relationships between Mallory and Deena from the other. After her conversation earlier in the week with Mallory, it was more important than ever that she walk the straight and narrow.

She had been in her room, minding her own business, when Mallory walked in and gave her the Spanish Inquisition about the "Talk of the Town" article. Being the practiced liar that she was, Nikki was able to deny any involvement with a straight face. Even so, she wasn't certain that Mallory bought her story, so she had to be careful from this point on, since it seemed that Mallory wasn't quite as innocent or naive as she'd imagined. Nikki watched her as she stood to the side of the large glass-enclosed main room of the boat's first level.

Mallory stood drinking in the intoxicating scene laid out before her, proud of the hard work that she, Eric, and the rest of the staff had done to get to this point. She wore a sumptuous satin dress with straps that crossed her chest and accentuated the beautiful sculpture of her shoulders and upper torso, plus a pair of silver evening sandals. The diamond pendant to a vintage necklace that belonged to her mother nestled just above her cleavage. Courtesy of good genes and an afternoon shuttling between Mario Badescu Facial Spa and Josephs Hair Salon on Sixtieth, she looked exquisite.

Beverly had called yesterday, asking Mallory to put her

name on the guest list. Though she usually stayed away from glitzy entertainment industry soirees, no one would know it from her appearance. When she walked up, Mallory did a double-take.

"My, my, my," she mused, taking Beverly in head to toe, "don't we look fabulous."

Beverly tried to play it cool. "Thank you, and so do you. Is that gown new? It's beautiful."

"Don't try to change the subject on me. Look at you." Mallory gestured up and down. "Who is he?"

"I have no idea what you're talking about."

Mallory had been after Beverly for years to spruce up the goods. Just last week they'd spent thirty minutes at Sephora, with Mallory telling Beverly what tools she needed to transform herself from a dowdy stepchild into a radiant Cinderella. Though Beverly had purchased the products, Mallory doubted that she'd ever really put them to use.

She had been dead wrong: Beverly looked amazing. She wore a fitted Isaac Mizrahi tube dress that showed off curves Mallory never knew she had. Her hair was worn straight, giving her makeup a sexy, dramatic flare.

From their vantage point they could easily follow all of the action, regardless of whether guests were braving the brisk autumn air on the outer decks, tucked away in the top tier opposite the heliport, down below in the main room, or in one of the more private bars hidden away below. Since the yacht came equipped with a prewired video surveillance system, Caché had set up roving spotlights and cameras throughout the party to illuminate clusters of guests and transmit the images onto five large screens placed throughout the boat, which also housed four full staterooms, complete with bath and bar.

"I see TJ at the bar with one of his newest acts," Beverly whispered to Mallory.

"They look kinda cozy to me. Isn't he married?"

"Since when does that stop a dog from chowing down?" Beverly said dryly.

Mallory flinched a little, as she thought about her rendezvous with Saxton.

"I think I'll go over and stir things up a little." Beverly took off toward the bar.

"Now, *this* is sexy!" Eric sauntered over to Mallory holding two frothy glasses of champagne.

She took one from him and clinked the other one with hers. "Here's to sexy," she said before taking a sip.

"Speaking of, you look awesome." He backed up a couple of steps in order to take all of her in before whistling appreciatively. Coming from a gay man, this was the ultimate compliment.

"Thank you, darling. And you don't look too bad yourself."

Eric was the picture of debonair, wearing a black casual tuxedo with a white handkerchief hanging loosely from his breast pocket and his tieless piqué cotton shirt open three buttons from the neck.

"If it weren't for the sex thing, we'd make the perfect couple." They both laughed, though they couldn't agree more. Since she joined *Spotlight* they'd become the best of friends.

"Speaking of the perfect couple, where are they?" Mallory asked, trying for a nonchalant tone as she scanned the room.

"If you mean Deena and Saxton, I haven't seen a sign of either one of them." Nor had Mallory, who had been keeping an eye out for Saxton since she arrived. The shame of her run-in with Deena was already receding, and the glow from their fabulous night together was burning ever brighter. Plus, it was as much her fault as it was his, and she hadn't been honest with Deena herself. If they met tonight, she only prayed that no one else would notice the sparks of electricity that flew between them.

"Tell me, Mallory, are you still in love with him?" Eric asked, watching her closely.

The question made her jump. "Of course not. Why would you ask that?"

"I can see it in your eyes," Eric answered. "And in his."

So much for no one noticing. She could only hope that Deena was too vain to see.

The pace of the party was being amped up by the famous DJ Jazzie B, whom they had flown in from London. He brilliantly mixed classic R&B with hip-hop, fusion, and dance music. Everyone on the yacht was either nodding his head to the funky beats or dancing on the floor in the center of the main room. Images of the sleek, writhing bodies moved seductively under a roving spotlight and onto the big screens for all to see. "Let's go up to the observation deck. See what's happening there," Eric suggested.

"It's a little too cold out there for me," Mallory answered, passing her hands over her bare shoulders.

"There's a glass-enclosed area just off the heliport. Come on, let's check it out." They snaked their way through the throng of hot bodies, up to the room looking out over the river and the gleaming lights on either shore.

They were leaning on the bar, taking in the spectacular view, when a crowd of people began to descend on them, spilling out onto the outer deck. Many were pointing upward. A detail of security guards in dark suits and earpieces also converged on the area. Mallory and Eric peered up into the moonlit sky and noticed a gleaming helicopter that was slowly hovering downward in their direction with a large spotlight trained directly on it. Just then the DJ lowered the music. Out of the speakers blared the theme song from the James Bond movie *Goldfinger*. Everyone stared in awe as the helicopter descended ever closer to the boat, whipping the crowd and the night air into a frenzy, blowing hair, dresses, and anything else that wasn't held down. As it prepared to land on the heliport at the far end of the yacht, they spied the helicopter's passengers. There sat Deena Ingram and her handsome fiancé, Saxton McKensie, preparing to make their grand entrance. Deena smiled broadly and waved to the crowd. Flashbulbs went off like magical fireflies flickering in the night.

After the helicopter had safely landed, six sailors in white stood on either side of the aircraft to assist the star and her fiancé onto the deck. She wore a white mink open over a long oyster-colored evening gown. Saxton was as dashing as 007 himself in an off-white tuxedo that dripped from his body, with a white shirt and black necktie. He wore a red carnation in his buttonhole. They walked arm in arm down a red carpet, into a throng of well-wishers. The media went wild. They loved it, which was just the effect that Deena and CoAnne had counted on. In the following days, numerous pictures would run of the dashing couple stepping out of the gold helicopter onto the sleek yacht.

Eric whistled. "Talk about a grand entrance."

"When I saw CoAnne in the office yesterday, I should have known that Deena was up to something like this."

The couple made their way along the observation deck down the outer stairs to the ship's main room. The excited crowd parted for the two, before swelling up behind them to become part of one throbbing entourage. Eric and Mallory took the interior steps downstairs and arrived in time to see Deena and Saxton conclude their impressive entrance at a microphone set up in the center of the room with a bright spotlight focused directly on them.

Deena reached for the mike. "Wow! This is phenomenal!" she said, still a bit breathy from the thrilling helicopter ride. "It's so good to see you all here to help Saxton and me celebrate the launch of the hottest new magazine to hit the newsstand since *Variety*." The audience cheered loudly and clapped enthusiastically.

"Without you all and our advertisers, *Spotlight* magazine would not be possible, but I'd be remiss if I didn't thank the exemplary staff of *Spotlight* for their tireless efforts to make the magazine and this night possible. I'd like to introduce, of course, the main person responsible for this, my fiancé, Saxton McKensie." He took a step forward and gave a short quick wave around the room. "And I'd like to thank our editor-in-chief, Eric Handley, who is the brainchild behind the premier issue, which we've gotten rave reviews for." Eric remained in place as the spotlight found him, and he waved his hand to loud applause. He then turned toward Mallory in order to clap for her introduction, which he assumed was coming next. "I'd also like to thank Morgan Nelson, owner of Caché, for pulling this fabulous party together, and my publicist, CoAnne Bernstied, for making sure that you all knew about it." The audience again gave another round of applause as Eric looked on in horror, and Mallory stood dumbfounded. Saxton's face, she saw, had turned to stone. "Enjoy the rest of the night." The DJ picked up the music and the party was amped up another notch.

"That bitch," Eric hissed. He took his silver flask from his breast pocket and tossed back a swallow of single malt.

"It's okay," Mallory assured him.

"No, it's not okay. You've worked harder than anybody here to pull this together, and for her to thank a party planner—and a publicist, for God's sake—and not thank you is unimaginable."

Just then Eric was swarmed by a swell of well-wishers, anxious to meet the new editor-in-chief of *Spotlight* magazine. Mallory quietly eased away from him while he was swallowed in a babble of conversation. As she headed to the other side of the room, someone grabbed her arm. When she turned around, there stood Saxton.

"Hi, Mallory." For such a celebration, his expression did not fit the mood. He had been mortified by their splashy grand entrance. He'd had no knowledge of it until their driver passed the piers and instead dropped them off at the Thirty-fifth Street heliport. By then it was too late to board the yacht on foot because it had already set sail.

"Hi, Saxton." The feel of his touch on her arm warmed her instantly. For a moment it was hard for Mallory to concentrate on what he was saying.

"Listen, I'm sorry about Deena." That simple statement

told a much more complicated story. Not only was he sorry for her malicious omission earlier, but what he really wanted to say was that he was sorry about Deena, period.

Mallory held her head down. "Hey, it's not your fault."

"No, it is. I hired you and it's my responsibility to make sure that you are treated fairly." He was still holding on to her arm as they were jostled by merrymakers. "If it weren't for your hard work and vision, none of this would be possible."

Mallory fixed him with a stern look. "Really, Saxton, it's okay. I don't have to have the spotlight, no pun intended. I just want to do my job, and do it well."

Saxton smiled, seeing her fierce expression. "You look amazing tonight."

Her heart fluttered. "Thank you."

At that moment Greg appeared at his side. "Man, this party is off the hook! Babes for days." He and Saxton hugged. "Seriously, man, it's great, and congrats." He held his martini glass upward in a silent toast.

Greg turned to Mallory and said, "Long time, no see. How've you been?" He embraced her, looking over her shoulder at Saxton and winking appreciatively.

"I've been good," Mallory said.

"Where's your girl?" he asked.

"Who are you talking about?"

"Beverly," he answered, rocking on his heels, his hands stuffed in his pocket. He was acting all nonchalant, but the slight tightness in his throat betrayed him.

"She's over at the bar. Why do you ask?"

"Just curious."

He was about to excuse himself and head off in that direction when he realized Beverly was headed their way. He almost raised his hand to wave, but stopped himself. Mallory and Saxton looked at each other questioningly. As far as they knew, Greg and Beverly's last meeting hadn't exactly been a scene from *Romeo and Juliet*.

"Wow," escaped from Greg's cloak of cool as Beverly walked up. "You look great."

"Don't sound so surprised," she chided lightly. "I told you that there was a lot about me that you didn't know."

"I see," he said, letting his eyes wander appreciatively from head to toe. "Well, tell me this: Can you dance?"

"I guess you'll have to see to find out."

Mallory and Saxton looked at each other with raised brows as the pair headed off in the direction of the dance floor with Greg's arm resting possessively around Beverly's waist.

When they were alone Mallory turned to Saxton. "Look, I wanted to apologize to you for putting all the blame on you. It was as much my fault as yours."

"Let's forget about it," he said, reaching for her hand. They held hands for a few precious seconds before they both knew that it was best to pull apart.

Nikki was observing this private exchange from her perch at the bar. She had first seen Mallory's and Saxton's images a few minutes ago as they were flashed onto the big screens. He'd been holding on to her arm as though in pursuit, and she had her head down modestly. Nikki also watched Deena, and the menacing glare that settled onto her face, as the images were shown. She quickly headed down below, no doubt trying to run away from what was right before her eyes.

Nikki headed down below as well, in search of Deena. She checked one of the smaller bars and was about to head into the bathroom when Deena bumped into her on the way out. "Hey baby, is everything okay?" she asked, running her fingers through Deena's layered locks.

"Sure," Deena lied, "everything's fine."

Nikki noted the lines etched across Deena's brow. "Are you sure?"

"It's nothing, really."

Knowing that it wouldn't take long, Nikki decided to poke around until she hit the right nerve. Pretending to change the subject, she asked, "Did you see Saxton and that chick in the lilac dress all huddled together?"

Deena nodded, and rolled her eyes. "That was Mallory Baylor, the new executive editor for *Spotlight*."

Nikki feigned surprise. "Oh, so she's the one that slept with her old boss."

Nikki could see the rage under the surface of Deena's cool demeanor. "She's the one."

Nikki snapped her fingers as though she was suddenly recalling an important detail. "Didn't I also read that she and Saxton had an affair?"

This struck the nerve that Nikki had been probing for. Deena nodded sadly.

Realizing that she'd caught Deena in a rare moment of weakness, Nikki reached for her hand. "Let's go in here, get out of the hallway." She led Deena into one of the four staterooms and locked the door behind them. Once they were inside, she held Deena's face between her hands and looked deeply into her eyes. "You know that you have nothing to worry about," she said. "She can't touch you. You are gorgeous, sexy, and brilliant, and if Saxton can't appreciate it, then he's a fool." She leaned forward and placed a light, teasing kiss on Deena's lips.

When she felt Deena respond, she pulled her closer into a passionate, steamy embrace. While their tongues tangled in a hot duet, Nikki gathered Deena's white silk dress in her hands, raising it from the floor to above her waist. Sliding down to her knees, she pulled the scant thong along with her. She buried her head beneath Deena's dress for a late-night snack. Their moans filled the room as the urgency of the stolen moments dissolved Deena's concern, scattering her caution to the wind.

After she returned Nikki's favor, they both freshened up and emerged from the stateroom still flushed from their hot encounter. They almost bumped into Greg, who was in search of the men's room. He watched as they made their way upstairs, anxious to blend unnoticed into the throng of people. He hoped that Saxton and Mallory had managed to pull themselves apart before Broom-Hilda swooped back into the main room, where he'd just left them.

23

THE SMOKING GUN

The Browns' situation had gone from very bad to much worse. They couldn't stay in the little house much longer knowing they were being tracked, for they were not sure who would be following in the detective's trail. Yet they did not have the money to leave.

The knock at the door froze Linda and Jonathan in their tracks. Thankfully, Dylan was still taking his afternoon nap. Jonathan put his finger to his mouth, motioning his wife to stay quiet, but the knocking continued.

"I know you're in there," a deep male voice said, "so either open the door so we can talk or I go straight to the police. Your choice."

Jonathan could feel the contents of his stomach begin to liquefy. This was the knock on the door that he'd dreaded since last year. At this point, he would much rather it be the police. At least then he'd be assured of his physical safety. If the mob was waiting on the other side of the door, though, all bets were off. Linda stood in the kitchen doorway with a petrified look on her face.

He parted the curtains an inch and craned his neck to peek out the window to see his unwelcome visitor. Oddly, the guy didn't look like the mob figures he'd seen on TV. He could have been an attorney or an accountant. "Who are you?" he mustered up the courage to ask through the door.

"I'm Bob Morris. I'm a private detective. I'm the one who called you a couple of days ago."

Linda's heart lurched in her chest. She hurried to the room where Dylan slept to close the door.

"Don't answer it," she whispered urgently.

Her husband ignored her and called out to the stranger, "How do I know that you aren't the cops?" The guy couldn't be from the mob. If he was, this conversation would already be over. "Let me see some ID."

The detective took out his identification and slid it under the door. "I just want to talk to you about Dylan."

At the mention of her son's name, Linda folded her arms tightly across her chest. After Jonathan finished studying the laminated photo ID, he opened the door for the tall, husky man to enter the house.

"What do you want?" he asked brusquely.

"Like I said in my message, Mallory wants to reestablish contact. Obviously she's worried about her son."

"Do you mean my son?" Linda snapped. "Perhaps you need to remind Ms. Baylor that she gave up her parental rights five years ago."

"She just wants to see the boy."

"Does she want him back?" Jonathan asked.

Linda looked at him in loathing. How could he even consider that as a possibility? "There is no way I'll ever give him up," she interjected before Mr. Morris could answer her husband.

"Honey, let's be reasonable." He was reaching for her, but she pulled away.

"All she wants is to talk. Would you meet with her?"

Linda turned her back to the two men, hiding the tears that welled in her eyes.

"Listen, we can do this in a civil manner and set up a meeting for you three to talk. Or I can make a few calls to some friends in the local FBI office."

That definitely got Jonathan's attention. "Don't do that. Just give us a day or two to think about it."

The detective weighed his options and said, "Okay, you talk it over. I'll be in touch the day after tomorrow, and by then, I want a date." He turned around and left the house without a glance back.

As the door closed, Linda started crying in earnest. "How could you even think of—"

"Mommy, what's wrong?" Dylan appeared at her side, still grumpy from his incomplete nap. Neither one of them had seen him come through the door.

Linda sniffled and wiped her eyes and nose with the back of her hand. "Mommy's okay, sweetie," she said, rubbing his head. "I'm just a little sad, that's all." She took his hand and walked over to the sofa, sitting down with him in front of her.

"Why are you sad?" He crawled up into her lap and wrapped his little arms as far around her as he could, in an attempt to comfort the one person who was always there to comfort him.

"I'm not sad anymore," she said, holding on to him. "You make Mommy feel much better." She hugged him tightly, not wanting to let go.

After Dylan, tucked safely in his bed, was drifting off to sleep, she trudged back to the small living room. Her husband sat on the tattered sofa with his head in his hands. She sat down next to him. "Jonathan, we can't do it."

"We have to. Think about the boy. He'll be much better off with his mother than he will be on the run with us," he reasoned.

"I *am* his mother," she insisted angrily.

"I know that, and so does he, but we have to give him back to Mallory. We barely have enough money to live on, much less to give him the security that he needs."

"You should have thought of that before you got us into this mess," she snapped. Through everything she'd been loyal to him. Losing her child, though, would be the last straw. She'd never give up her boy.

Mallory was getting ready for a dinner date with Beverly when the phone rang. She picked it up on the second ring.

"Mallory, it's me." This time she recognized his voice right away.

She sat straight up immediately, bracing for news. "What is it?" she asked without the preamble of pleasantries.

"I just spoke to the Browns. They'll meet with you, probably within the next few days."

Mallory was so stunned by the news that she felt as though she were having an out-of-body experience. She had dreamed of this moment for so long. "Ohmigod, ohmigod," she repeated.

"I can't promise anything, but the husband seemed really anxious to turn him over to you—I mean permanently," Mr. Morris said. "But he'll have to get past his wife first. She was adamantly against it." He paused, obviously hesitant to ask the next question. "Would you want the boy back? Permanently?"

"Of course I would."

Mallory hung up the phone in a fugue state. All of these years she'd only asked for contact with her son, while not admitting to herself how much she longed for him. She wouldn't allow herself to hope that more would ever be possible. And now it was. She might finally get her son back. Now she only had to figure out how to explain the appearance of a five-year-old boy to her relatives, to her friends . . . and of course to Saxton.

With one eye Nikki watched Mallory leave the apartment. Nikki sat masterfully applying a coat of MAC foundation to her dark chocolate skin, adding just a touch of concealer under her eyes to hide the cumulative effects of age, alcohol, and staying out all night the evening before. A swath of blush along her prominent cheekbones was her final touch. Once she was pleased with her makeover, she headed over to her closet to find the perfect outfit for this evening's meeting with Yvette. One little confrontation with Mallory wasn't going to stop her.

Though Yvette was a syndicated columnist with the *New York Gazette*, she had not been put on the media list for *Spotlight*'s launch party. So she'd called Nikki to see if she'd gotten any juicy gossip from the event. Plus, it was time for one of their little chats anyway, since she never knew what tasty little nuggets Nikki's loose tongue would drop. Nikki was more than happy to oblige, especially now that Deena was moving her wedding date up to January.

When she and Deena had returned from their secret tryst, they had gone back up the main stairs to find Saxton still hovering over Mallory.

"So what do you make of that?" Nikki asked.

Deena, recovered from her moment of vulnerability, had her suit of armor firmly back in place. "I'm sure it's nothing," she lied, though she was seething inside. How dared he make such a fuss over Mallory in front of everybody?

Nikki crossed her arms over her chest. "I wouldn't be so sure."

Deena's head snapped around like that of the sick little girl in *The Exorcist*. "Why do you say that?"

Nikki gave her that I-didn't-want-to-tell-you-this-but look. "They looked pretty cozy to me. That's all."

"It's nothing to worry about," Deena said nervously. "I'm sure that they are just discussing business, probably the next issue of the magazine. Besides, Saxton wants to move the wedding date up to January fifteenth. Not exactly the kind of thing a man would do if he were up to something."

Nikki had been really irked by this revelation. But even as the lie rolled smoothly off Deena's tongue, Nikki was sure that moving the wedding date up was Deena's idea, definitely not Saxton's. She couldn't understand why Deena continued to put up with him, since Nikki was sure after watching him and Mallory together that he was not really in love with Deena. To confirm her suspicions, she had also noted how strange Mallory had been acting lately. She seemed withdrawn, anxious, and even secretive. Nikki figured that the two lovebirds had rekindled their affair. And if Deena was too stupid to see the obvious for herself, it was up to Nikki to show her. After all, what were friends for? Even Mallory should thank her for her efforts, since she was making it easier for her to get her man back.

After flipping through the hangers in her junky closet, she decided to play the diva role. She'd wear a short leather miniskirt and her black leather Prada knee-high boots. At almost the same moment she realized the black fitted turtleneck she liked to wear with that outfit was in the dry cleaners. But before she discarded the idea altogether, she remembered that Mallory had a similar one that would work just fine. Even though she did not have permission to wear the sweater, or even to go in Mallory's room, she walked in anyway. She headed directly for Mallory's closet and began her search. When she didn't see the sweater folded on the shelf above the rack of hanging clothes, she stooped down to the chest of drawers to rummage some more.

Drawer by drawer she pilfered through Mallory's things. She was about to give up the idea when she spied the black turtleneck neatly folded under a stack at the very bottom drawer. When she tugged it free from the other sweaters that lay on top of it, she saw the edge of a manila file folder peeking out from beneath the pile. What on earth was a file doing buried in Mallory's sweater drawer? Nikki's curiosity was piqued, leaving her no other choice but to see for herself. Carefully she pulled the file free. Mallory had handwritten the words THE BROWNS across the label tab. "What do we have here?" she said out loud to the empty room.

Getting comfortable, Nikki sat down cross-legged on the floor and opened the mysterious manila file. After she had riffled through the documents and notes inside, it took her but a minute to put all of the pieces together. When she did, she was shocked. Mallory the saint had borne a baby that she'd given up for adoption.

As this startling piece of information seeped into Nikki's devious brain, a more titillating question arose from it. Who was the baby's father? She quickly sifted through the paperwork again, looking for clues. When she found the birth certificate, she was disappointed to see that the line for the father's name had been left blank. But then she saw the date of delivery: June 7, 1997. That was before Mallory moved to New York and after she had left Atlanta. Nikki thought long and hard and remembered that Mallory had mentioned spending some time on an internship in Philadelphia. According to the papers, that's where the adoption had taken place. The wheels in her mind were turning freely now. Nikki recalled all of Mallory's conversations about her past relationship with Saxton and the hows and whens of its beginning and end. She quickly added up the dates, and Saxton's sudden departure, and Mallory's falling in love with him again. The father of Mallory's child could be none other than Saxton McKensie. *Oh, my God!* she thought.

She sat on the floor in a stupor, holding on to the ticking time bomb that she'd just unearthed. It all made complete sense to her now—Mallory's closeness to Saxton, why she never wanted to get involved with anyone else. It also explained the weird phone call that Mallory had received last week from the detective agency. But what exactly did that mean? Was Mallory now searching for the child so that she could get Saxton back? Did Saxton even know about the baby?

Talk about a bombshell. This would rock the media world to its core, and the collateral damage would be just what Nikki needed to further her own agenda. She could not believe her good fortune. She kissed the folder madly. Nikki was so excited she could barely contain herself. She skipped around the room, waving the file in the air. "Wait until Deena finds out about this."

She quickly tidied the closet, even putting the black sweater back in place, covering her tracks. Then she dressed in a hurry. She had to get out of there and get back to replace the file.

Now she had another stop to make before her meeting with Yvette. She had to get to Kinko's, quick!

24

A FRIENDLY WAGER

The two men were posed on the pristinely manicured green at the eleventh hole of Rio Sacco golf course outside Las Vegas. It was their yearly boys' weekend away. They'd been at this travel ritual for the last eight years, ever since they had each reached a point in their career where money was no longer an object. They usually traveled beyond the East Coast for a long weekend of nonstop golf, drinking, bragging, and back in the day, even a little tail chasing.

After Greg putted for bogey, Saxton began to line up his own putt for a birdie. He crouched low, analyzing the roll of the green. "So what's up with you and Beverly?" he asked, not taking his eye away from the lie.

"Beverly? What do you mean, what's up with us?"

"It's just that you two looked awfully cozy at the party last week."

"I was just being social—that's all." He shrugged. "She's a nice girl."

"I know. That's why I didn't think she was your type." Saxton chuckled. He stood up to take his stroke.

"Funny," Greg said. "You know me. I'm not trying to get involved with anybody long-term, especially a 'nice girl.' You know how they are. You can't exactly treat a girl like that—"

"Like the young and clueless ones you normally date."

"Hey, whose side are you on?"

"I'm like Switzerland. I'm completely neutral. I'm only making an observation—that's all." He stifled a smile. It felt good to goad Greg, after all the heat he'd taken about Deena.

"I don't know what you think you've observed, but it's all a figment of your imagination."

"If you say so."

Saxton began to concentrate on his shot, with a cigar dangling between his teeth.

"A hundred bucks says you two putt it."

"Man, I don't want to take your money like that." Saxton handed his cigar off to Greg. After methodically lining up the putt, which was fifteen yards out and uphill with a right slope, Saxton took a precise stroke and sank the little white ball in the cup. "Yessss!" he yelled, pumping his fist.

Greg shook his head. "You're a lucky man."

"Luck don't got nothin' to do with it," Saxton boasted, buffing his nails on his Sea Island cotton golf shirt before blowing across their surface. "It's all skill, my brother."

It was a great day for golf. The skies were clear blue without a cloud visible. There was a slight breeze, but not a touch of humidity, so they happily chased the little white ball, talked shit, and told lies. On the eighteenth hole, before Saxton led the charge with the first tee shot, they wagered a little bet. "Whoever finishes this hole with the most strokes buys drinks tonight," Saxton challenged.

"Better yet," Greg said, raising the ante, "whoever finishes with the fewest strokes calls the shots for tonight's entertainment." This trip was dedicated to the end of Saxton's bachelorhood, so Greg was anxious to get him into a little trouble. Besides, he felt like his mack-daddy muscles could use a little flexing, especially since Saxton's comment about him being interested in Beverly. She was cool and all, but he knew the type. She was not the kind of girl he could casually date. And forget about booty calls—they were totally out of the question.

"Nah, man. If you win, there's no tellin' where we'll end

up." Saxton already felt guilty enough about his fling with Mallory. He was committed to trying to stay on the straight and narrow, even if it did lead to the wedding altar with Deena.

"Sounds to me like the birdie-man has turned a little chicken," Greg teased, flapping his arms and yelling, *"Baaac, baac, baaaac!"* as he strode around the championship tees.

Saxton took a puff of his half-smoked stogie and floated a deal. "I'll tell you what," he said. "If you win, no questions asked, we'll do whatever you want tonight, but if I win, you have to lay off the hoochies for a whole month." Taking another puff, he expelled the smoke toward the wispy sky.

"What?"

"One full month of celibacy."

"You've got to be kidding me." Greg was mortified by the thought.

"Oh, okay, I understand. If my game was as shaky as yours, I wouldn't be quick to bet either."

"Shaky?" He'd hit a nerve with Greg. "Man, you may not know what to do with a lob wedge, but you can sure talk some shit."

"Put your Big Bertha where your mouth is," Saxton said.

Greg held his palms up in surrender. "Bet," he said, taking his Big Bertha Calloway driver up to the tee box.

It was a 525-yard par five over an imposing hundred-foot-long body of water that stretched 180 yards from the tee, followed by a narrow tree-lined fairway, leading to scattered bunkers on the approach to an uphill green. After taking a practice swing, Greg settled into his stance. He swung the club in a perfect and powerful arc, sending the ball soaring. His strategy was to clear the water in order to get a head start on the fairway shots. The ball, which sliced a little to the right, floated in the sky for several seconds, making it hard to determine whether he'd be taking a dip in the lake or heading off to the races. It was close, but the ball, helped along by a bit of breeze, landed just on the other side of the water, off to the right in the rough. Not a bad shot, but getting out of the rough smoothly could cost him the stroke that he saved by not laying up his shot.

Saxton followed him to the tee box, swaggering all the way with his TaylorMade five iron over his shoulder. A very talented golfer, he played the game with great athleticism, which accounted for some pretty miraculous shots. From time to time, his drive was less controlled, making him prone to an occasional errant shot. But his short game and putting were usually spot on. He was also very strategic and fully aware of his shortcomings, so he decided to lay up. After taking a practice swing, he placed the ball right in the sweet spot: ten yards before the water. It sat waiting for him to send it sailing to the fairway on the other side. Pleased with himself, Saxton pimped over to the golf cart.

Greg dropped Saxton off near his ball with a three wood in hand. He then headed over the wooden cart path to the other side of the lake to prepare for his own second shot.

Saxton easily cleared the water, dropping his ball in the middle of the fairway, leaving him two hundred yards out from the flag. Because of his awkward lie in the rough, Greg was forced to chip out with a pitching wedge. Even though he had cleared the water on his first shot, he paid for it with yardage on his second.

But he put some muscle into his third and came to within 125 yards of the green, managing to avoid two of the three strategically placed sand traps. Next up, Saxton played it safe, using a nine iron to sit his ball just ahead of the sand bunkers, planning to chip over them on his approach to the green. Then he finessed his pitching wedge, lobbing his ball past the flag, letting it roll back toward it on the downhill side. It stopped fifteen yards out. Not to be deterred, Greg confidently chipped his ball onto the green as well. It rolled to a stop twenty-five yards to the left. They were both at the party now, though Saxton sat prettiest. Both were even at four strokes. It would all come down to the putting, as it usually did: drive for show and putt for dough.

"Feelin' the heat?" Greg teased, pulling on his brimmed golf hat.

"It's all good," Saxton answered.

"It'll be even better when we are sittin' with some honeys tonight," Greg said, removing the flag from the hole. He'd already thought of two hot chicks for them to party with. He figured they'd hit the casinos before checking out a hot new club in town.

They both knelt on one knee to get a read on the green. Being farther out, Greg set up with his Phil Mickelson putter and smoothly stroked his ball toward the hole. He called the break from left to right, and the ball rolled straight up to the hole. When it looked as if it would run out of steam, it just dropped in.

Greg was ecstatic. "Whatchu gonna do with that?"

"Look and learn," Saxton said, lining up for his own par shot. He gave the ball a solid stroke, and it rolled directly for the hole—until the last second, when it drifted off to the left, leaving Saxton an inch shy of a draw.

"You see that shit?" Saxton screamed, holding his arms straight out in proclaimed innocence. "I was robbed!" he shouted. "That should be a gimme," he said, looking to Greg for sympathy.

"Yeah, gimme a break," Greg laughed, breathing a sigh of relief. "Now we're going to party the right way. My way."

25

THE PAPER TRAIL

Today was the day that Mallory had been waiting for even before she realized it herself. Prior to the Browns' disappearance, she had convinced herself that she could live the rest of her life without ever seeing her son again. He was better off with a stable two-parent family. She had done the right thing and could accept the consequences. But she'd always carried around an empty place in her heart that yearned to be filled by the child she had borne. Out of respect for his well-being, she had never planned to reenter his world, but now that the pieces were in place for it to happen, she realized that her life would never have been complete without him.

She was anxious and jittery as she and Mr. Morris left Buffalo's airport, heading for the visit with her son. Mallory clutched the letter that she had received by FedEx earlier that morning containing a note from Ms. Brown:

Dear Mallory,

I'm sorry that things have come to this. Please know that Jonathan and I love Dylan with all of our hearts and never planned to put him in harm's way. I've asked myself over and over again just how our lives have spiraled so drastically out of control. Though I still don't have all of the answers, as a mother, I do understand your pain and your need to see Dylan.

> *Yours truly,*
> *Linda Brown*

Tears had rolled down Mallory's face as she read the letter. Along with the letter, there was a picture of Dylan. He was on the floor in what looked like a living room, happily playing with a bright red fire truck. He looked older, more boy now than toddler. He also looked very much like his father. The package also contained the address and directions to the house.

Mallory held the note in one hand and a tote bag in the other. She'd filled it with juice, fruit, cut-up vegetables, and Legos, and she'd even thought to bring along a few kids' books she'd picked up a couple of days before. As she shopped for them, she realized how little she knew about her own son.

Something else was weighing on her as well. She hadn't yet figured out how to break the news of Dylan's existence to her friends and family. After wringing her hands over the matter, she finally decided that, if a picture was worth a thousand words, flesh and blood must be worth a million. So she would just wait until she had him with her and let the rest speak for itself. No longer twenty-four, she was much less concerned about what other people thought about her. Her main concern was for the well-being of the child she'd brought into this world.

"The house is just up over the hill," Mr. Morris said, squinting through a pair of dark, silver-rimmed aviators. He was a serious, take-no-prisoners kind of guy, Mallory thought. Not the warm-and-fuzzy type, but definitely capable.

Her heart quickened, until she could hardly catch her breath. Seconds later they pulled into the driveway of a small wood frame house set alone on a hill surrounded by tall pine trees. Before the car even rolled to a stop, Mallory had unsnapped her seat belt and was reaching for the door handle.

"Mallory, you need to wait here," Mr. Morris said firmly.

She was about to object when he added, "It's not open to debate. We don't know what's on the other side of that door. And until I know it's safe, you stay in the car."

As he walked toward the house, Mallory saw him reach for the pistol that he'd had to register with airport officials. The sight of it gave her the creeps. She held her breath as he approached the house and knocked on the door. When there was no answer, he turned the knob with the gun at his head pointing skyward. He slowly eased the door open and entered the house. Malloy's heart was pounding in her chest as she sat with her face almost touching the windshield, waiting with her hand poised on the door handle.

A minute later, he appeared in the doorway again, but without Dylan.

She jumped out of the car and ran to the empty-handed detective. "Where is he?" she cried. "Where's my baby?"

He grabbed her forearms to steady her. "They're not here." She tried to free herself from him, but his grip was too strong. "Mallory, listen to me. They left, and they took the boy with them."

By now Mallory wasn't struggling against him. Instead she turned limp, nearly catatonic. "But she promised." She stared blankly through the door, able to just make out a threadbare sofa and a table with a lamp.

"They did leave a note." He ushered her into the house. On the table was the second letter that she would receive from Mrs. Brown. It read:

Dear Mallory,

Again I have to start a letter to you with an apology. We have left the area for good, so do not bother looking for us. But don't worry about Dylan. I know you're disappointed and hurt, but no more so than I would have been to have to give him up. Remember, I'm the one who's nurtured, loved, and cared for him all these years. Please understand.

Linda Brown

Mallory dropped to the floor, overwhelmed by grief for her lost child. Sobs racked her body, and hot tears streamed down her face. She cried for Dylan and for herself. She cried for the five birthdays that she had already missed and for the fact that she didn't even know what his favorite bedtime story was.

Mr. Morris gathered her in his arms to help her start the long trip back to Manhattan, but she pushed him away. "I just need to be alone for a few minutes," she said in a hoarse voice.

He backed away to give her space to mourn. While she sat there staring at images that he could not see, he went through the small house, searching for clues. He looked through the garbage that remained in the kitchen and bath, in the drawers of the bedside table, and on the floor of the closets. He even lifted the bed's mattress and peeked into the shower. Aside from mundane evidence of everyday life, he found nothing. No personal traces that showed him that the Browns had ever even been there or where they were now headed.

"Let's go, Mallory," he said as he reentered the living room. He held her hand as he pulled her up from the cold hard floor.

Deena sat in her spacious office, drumming the desktop. She was contemplating her next move. Now that the stakes were so high, she could not afford to run off half-cocked. Instead, she was going to carefully load up her ammunition and aim as accurately as an Olympic sharpshooter. The biggest question she had was who exactly should be her target, since there were so many standing right there in her line of fire.

Her day had gotten off to a testy start. She was half listening to WBLS as she dressed for the office. After hearing Saxton's name on the radio, she froze midway while putting one leg into her pants. Her ears perked up immediately. The DJ was in the middle of a lively interview with a famous rapper known as SamTheLover, who was flossing on the airwaves about his wild weekend spent carousing in Las Vegas during the big Lennox-Lewis fight.

"Yeah, man, me and my dawgs was flowin'."

"So you guys were raisin' the roof out there, huh?"

"You know how we do—we hit all the hot spots."

The DJ then said, "Sounds like it was off the chain."

"It was on! Me and my homies were packin' the heat up in the G Spot," he laughed salaciously.

"Tell the listeners who was rollin' with you?"

"You know my peeps: Ja Rule, Nelly, Eminem, the ballers Vince and Shaq, and even my homeboy Saxton."

"You mean Saxton McKensie? Isn't he engaged to Deena Ingram?"

"He might be, but he was flowin' freestyle that night."

"Sounds like y'all were having too much fun out there in Vegas."

"It was real."

Deena was mortified. Not only was Saxton up in a nightclub—she would expect no more from him and Greg—but he was hanging out with a bunch of rapper thugs! As soon as she walked into her office, she'd nearly punched the digits through the phone as she dialed Saxton's extension. Cindy picked up the line. "Mr. McKensie's office," she sang out.

"I know whose office it is," Deena snapped. She didn't know why the heavyset heifer couldn't bother to look down at the phone's display and see that the call was from her. Was that too much for her to ask?

The sunny smile left Cindy's voice. "I'm sorry, Ms. Ingram. I didn't realize it was you."

"If you'd taken the time to look at the— Oh, never mind. Where is Saxton?" she demanded.

"He's not back from his trip yet, but his flight is due in at two and he's coming straight here from the airport."

"You call me the minute he walks in. Do you understand?" She hung up before Cindy had a chance to reply.

When the call finally came, she marched straight to Saxton's office, her anger mounting with each step. By the time she made it to his door, her stride was more like a charge.

Saxton's back was to the door. He was hanging up his overcoat in the closet when she stormed in. "Hey, babe," he said.

"Don't you hey-babe me." She had both fists planted firmly on her hips.

He was surprised by her anger. "What are you talking about?"

"Does the name G Spot ring a bell?" she asked, cocking her head to one side.

For a few seconds Saxton looked perplexed. He had no idea what she was talking about.

"Maybe you need a picture painted. How's this: Vegas, a club, and you 'rollin' freestyle' with that ghetto rapper SamTheLover."

The night all came back to him then. He and Greg had hung out at the club with a friend of Greg's and her girlfriend. They had run into SamTheLover, but there was nothing to it. "What's the big deal? Greg and I were just hanging out, you know, hitting some of the new clubs in Vegas. It was no big deal." Saxton turned around to close the closet door.

"Well, it may not be a big deal to you, but it is to me. Especially when, thanks to WBLS, the whole world knows that my fiancé was carousing around Vegas."

"I was not carousing." Saxton was beginning to get angry.

"Are you telling me that you and Greg were alone?" she asked, pinning him with a penetrating glare.

His first impulse was to tell a half-truth, but he remembered the disaster that resulted the last time he tried that ploy, so he thought better of it. "A friend of Greg's was there, along with her girlfriend. But it was strictly platonic."

"That's what you first said when I asked you about your relationship with Mallory," she spat at him. "I suggest you figure out quickly where your priorities are, because I won't stand for this humiliation."

"Deena, I told you that nothing happened. I don't even remember the girl's name."

She shook her head. "You don't get it, do you? It doesn't

really matter whether something happened or not. What matters is the perception that something did. What do you think this will do to my ratings?"

For once Saxton was speechless. Deena cared more about her ratings and her public image than she did about him or their relationship.

She spun on her heel and made an exit as dramatic as her entrance had been only minutes before.

Still fuming, she headed back to her office, grabbed her coat and handbag, and headed out the door without so much as a word to Hazelle.

"Ms. Ingram, I don't see anything on your schedule. What should I tell callers?"

"Tell them that I am indisposed," she said, not looking back.

There was a reason that she did not want anyone to know where she was going. Nikki had called insisting that they meet face-to-face. She said she had something to show her that she would definitely want to see, and it concerned Saxton. They'd decided to meet at a small café down in Alphabet City, an area where neither would likely be recognized.

When Deena walked in, she saw Nikki sitting at a table in the corner, flipping through papers in a file. "What's up?" Deena asked, getting right to the point.

"Hello to you, too," Nikki said, a little put off. Here she was doing Deena a major favor, and the diva was copping an attitude.

"I'm sorry. It's just been a hell of a day."

Well, it's about to get worse, Nikki thought cheerfully. "Sorry to hear that, especially in light of what I have to show you, and believe me, I take no pleasure in doing this. In fact, it breaks my heart."

Deena leaned forward, now more curious than ever. When Nikki had first called, she figured it was the usual Nikki melodrama. She agreed to see her really just to get out of the office, but this was beginning to sound important. "What is it?"

Nikki slid a file containing the copied adoption papers

across the table to Deena, who quickly grabbed the folder and opened it. As she scanned the first page of the document, a frown appeared on her brow. Nikki could almost visualize the wheels in her brain as they churned through the unfathomable.

When Denna first saw Mallory's name on the papers, she stiffened. As she continued to read, she was startled to realize that these were adoption papers. That was the last thing that she expected. Not until the third page, where the birth father's name was requested, did the full impact of what she was reading begin to sink in. To help it sink faster, Nikki had highlighted the date of birth and had made notes in the margins recounting Deena's conversation to her about Saxton's recollection of meeting Mallory, complete with the time frame. It didn't take a rocket scientist to figure out the obvious. Mallory had had Saxton's baby.

"Where did you get this?" Deena hissed.

Nikki looked at her solemnly. "Let's just say that a friend of mine from Philly told me about the child after the 'Talk of the Town' piece ran. At first I thought it was just gossip and didn't want to upset you with it. But then she told me that she had proof. She works for the lawyer who handled the adoption. So I asked her to get it, figuring that you'd want to know."

Deena's fury began to spin out of control. There were so many questions. The most important to her was if Saxton knew about the child.

"There's one more thing," Nikki said.

Deena looked up questioningly.

"Mallory is trying to get the baby back. She's hired a private investigator. Apparently, she called the attorney in Philly to get a referral."

That could mean only one thing. Mallory was trying to get the baby back so that she could use him to get Saxton. *Over my dead body,* Deena thought. Two could play that game.

After she stumbled back into her office an hour later, she picked up the phone and called in a favor. "Hi, Steve? This is

Deena Ingram. We met when you were on my show about missing and murdered children."

She nodded as the detective talked on the other end of the line. When the pleasantries were over, she said, "Listen, I need a favor. . . ."

During the short flight from Buffalo to JFK, Mallory sat hiding her puffy eyes behind a pair of black Christian Dior sunglasses. The small blue tote bag on the empty seat next to her was a constant reminder of Dylan's absence. She had started the day barely able to contain her excitement. During the trip upstate she was consumed with nervous anxiety. By the time they pulled up to the house, her heart was pounding against her chest. But when he emerged empty-handed, a heavy sadness fell over her. Staring out of the window as the plane descended for its landing, she felt numb inside.

She said her good-byes to Mr. Morris curbside before grabbing a taxi to head into the city. She'd taken the day off work, saying that she had personal affairs to attend to, but decided to swing by the office to pick up a press file she'd left on her desk the night before. The following morning she had a breakfast meeting scheduled with one of William Morris's agents, so she wanted to be prepared.

She didn't arrive at the office until after eight o'clock, so it was a ghost town, quiet and empty. As she headed toward the back, she could smell the smoky oakiness of a fire burning in Saxton's office. But when she looked down, she didn't see light coming from under the door. She started to walk on by, but then she asked herself, *What if everyone has left without putting the fire completely out?* It wouldn't hurt to check, and it would sure make her sleep easier—she had enough on her mind as it was.

She knocked quietly on the door, and when she didn't get an answer, she opened it to the low illumination of red-hot embers and a small desk light. Assuming that Saxton was gone, she decided to make sure that the last of the coals was pushed to the back of the fireplace. She picked up a poker and prodded the remaining pieces back against the far wall. As she was replacing the wrought iron utensil, she heard a movement behind her. She turned to find Saxton looming over her.

She jumped. "You startled me," she said, clutching her heart. Her nerves were still frayed by all of the day's events.

"I'm sorry. I didn't think anyone else was here. I was in the bathroom," he said, motioning toward the back of his office. "Besides, I thought you were off today." He was smiling, happy to see her. She'd been avoiding him lately.

She held her head down, not wanting to make eye contact. "Yes, I was off, but I'm meeting with Susan Turner in the morning to discuss some potential stories for her clients, so I needed to pick up my file." She glanced at her watch. "I've got to get going."

Saxton examined her more closely. Even though the light was dimmed, he could see her eyes were puffy. A shadow had fallen over her delicate features, illuminating a pall of sadness that he'd never seen there before. "Mallory, are you okay?"

"Yes, I'm fine," she answered, looking up into his eyes, wondering what trace of her secret life he had glimpsed.

He gently held her at arm's length to get a better look at her. Something that he saw worried him. "Come with me. Let's go grab a drink," he said, turning around before she had a chance to answer him. "I've had a rough day myself."

"I've got to get home," Mallory said, checking her watch. She wasn't sure that she had the energy to deal with Saxton.

"Oh, come on, Mallory, a quick drink will probably do us both some good. I know I could certainly use one." When she didn't answer right away, he grabbed his coat and headed for the door, then turned to look back at her. "Come on, don't make me drink alone."

Mallory followed him out of the door. "Let me grab my things and I'll meet you in the lobby." As she headed to her own office, she knew that she should be going home instead. She'd had enough drama for one day. After grabbing her file, she stuffed it into the tote bag and headed to the reception area, where Saxton stood waiting.

Outside, he waved down a cab and held the door for her once it had cruised to a stop. "Madison and Thirty-sixth Street." Then he turned to Mallory. "I thought we'd grab a drink at Asia de Cuba, and if you want something to eat later, we can order dinner or appetizers there, too."

Great, Mallory thought. Asia de Cuba was just four blocks from her apartment. She could have a drink, then excuse herself. "I'll just have a quick drink, but then I've got to get home."

"Cool," he said as he settled into the cab next to her. "So which of Suzy's clients are you thinking about for *Spotlight*?"

She relaxed a little, happy to be discussing a safe topic. "Not exactly sure who I'd be most interested in, but I did want to go over her roster to find out who has big projects coming up soon and which of her clients might be good general-interest subjects."

"Who do they handle?"

"They handle the actress Lena Moore, the Golden Globe winner Will Swan, and a bunch of Grammy winners. Really a good lineup, and right now I need to solidify our cover and feature stories for the next six months out. So I'll sort through her client list to see which of them make the best fit for our readers and editorial slant."

"That sounds good," Saxton said, impressed, as always, with Mallory's dedication and her laser vision where pop culture was concerned.

As the taxi cruised to a stop in front of the Morgan Hotel, Saxton slid a ten through the open partition and said to the driver, "Keep the change." They walked past the line that had formed at the restaurant's velvet rope, right up to the bouncer, who unleashed the hook allowing Mallory and Saxton to enter the hip, cozy nightspot/restaurant.

After speaking to the host, they were quickly escorted to a very private table on the balcony upstairs that overlooked the communal dining table below. When their waiter appeared for their drink order, Saxton asked, "Are you in the mood for champagne tonight?"

"No, it's not that kind of day," Mallory answered. If she'd seen Dylan, there would be plenty to celebrate, but she was certain that she wouldn't have been doing it with Saxton. She still did not know what she would tell him if she got back in touch with Dylan. "I'll have a glass of cabernet sauvignon."

"I'll take a vodka gimlet. In fact, make that a double."

Mallory looked at Saxton, surprised. "Someone besides me did have a rough day," she said, wondering what office antics she'd missed. "Didn't you just get back from a golf weekend? Aren't you supposed to be all tanned and relaxed?"

"Let's just say that my homecoming quickly erased any relaxation that I enjoyed during the trip. In fact, you could say that I'm now operating in a very deep deficit in that area."

Once their drinks were served, Mallory said, "So tell me about it." When he hesitated, she teased, "This is your one chance for free therapy. Take it or leave it."

Saxton picked up his highball glass and held it up halfway between them. "Here's to free therapy."

She clinked his glass and took a deep sip of the dark ruby wine. She closed her eyes momentarily, enjoying the taste and feel as it flowed down her throat, warming her body and relaxing her mind.

Saxton watched her, wishing that he could open the door to the secret place that he had been shut out of so long ago. He could only stand on the other side of it, like a hungry kid with his nose pressed to the window.

She opened her eyes. "So tell me all about it," she said, feigning the tone of Lorraine Bracco, who played the therapist on *The Sopranos*.

Saxton slid down slightly into the soft leather of the cozy couch. "Well, Dr. Baylor, the trip itself was great. It was only the aftermath that I could have done without."

Keeping in character, she said, "Uhhhhh-hmmmm. Tell me

exactly what happened." Mallory shifted in her seat to listen. It took her mind off her own problems.

"Let's just say that Deena got wind of a night out in Vegas—one that included a little club hopping, some female friends of Greg's, and some rappers."

"Go on," Mallory encouraged him, keeping her tone professional, though a pang of jealousy swept through her.

"It's all a big misunderstanding. Greg and I made a bet on the golf course. If he won, he got to be in charge of the night's entertainment, and unfortunately, he did. So he invites an ex-girlfriend to hang out and she brings along a friend. But it was nothing. I don't even remember her name."

"Hmmmm, I see," she said.

"It gets worse." Saxton took a long sip of his drink. "While we're hanging out at a new club called the G Spot, in walks SamTheLover and his crew, who come right over to my table like we were all homies. Come Monday morning, he ends up back in New York on a morning radio show and proceeds to paint a picture of Sodom and Gomorrah with me in a starring role. And of course who happens to be listening but Deena?"

Mallory took a sip of her drink, too, pretending not to be bothered by the unseemly picture he'd painted. "It's perfectly normal for a guy to have a little fun every now and then, but how did you explain this to Deena?"

"Well, let's just say that I didn't have the chance. By the time I reached the office this afternoon, I had been tried and convicted. I only needed to show up in person for the sentencing."

"That's a little bit of an overreaction, wouldn't you say?"

"Oh, she felt she was right."

"I'm sure she did," Mallory said. "By the way, what would have happened if you'd won the bet?"

"Greg would have been sworn to celibacy for a complete month."

Mallory laughed. "Do you think he's capable?"

"He talks a good game, but we both saw how he was checking out Beverly at the party."

This sparked Mallory's interest. She too had been wondering about that night. "I know, but she claims there's nothing to it."

"So does he, but he's not known for going for her type, which means something must be going on."

"Maybe."

Saxton settled back contemplatively in the sofa and lightly placed his hand over Mallory's. "Let me tell you some news you might not know. The reason that Greg wanted to get away this weekend is because I let Deena convince me to move the wedding date up to January. Greg doesn't like Deena, in case you didn't know." He felt Mallory's body tense up. "But after the blowup today, I've been rethinking whether or not I want to marry her at all—in January or ever." He had never said those words out loud before, though they had been whispered many times in the recesses of his mind. But holding Mallory's hand and feeling his attraction to her made him want to explore alternatives for the first time in a long while.

Mallory didn't know what to say. She was dismayed that the wedding date had been moved up. Yet at the same time she was very relieved to hear that he wasn't sure he wanted to marry Deena in the first place.

Seeing her troubled face, Saxton decided to probe further. "Enough about me. How are you?"

Mallory gave him her stock answer. "I'm fine."

The fake cheeriness didn't work on Saxton. He raised his eyebrows. "I don't have a couch here, but I can offer you an ear. Come on, Mallory. I know that something's wrong, and it bothers me to see you so unhappy. Is there anything that I can do to help?"

Mallory looked into those beautiful eyes. How could she ever begin to tell him her problems? How could she tell him that she'd had their baby, and oh, by the way she'd then given the child away, and oh, guess what else? Today she'd lost him again. There were just no words to say all those tragic things over a glass of wine. A part of her longed to unburden herself of the heavy load she had carried alone for so many years. She yearned to tell him everything so that together they could find the strength to locate Dylan. But on the other hand, she knew the mess that the existence of Saxton's son would stir up in the media. Deena would make her and Dylan's lives a living hell. Besides, she had no idea how Saxton himself would react.

"It's been really tough," she finally admitted to him. "I'm deeply troubled right now." When he didn't interrupt her, she dropped her head into her hands. It was easier to not look at him as she continued softly. "A long time ago I gave away something that meant a lot to me, even though at the time I didn't realize how much. Since then I've been trying to get it back, but undoing some things is a lot easier said than done." She took another sip of her wine and, facing him, plowed ahead. "Recently, I thought that I would be getting this special thing back, until today when I learned that I may never see it again." Her voice cracked, and she covered her mouth with her hand, trying to hold back her tears.

Saxton was alarmed. He'd never seen Mallory so upset. "How can I help?"

Mallory almost laughed at the rich irony of that question, her baby's daddy wanting to help her when she didn't even know where his son was. Nor had she ever told him that he existed. But she gathered what was left of her composure and said, "No. It's something that I'll have to work out all by myself."

"Isn't there anything that I can do?" he pleaded.

Mallory looked past him with a thoughtful expression on her face. "If you ever find something beautiful, hold it tight, keep it close, and never let it go."

He looked at her, desperate to understand her cryptic code, but she didn't offer any further explanation.

"I better be getting home," she said abruptly. Suddenly the melancholy of the day's events seemed like too much.

After Saxton settled the tab, he insisted on walking her home. When they stepped outside the restaurant, they were both surprised to see large flakes of snow floating magically to the ground. Mallory pulled the collar of her coat up over her ears and pulled it tighter. Saxton wrapped his arms around her to help keep her warm.

Even in her melancholy, Mallory couldn't help but feel hopeful, even a little joyful, as they walked arm in arm through the flurry of snow. Many people who grew up in the North dreaded nights like this, but for Mallory it was magical. In Atlanta the threat alone of snow was enough to close schools, leaving children giddy with excitement over the possibility of a free day at home. For Mallory snow meant the promise of unexpected pleasures.

By the time they reached the gaslamp outside Mallory's apartment, their heads and shoulders were covered in a thick dusting of white powder. When Mallory turned to Saxton to say good night, he playfully ruffled her hair, causing snowflakes to descend on her face and nose. When she laughed, he gently brushed the powder from the tip of her nose. She gazed up at him and he leaned down to kiss her on her lips.

Kissing him under the light of a streetlamp, while flakes floated quietly from the sky, seemed like the most natural thing in the world to do. She did not hesitate at all, but opened her mouth to taste his hot, probing tongue. The thought of being seen by someone didn't keep her from letting him pull her close to his body—close enough that she could feel the urgent outline of his penis pressing against the fabric of his pants. Discretion did nothing to keep her from rocking her hips against his groin, teasing her own hot sex with his.

A taxi drove by, sloshing through the snow, breaking the tranquility of the spell. Mallory pulled away, catching her breath. "I should be getting inside," she said, thankful to the cab driver for bringing her to her senses.

Saxton held on to her hand. "Mallory . . ." he started. He wasn't sure what he wanted to say to her, only that there was so much left unsaid between them.

She didn't trust herself. She had to get away. Otherwise, she'd risk a repeat of the night in Saxton's office. "I have to go," she said, retreating hastily. She fumbled with her keys and didn't look back at him, standing forlornly on the sidewalk, until she was safely on the other side of the door.

26

THE WAR OF THE RATINGS

By the seventh round of the thirteen-week showdown between *The Ingram Hour* and *The Gina Davis Show*, all bets were off. While Deena had managed to maintain her twenty percent ratings lead over the tabloid host for the first few weeks, the blind article about Saxton's hiring of his ex-girlfriend, Mallory Baylor, had a huge negative impact on Deena's image, sending some of her viewers scrambling to *The Oprah Winfrey Show*, and others off to Gina's, effectively cutting her lead to less than twelve points. The publicity bounce that resulted from the splashy *Spotlight* premier party was a huge help to Deena, allowing her to pull ahead of her rival by seventeen points. Not as much distance as she wanted, but a respectable lead nonetheless—that is, until the syndicated radio show told the world that her fiancé, Saxton McKensie, was seen hanging out in Vegas with a bunch of hardcore rappers and skanky women. This was not the image that her viewers had of her. Now Deena was desperately trying to hold on to a measly six percent lead.

"Listen, people, we have to figure out how to pull away from that trailer park witch once and for all, and in case any of you haven't noticed, we only have five weeks left to do it in." Deena was on the prowl, while Saxton, Tom, Ralph, and

CoAnne sat around the conference table trying to figure out a way to contain the damage.

"Who do you have lined up for the next few weeks?" Tom asked. "If the shows are really great, maybe we can press the network for an extra promotional push behind them." He poised his pen over his legal pad, ready to make notes.

Deena sat on the edge of the table with her arms crossed tightly. "My lineup is not the issue here. It's always excellent." She turned to face Saxton. "In case you haven't noticed, the issue lately has been a nonstop barrage of bad publicity."

Saxton leaned forward. "While we may not be able to control all publicity, especially that written in a gossip column, what we can control is the content of your show and how we choose to promote it."

Tom spoke up. "Saxton's right. Bad publicity may be a part of the problem, but for now let's focus on the show's lineup first so that we can make sure we're doing everything that's possible to capitalize on it. Later we can figure out how to change the direction of publicity."

Reluctantly Deena reached for her file with the show's lineup for the next three weeks. "I've got guest interviews and performances by Janet, Denzel Washington, and a retrospective and performance by P. Diddy. For the first time ever Michael Jackson's making an appearance on my show with his kids, and we've got a blockbuster diva show scheduled starring Whitney, Mary J., Mariah, and Christina Aguilera. There's also a cooking show slated with Colin Cowie and a special on living with anxiety with renowned psychotherapist Dr. Julie Evers. I also have an interview set up with Jesse Jackson's baby's momma, and Bill and Hill together." She closed her notebook, effectively saying, *Any questions?*

"Nice lineup," Ralph said.

Now that she was vindicated, she closed her file and refolded her arms.

"One thing that we've got to do is figure out how to put

as much marketing and publicity ahead of these shows as possible."

"I have an idea," Saxton said. "The December issue of *Spotlight* hasn't closed yet. We can add a page with an *Ingram Hour* calendar that shows which guests are confirmed for appearances. This one will hit the stands in two weeks, which can help us with the last three weeks of rating comparisons."

"That sounds great," Tom said, making a note of it.

Ralph turned to CoAnne. "We need you to get some positive human-interest press for Deena in the major newspapers at least once a week. Maybe cover some of the charity work that Deena does."

CoAnne sat back in her chair. "That would be fabulous if she ever did any." Deena cut her eyes malevolently in CoAnne's direction. "Hey, honey, I'm just telling it like it is."

Tom said, "Deena, you need to get on the phone today and figure out how to attach yourself to somebody's charity, and once you've put a check in the mail, CoAnne, you need to tell the whole world about it."

"No problem there."

"We also need to draw up some papers to start a Deena Ingram Foundation for underprivileged children, the environment, animals, or something. Those things always manage to get great publicity," Tom said.

Ralph made a note of that. "I'll start drawing up some papers right away."

CoAnne cleared her throat. "Since we're talking about publicity, we have to do something to stop all of these leaks about Saxton. It's killing us."

He leaned forward. "I've given that a lot of thought, and I think it may be necessary to have everyone on staff sign a letter of confidentiality. Hopefully that'll scare whoever is responsible into keeping their mouths shut." Everyone nodded in agreement.

"While we're on that subject, is there anything else that we should know about?" Deena asked, fixing Saxton with a cold glare.

"Not that I'm aware of," he said flatly.

"Well, back to more positive press opportunities: the wedding," CoAnne said. The room grew silent as she looked around. "Well, don't all speak at once."

Deena said, "It's scheduled to take place in four weeks."

"Good, that'll give us just the tailwind we'll need going into the last two weeks of the ratings war. It'll work like a charm just the way we discussed." When she looked over to her co-collaborator, Deena dropped her head.

Saxton could not believe what he was hearing. Deena had made the idea of moving their wedding date up sound like an impulsive romantic notion brought about by her love for him, while all along it was nothing but a media ploy concocted to help drive up her ratings. He should have known better. Extremely irritated, he excused himself from the table. "Is that all? I have some things to tend to."

"I think we've about covered everything," Tom said. "Let's all meet again next week to assess where we are, and of course I'll keep tracking the ratings and sending out e-mails to keep everybody updated."

Deena headed back to her office and closed the door behind her. "Hazelle, I need you to hold all my calls," she instructed through the intercom. She sat in her desk chair, massaging her temples, trying to drive off the clawing tendrils of a major migraine that was beginning to take hold. She had seen the hurt look on Saxton's face when CoAnne opened her big mouth. She couldn't understand why he was being so sensitive. It was his fault, on many levels, that they were in this position to begin with.

Preying on her mind was the latest Mallory situation. If she hadn't seen the adoption papers with her own eyes, she wouldn't have believed it. Though Saxton's paternity was based on all circumstantial evidence—there was no smoking gun—it was enough to convince Deena, especially after seeing the photocopy of the grinning three-year-old. He looked exactly like old pictures she'd seen of Saxton.

She hated Mallory. She was convinced that the only reason that the conniving bitch had suddenly grown a maternal instinct and was searching for her long-lost kid after all of these years was so that she could use the poor child as bait to lure Saxton back. She would never let that happen. If the media ever found out that they had a kid together, forget about a syndicated network show. Deena would be lucky to walk away with a late-night cable spot hawking astrology.

But what really kept her up at night was wondering whether Saxton knew about the child. She really didn't think so. He was the sappy type who'd insist on "doing the right thing." He would have looked for the child himself rather than leaving it up to Mallory and some private detective. On more than one occasion Saxton had expressed his desire to have a couple of kids. She'd let him assume that she felt the same way, when honestly the thought of dirty diapers, sleepless nights, and a whining brat made her physically ill.

The more she thought about the lurking time bomb, the more she was convinced that Mallory was waiting to spring the news of their child on an unsuspecting Saxton once she found the boy. She no doubt had starry visions of the three of them walking off hand in hand into the sunset, living happily ever after. But as long as Deena drew breath, there was no way that she would ever let that happen.

She picked up the phone to call Steve, the private investigator. "It's Deena," she announced over the crackle of static from his cell phone.

"Who is it?"

"I said it's Deena, Deena Ingram," she nearly shouted.

"Oh . . . Deena . . . got . . . lead . . . to Buffalo . . . kid." She was unable to make out much of the static-filled conversation, but from the few words that she was able to piece together, it sounded like he was making some progress.

She nearly screamed into the phone. "Call me when you have some details about the kid. It's urgent."

After she hung up, exasperated, she looked up to see Saxton standing there with a puzzled look on his face. "Who was that?"

Deena nearly choked with fear, but the talented actress in her found words and even managed to deliver the lines. "Oh, nobody. That was my mother."

"What kid were you talking about?"

Deena expelled a long breath. "Since when do we listen in on each other's phone calls?" The best offense was a good defense, she thought proudly to herself.

"I didn't have to listen in. In case you didn't know it, you were shouting." He sat across the desk, facing her.

She rolled her eyes. "Her cell phone frequency was bad." When he didn't reply, she realized that she'd have to answer his question. "It's really nothing. A friend of the family just had a baby and I wanted to get a gift, but of course, Mother didn't have any information. I don't even know if it's a boy or a girl. Oh well." She shrugged, trying to make light of the situation. "Did you need to see me?" she asked, adeptly changing the subject.

"In fact, I did," he said, crossing his legs. "I'm really not comfortable with this ploy to use our wedding for ratings points."

"Neither am I," she lied effortlessly. "That was all CoAnne's idea. I didn't know that she was planning to do that until today."

Somehow, Saxton had trouble believing this. "Just make sure that you manage that woman. I won't stand for a media circus on my wedding day." He got up to leave.

When his back was turned, she mimicked him by mouthing

the words that he'd said. She'd pull a fast one on him, just like their entrance to the *Spotlight* party. Besides, he would stand for whatever she decided. He'd obviously forgotten which of the two of them laid the golden eggs. The last time she checked, it was clearly she.

27

THE UNINVITED GUEST

Eric walked into Mallory's office like a crowned king. "Everything's set. J. Lo's agreed to do the cover, but only under a couple of conditions." He had been working on getting her committed for three weeks.

Mallory braced herself. "So should I sit down?" From dealing with the celebrities they covered at *Heat*, she was used to the diva act, and she had heard through the thriving media grapevine that J. Lo was the mistress of divadom.

Since Deena's horrible experience with the Blondie interview, she had decided that she wanted no part of interviewing other celebrities for *Spotlight*. Instead, her sole contribution to the publication would be a quick question-and-answer page on which she would respond to inquiries from readers each month. So it was left up to Mallory to either assign or write the magazine's cover stories. She had decided to write the story about Jennifer Lopez herself.

Eric gestured excitedly with both hands. "No drama. Actually, for her it's pretty benign. She just wants to make sure that the photo shoot is done at her home in Miami, and because of her filming schedule it's got to happen this weekend, which means we need to get down to Miami tonight for preproduction."

"That's not a lot of notice to get a top photographer." As a writer, Mallory knew that the editorial content was important, but as an executive, she now understood that the accompanying art, especially with a subject like Jennifer Lopez, could make or break a story.

"Don't worry about that." Eric waved his hand. "I'll have Deena or Saxton pull some strings to make sure that we get either Marc Baptiste or Ernest Washington."

"Cool. Now we just need to get hair and makeup set. I'll get with Kevin and have him make a few calls to some of the top people."

Eric waved for calm again. He had everything under control. "Don't worry about that either. I'm sure she'll want to use her own hair and makeup people. But of course she'll also want to send us the bill," he laughed. He'd been down this road once or twice before.

"Well, I'll work on our travel arrangements."

After Eric left her office, Mallory picked up the phone to call Vickee. "Listen, Eric, Kevin, and I will need a flight out to Miami tonight. We'll also need reservations for a photographer and one assistant. Not yet sure who we'll be using, but I'll keep you posted. Add to that hotel rooms booked through Sunday and a couple of rental cars. No, make that one van and one car," she said, thinking through the logistics as she spoke.

She hung up the phone and turned her attention back to the copy that she had been in the process of editing for the upcoming issue. Running a magazine was a never-ending process—closing one issue and immediately ramping up production for the next—but she loved every second of it. Working under Eric had been a great learning experience. In the past few months she'd been exposed to more of the details of the publishing business than she ever would have working for Chad at *Heat*.

She shuddered to think of working for him. In fact, she'd recently gotten word that he'd had the nerve to predict that *Spotlight* would fold after the first issue, due to lack of newsstand support and no ad sales. Nostradamus he was not, since both of his predictions had proven to be way off base. Not only were their subscription rates soaring, but *Spotlight* was also blowing through boxes of thick ad-laden magazines at the newsstand. Meanwhile the staff at *Heat* was jumping ship like a horde of starving rats. She had taken more than a few calls herself from ex-colleagues looking for jobs, and so had Eric. There was definitely trouble in paradise. Rumor had it that Richard was even looking to sell the publication.

Her phone rang. "Mallory here," she said, not taking her eyes off the computer screen.

It was Vickee. "I just finished speaking with Linda at the travel agency. She said that Mr. McKensie is taking the corporate jet to Miami this evening for *Newsweek*'s CEO conference, and she thought it would make sense for you guys to fly out with him. It would save a lot of money."

Mallory squirmed in her chair, feeling very uncomfortable with the idea. Yet what was she supposed to do? "Vickee, do me a favor and ask Cindy to check with Mr. McKensie. If he says that it's okay then it sounds good to me." She hung up, feeling uneasy. She knew that this development would not go over well with Deena. There was no way that this could appear to be Mallory's idea.

Minutes later, Vickee was back on the line. "I just spoke to Linda, and she said that it was fine with him. In fact, he thought it might be a good opportunity for you guys to catch up on some *Spotlight* issues."

"Cool," she said, though her pulse began to race. The thought of traveling with Saxton was definitely making her hot under the collar and other places.

Before she hung up again, Vickee added, "He's staying at Turnberry Isle Resort in Aventura, and Cindy suggested that I book you guys there as well. Apparently, she was able to get a really good rate."

"That's fine," Mallory said, though inside butterflies were in full flutter.

* * *

During lunch she hurried home to pack. She refused to dwell on the fact that she and Saxton would be traveling out of town and staying in the same hotel together. There would be other people on the trip, she kept telling herself, and once there, she'd be crazy busy with the photo shoot and the interview, and he'd be totally consumed by the conference. So she had nothing to worry about.

Nonetheless her emotions were in high gear that evening as she boarded the Gulfstream IV at New Jersey's Teterboro Airport. She was excited about the trip. All she had to do was stay away from her soon-to-be-married ex-lover.

When she stepped into the elegant burl wood–trimmed interior, Eric was already ensconced in a supple cream leather chair with a glass of chardonnay in his hand. She headed for the seat next to him. "Not a bad way to travel, huh?"

"I could certainly get used to it," he answered, slowly swirling his glass. An attractive, smartly dressed flight attendant walked through the velvet curtains and took Mallory's coat before storing her luggage. "Can I get anything for you, Ms. Baylor?" she asked, smiling brightly.

Why not? Mallory thought. *I could sure use a drink.* "Yes, I'll have a glass of cabernet."

"My pleasure," the stewardess said.

Eric turned to Mallory. "You certainly don't get this kind of attention traveling commercial—not even on the Concorde."

"You're right about that," Mallory said, reclining in the plush leather seats.

The passenger door opened again and in walked Ernest Washington, the photographer, and his assistant, Angela. They were both carrying several heavy black bags full of photography equipment. They were greeted and assisted by another immaculately clad, perky stewardess, who was all smiles. Pleasantries were exchanged as the pair took seats across from Eric and Mallory.

Saxton walked on board several minutes later and was warmly greeted by the first stewardess, who managed to ratchet up her ultrabright smile another notch. "Mr. McKensie, it's such a pleasure to have you aboard."

"Thank you, Sarah."

"Your regular?" she asked, showing him to the head seat.

"That sounds fine," he said, and she sashayed off to retrieve his martini, which was already chilling in the shaker.

When Saxton was settled with drink in hand, Eric leaned forward and said, "Thanks for the lift," and clapped the other man on the shoulder.

He smiled at Eric and Mallory. "I'm happy to have the company."

The engines had roared to life, and the pilot and copilot were going through their checklists, when the cabin phone rang shrilly, breaking the preflight calm. One of the stewardesses picked up the phone. "Good evening, Ingram Enterprises." After a second, she put the caller on hold and took the portable phone over to Saxton. "Mr. McKensie, the call's for you. It's Ms. Ingram."

"Hello?" he answered with all warmth absent from his voice.

"It's me, honey. I need you to hold the flight. My taping ended early, so I'm headed up Route Seventeen and should be there in fifteen minutes. Don't leave without me."

After he hung up, disappointment was written on his face as he turned around to face Eric and Mallory. "Deena's joining us. She should be here soon."

Twenty minutes later, a frazzled Deena appeared breathless at the top of the gangway, awkwardly making her way onto the jet with shopping bags dangling from every inch of arm space. "Good evening, Ms. Ingram. Let me help you with those bags." The stewardess unloaded several shopping bags full of last-minute purchases for the trip. Once Deena realized that she didn't have time to make it to the apartment to pack, she ran through a couple of shops in SoHo as though they were her remote closet. She had no intention of missing this flight.

After she'd handed off her bags, she strutted down the aisle headed to the seat next to Saxton. When she eyed Mallory, she said snidely, "I'm glad that I could join you on your little weekend getaway."

"So am I," Mallory said, ignoring her sarcasm. Eric took a quick gulp of his drink, as did Saxton.

"Are you comfortable? If not, there are plenty of couches in the next cabin. I know how fond of them you are." Not waiting for a reply, Deena swung her hair and continued down the aisle.

Eric leaned over to Mallory and whispered, "Make sure you buckle up your seat belt, honey. This is going to be a very bumpy ride."

28

THE LOVESICK DOCTOR

What am I doing here? Beverly wondered as she stepped out of the taxi and headed into Park Avalon, a trendy restaurant on Park Avenue South. She removed her dark mink coat and handed it to the hostess. "I'm meeting Greg Donner," she said, briefly scanning the room.

"Right this way." A second hostess led Beverly past the bar and into the cavernous candlelit dining room.

When they approached Greg's table, he jumped up to greet her. In the process he nudged the table hard enough to nearly topple a glass of water. "Hi, Beverly. You look great."

She wore a pastel print Diane vonFurstenberg wrap dress with a pair of dark chocolate Jimmy Choo calf-length fitted boots. Her dark brown hair was loosely layered, falling just past her shoulders.

"Thank you."

Greg seemed nervous, Beverly thought, although she didn't know why. As far as she was concerned, she was the one who should be a complete wreck. After all, he was a noted player—not at all the type of guy that she normally dated. She had been shocked when he phoned her last night to invite her to dinner. She'd given him her number at the *Spotlight* party, but never expected for him to call. She figured he asked for girls' phone numbers just to keep in practice.

She took the seat opposite his, hoping that her choice of dress was appropriate. It was sexy, given the deep V-neck that the wrap created, yet a Diane vonFurstenberg was always a sophisticated choice.

After the hostess left them alone at the table, Greg squirmed in his seat. "You really look amazing."

"You say that as though you're surprised," she said lightly. "Didn't think that a woman could have brains and looks at the same time?"

"Th-that's not what I meant," he stammered.

"I'm teasing. It's just that I was a little surprised when you called. After all, I am definitely not your type."

"I wouldn't say that," Greg defended himself. "It's just that the type of girl you usually see me with is more for convenience."

"Convenience?"

"Yeah, you know, I don't really have to think when I'm out with them," he explained.

"It's clear why," Beverly mumbled under her breath, but loud enough for him to hear.

He chuckled. "Be nice."

"I just don't get the 'convenience' angle. What's so convenient about dating a string of airheads?"

He had a ready answer for that. "For one thing, I never have to think about what I say. As long as I take them to good restaurants and show them a good time, I get what I want, and they get what they want, no strings attached."

"So, Mr. Convenience, why call me?" Beverly asked, holding his gaze.

Greg looked thoughtful. "You know, that's a good question. I'm not really sure why."

"That really makes a girl feel special," she said wryly.

"No, I don't mean it like that. It's just that you're different."

"So is a case of the chicken pox, but that doesn't mean it's good for you."

Greg looked pained. He wasn't his slick self at all tonight. "What I mean is that I know I can't treat you the way that I treat the 'convenient' women that I usually date. I guess that means that I'm ready for a change."

Beverly was now enjoying his discomfort. It was kind of cute. "Do tell," she said, leaning forward, resting her chin in her palm.

He smiled. "Don't tell Saxton I said that. I have to maintain some level of playa quotient, or I'll never hear the end of it."

She didn't like the sound of that. "What are you talking about?"

"When he saw us talking at the *Spotlight* party, he was sure that I was turning over a new leaf or something. And of course I denied it adamantly. So when he gets wind of this date, I can hear him now: 'The Love Doctor must have thrown away his own secret potion.'"

"Well, have you?"

His eyes twinkled. "Let's just say that I'm ready to try a new kind of therapy," he said, leaning forward to reach for Beverly's hand.

She smiled at his light touch. "I don't know how I feel about being an experimental treatment."

He gently worked his fingers in between hers. "Don't worry. You're in good hands."

She could feel her skin grow warm. He knew exactly what he was doing. "From what I can tell so far, you do have a pretty good bedside manner."

"You haven't seen anything yet."

Thankfully, the waitress appeared to take their cocktail orders. Beverly was beginning to get a little uncomfortable with the direction of their conversation. Now she knew why Greg had a bevy of females in line to date him. The brother was definitely smooth when he wanted to be.

After dinner orders were placed, they settled into chatting easily on topics ranging from the media's influence on race relations and political strategies and their effects on the current social structure to film, literature, and the best places to stay in the South of France.

Having an intellectually stimulating conversation with an attractive female was a new experience for Greg. It was like talking to a best buddy who also happened to look like a million dollars.

Later, when the bill was presented, Beverly reached into her Fendi evening bag for her wallet.

"What are you doing?" Greg had never seen that before. Usually the chicks he dated ordered every expensive thing on the menu, as though it was their first meal in an age and could be their last. He was lucky if they had cab fare back home.

She pulled out her American Express Platinum Card and placed in on top of the leather folder. "This is for half."

Greg slid it back over to her side of the table. "That's not necessary. Remember, I invited you out to dinner. So it's my treat," he insisted.

"Only on one condition."

"What's that?" he asked, motioning the waitress over to pick up the check.

"That I treat next time."

He smiled broadly. "I like that idea."

"Oh, really. Why is that?"

His hand slid out to cover hers again.

"Because that means that there will be a next time."

29

MIAMI VICE

The next couple of days were much smoother than their takeoff had been. On Friday and Saturday, Saxton spent both days at the media and technology conference listening to the gospel according to Bill Gates, Rupert Murdoch, Ken Chenault, and Dick Parsons, while Deena had every spa treatment that Turnberry had to offer. Eric and Mallory oversaw the setup and execution of Jennifer's photo shoot, while Mallory conducted the interview in three two-hour sessions over the course of the two days.

She was really looking forward to Sunday to relax and have a late breakfast before they took off in the afternoon after Saxton's last conference. She realized that she had worried needlessly about traveling with him, since she hadn't seen him once since they landed. She guessed that Deena had co-opted any free seconds that he had.

She soaked leisurely in the Jacuzzi in her room, letting the stress of the last two days seep out of her tired and tense muscles. When she stepped from the tub onto the thick twisted cotton bath rug, she smoothed on her Annick Goutal's body oil before putting on a thin cotton two-piece night set. She decided to enjoy the warm night air, which was now just a faded memory in New York City, since winter had taken a much firmer hold. She poured a glass of red wine and opened the double doors leading out onto the adjacent patio. It was a beautiful bright night. The tropical breeze was like a thick warm blanket that sent a trace of chills down her spine. She was relishing the calming night air when she suddenly heard a light rap at her door.

Since she hadn't ordered anything from room service, she used the peephole to glimpse the person on the other side. When she opened the door, there stood Saxton wearing a pair of white linen pajama pants and a breezy collarless shirt. At the sight of him, she was jolted. All of her reasons for staying apart vanished in a flash. "Can I come in?" he asked.

She stood to one side as he entered. There was no need to say anything. Once he was inside, she melted like warm butter in his open arms. There was no hesitation, nor were there any second thoughts. He held her tenderly but tightly as their lips met and parted in a silent agreement. This time there would be no turning back for either of them.

"I've missed you," he said.

Lost in a haze of passion, Mallory ran her hands up his thick sinewy biceps and found her way back down his muscular back. She caressed the rippling density of his body, committing each ounce of his flesh to her memory. She could have spent hours exploring the touch and feel of him, while he tasted her the way one might an exotic liqueur. He became a connoisseur of her swollen lips and darting tongue. Catching his breath, he stood back, drinking her in. His fingers began to unbutton her light airy top. She stood unwavering before him, challenging him to use his fingers, hands, tongue, and teeth on her. In response, he bent low enough to run his caressing tongue over her hardened brown nipples. She took a long, deep breath as he fed himself. Mallory's head lolled back as she focused on the intense pleasure of his flicking tongue.

He stood up and turned her around. Pinning both of her hands over her head against the wall, he started a hot trail of kisses at the base of her neck. Mallory turned her head urgently from side to side in weak, feeble attempts to escape.

When she was panting hoarsely, his kisses trailed southward, down her tingling spine. He pulled her bottom along for the downward ride before traversing the smooth roundness of her full hips. There he paused and took long licks and deep kisses, while his large hands kneaded her soft, supple flesh. When he'd loved and licked every inch before him, he parted her legs wide and dropped to his knees eager to taste her wet, ripe essence.

He lapped her hot sex in long, slow, sensual motions, beginning at her highly sensitive bud and finishing toward the back of her, taking a teasing and languid dip midway. Mallory's moans filled the room and floated freely through the patio doors and out into the warm night air. After her song reached an unmistakable crescendo, Saxton stood up, leaving his pants and underwear on the floor next to hers.

In a state of bliss, Mallory turned again to face him, but this time when they came together, there was nothing between them. No troubled past, no complicated present, and no underwear. She felt the entire length of his burning hot flesh throbbing urgently against her thigh. Holding him in her hand, she stroked the smooth shaft, marveling at its length and hardness. He took her hand and led her to the bed, where she lay back with her legs spread wide, the soles of her feet planted flat and her knees bent, waiting on him to fill her body completely. He gripped his long, hard shaft and held it poised at the tip of her slickness, feeling the heat rising from her hot sex even before he eased himself into her. His throbbing grew stronger, and his mass longer and harder. Her quivering muscles tightened their grip, holding on to every inch that he gave her.

As sweat pricked through his pores, a gasp caught, then was released deep in his throat. Her feverish body demanded more, quickening its upward thrusts, anxious to meet his powerful probing. Mallory looked through lust-covered eyes into Saxton's very soul as they held on to each other tightly and took a ride that ended somewhere over the moon.

After their breathing slowed, Saxton pulled her close to him, wrapping the light down comforter around them both.

Snuggled tightly together, she nestled into his chest, inhaling his masculine scent.

He kissed her forehead. "Do you know how much you mean to me?" he whispered in her ear.

"I can't say that I do," she answered. Her eyes were still closed, savoring the delicious afterglow.

"Let's just say that nothing will ever be the same for me," he said quietly. "You are like an addiction that I'll never be able to get enough of."

"That's not necessarily a good thing, you know."

"Only the withdrawal from addiction is bad, and I have no intention of ever letting you go again."

30

THE TABLES TURN

Deena was exhausted after a hellish weekend that had turned into an even less enjoyable Monday. And unfortunately, it was not over yet. She had just concluded a nauseating three-hour-long meeting at the Four Seasons with the executive producers for FBC. They had discussed her erratic ratings and ideas for her upcoming shows. Of course, the whole meeting was laden with veiled cryptic warnings and sharply qualified praise. Given the unmitigated disaster that Saturday and Sunday had turned into, how could she have expected for Monday to be any better?

What had started out on Thursday afternoon as a coup—her dropping in on Mallory's little getaway with her fiancé and thwarting the little hussy's plans for a weekend tryst—had not worked out as well as she planned. On Saturday afternoon, after she'd finished her herbal body wrap, she had gotten a frantic call from her mother on her cell phone. The woman was nearly hysterical. In between incoherent blather, Deena learned that her father was having chest pains and was being rushed to the hospital. She hopped on the jet immediately, again without packing, and landed at Boston's Logan Airport. Then she took a chartered helicopter to the city's east side heliport to be at her father's side. She had insisted that Saxton join her, but he had scheduled a lunch meeting with Rupert Murdoch and thought it wiser that she go on ahead of him and then send the Gulfstream back. He argued that given the state of their shaky relationship with FBC, Rupert was a contact that they could need sooner rather than later. He would follow should her father's condition prove to be serious. She had her reservations about leaving him, but at that point her father's condition was all that really mattered. So she left Saxton, she thought, dangling within claw length of Mallory's clutches.

By the time she arrived at her father's bedside, she was relieved but a little pissed off to see him sitting up in bed sipping ginger ale through a straw. According to the doctors, he had only suffered a nasty case of indigestion. Her mother sat perched at his side, totally ignorant of the fact that she could have just cost Deena her fiancé. Worse yet, before she could do any spin control and call Saxton, she found out that he'd already called the hospital himself and been told by her mother that his future father-in-law to be was doing just fine. Shit! Not exactly the plan that she had in mind. So she had been forced to sit idly by in Boston while God, Saxton, and Mallory only knew what was going on down in Miami.

She'd called him back around five thirty and caught him on his cell. He'd just left the last seminar for the day, he said, and he was planning to grab a bite with a few other conference attendees a little later on. He expressed his relief at the good news of her father's health and said that he would see her Sunday night back in New York City. She'd tried him again later that night and didn't get an answer, not in his room or on his cell phone. When she asked to be connected to Mallory's room, she heard what she assumed to be the sounds of a sleepy postcoital female. In her agitated state she imagined Saxton lying naked at her side.

When Saxton returned home on Sunday night, she was waiting when he walked in.

"So how was the rest of the conference?" she asked after kissing him at the door. She felt a slight hesitation on his part, a split second of resistance before he snapped back into his role as her fiancé.

"It was good. Very informative," he said, removing his coat and setting down his Louis Vuitton luggage. He walked past the foyer to the bar in the corner of his study. "Can I pour something for you?"

"No, I'm tired from dealing with my mother all day. Plus, I have an early morning tomorrow."

"How are your parents?" he asked.

"Physically, they are fine, but now they're both as agitated as a pair of rattlesnakes. Apparently word of Dad's emergency trip to the hospital got back to Washington, and there are rumors that his name may be removed from the short list of candidates for the Supreme Court."

"I'm sorry to hear that," Saxton managed to say. In truth, he didn't feel as if the country needed another Clarence Thomas, future father-in-law or not. "Well, I think I'll have a little nightcap," he said, pouring himself a snifter of port.

"So what did you do last night?" She tried to make the question sound casual, but they both knew that it was fully loaded.

"Nothing special, really," he lied. Flashes of Mallory flew through his mind as he sat on the sofa that faced the fireplace. "I had a late dinner with some of the guys and then called it a night."

She stood in front of him with her elbow resting on the mantel. "I tried to call you." It was a statement, a question, and an accusation all wrapped into five words.

He chose to ignore two of the three alternatives. "What time was it?"

"Just after midnight." She observed him carefully, waiting for a flinch that would give him away.

It didn't happen. "I was probably already in bed."

I'm sure that you were, she thought, *most likely right beside that bitch Mallory Baylor.*

* * *

Mallory barely remembered the plane ride back to New York on Sunday. It was all a blur. After falling asleep nestled in Saxton's arms, she had dreamed of blue skies and green waters, a thatched roof on a deserted island, orange sherbet on a hot summer's day. . . . She was lulled in and out of sleep by the strong, melodic beat of his heart as she rested her head against his chest. Each time she awoke, she was pleasantly surprised to see that her favorite dream was still in fact real. When he left her room early the next morning, she hugged the pillow that had held his head and drifted back off to sleep.

Once she boarded the Gulfstream, Eric regarded her astutely. "Something is different about you." He contemplated her appearance as he pulled his sunglasses down a notch to peer at her over the designer rims.

"I can't imagine what," she answered, blushing and putting her own sunglasses in place. She didn't want him, or anyone else, to see the new sparkle in her eyes, though the dewy glow on her face was pretty hard to miss. She shifted around before reclining in her seat, stifling a smile.

But Eric was not so easily fooled. "All I can say is that it must have been good." He then pushed his sunglasses back into place and turned his attention back to the copy of *Radar* magazine that he had been reading. He'd decided to mind his own business, for now. But the fact that Deena had been missing since the day before did not escape him either. He simply nodded his head and smiled.

Saxton was the last passenger to board the aircraft. As he passed down the aisle, he and Mallory exchanged a private smile that caused her heart to flutter. She would have expected, after the night before, to be worried about Deena, regretting the intimacy they'd shared, or simply anxious about the future, but amazingly she felt none of those emotions. Only bliss.

Once she was back in *Spotlight*'s office on Monday morning, she was forced from the clouds. She was swamped with a slew of copy flowing in from writers. She had to funnel it all to her team of editors for a first round of review, before it eventually ended up back with her for top-editing. The growing pile amassing on her desk was a welcome distraction for her. It kept her mind from wandering back to the steamy hotel room in Miami or just next door, to Saxton's office.

She was further distracted by Vickee's voice coming through the intercom. "Mallory, Beverly's on line one."

She set aside the stack of papers and picked up the phone. "Hey, what's up?"

"Just checking in. How was your trip?"

"It was very eventful."

Beverly noticed the catch in her voice. "Hhhhmmmm. What does that mean?"

"Let's just say that it was a very busy weekend." Not wanting to say more, she changed the subject. "How was yours?"

"Interesting, very interesting," Beverly said.

Mallory perked up, hearing a note in Beverly's voice that wasn't usually there. "What happened?

Beverly was bursting to tell her. "I went out with Greg."

Mallory nearly sprang from her chair. "I knew it!"

Beverly smiled. "Knew what?"

"I knew there was something going on between you two. Why didn't you tell me?"

"There was nothing to tell. There still isn't. It was only dinner."

"Yeah, yeah, yeah," Mallory said, disregarding Beverly's claim. "For you two to be out together, there has to be something to tell."

"Let's just say that the Love Doctor may be reforming his ways."

Mallory could hear the excitement in her friend's voice, and she recognized it as the same thrill that she felt after her weekend with Saxton. "Tell me more." She settled back in her chair, waiting for the juicy details.

"I'll tell if you tell." Beverly was nobody's fool; she knew that there was more to Mallory and Saxton's relationship than Mallory had let on.

"Let's get together later," Mallory said, not wanting to discuss anything personal here in the office. As far as she knew, Broom-Hilda could have her phone tapped.

After plowing through the morning, she took a break from reviewing copy. She headed to Eric's office to discuss the best editorial slant for a story they were doing on the socioeconomic consequences of the large number of wealthy black men choosing to marry outside the African-American race. She was deep in thought about the issue when suddenly she found Deena blocking her passage in the hallway. When she stepped to the side, so did Deena. After they repeated this awkward two-step, Deena put her hands on her hips. "You know, you really need to stay out of my way," she said, giving Mallory a scathing look.

As much as Mallory loved her job, at that moment it occurred to her that she probably needed to start updating her résumé.

Deena was still fuming over Mallory and Saxton when Nikki showed up to meet her for a quick drink.

"Hey, girl, how was your meeting?" Nikki asked, plopping down on the sofa next to Deena.

"You don't want to know."

"More drama?" Nikki was casually scoping out the room to make sure that Mallory was nowhere in sight, since she knew that the Four Seasons bar was also one of her hangouts. But after a long weekend shoot, she figured that her roommate would most likely be too tired to have drinks on a Monday night.

"Instead of a talk show, I should have a soap opera." Deena recounted the weekend's events to a totally absorbed Nikki. "Can you believe that shit?" she asked when she was finished telling the story.

"Well, I'll be damned," Nikki said. That explained the dreamy look that Mallory had been wearing around the house all last night, she thought. "So what are you going to do?"

Deena took a sip of her Belvedere martini and paused before speaking. "I have to play it really close. I need Saxton right now more than ever."

"I don't get it. Why?"

"I need the public to see a perfect picture of me, complete with a smart, handsome husband."

Nikki rolled her eyes and neck at the same time. "Girl, you're better off without him."

"Eventually maybe, but not right now."

"But what about the baby?" Nikki had been sure that that would be the straw to break the camel's back.

Deena snapped. "I have to look at the bigger picture here."

"Well all right, then." Nikki was beginning to be alarmed. Things were not working out the way she had planned. She had hoped that Deena would have gotten rid of Saxton by now.

While she was tangled in her own twisted thoughts, she heard Deena say, "There's that fuckin' skank bitch." The harsh bitterness in her voice sent a shiver down Nikki's spine.

When she turned around to see who was the subject of Deena's wrath, she spotted Yvette walking through the bar with a couple trailing closely behind her. Nikki slid down into the sofa, wishing that she could disappear. The last thing she needed was to be called out by the gossip columnist in front of Deena. When she had composed herself sufficiently, she asked, "Who are you talking about?" as she looked around the bar.

"The chick in the corner with the nasty dreads is Yvette Boynton, the gossip columnist over at the *New York Gazette*. She writes that rag sheet called 'Talk of the Town.'"

"Oh, really?"

"I hate that bitch," Deena sneered.

Nikki looked at her quizzically. "Tell me how you *really* feel." She did not expect for Deena to be happy with the things that Yvette had written about her, yet she hadn't expected such venom. Business was business.

"No, you don't understand. When we were in graduate school together, Yvette and I were good friends for three years,

until she caught me having sex with the guy that she assumed
was her boyfriend. Unfortunately, he hadn't made the same as-
sumption." She shrugged.

Since they'd been out of graduate school for years, Deena
thought that they had both outgrown that unfortunate little incident and didn't even cause a stink when the organizers for the
Women in Media awards dinner placed Yvette at her table.
Given the personal attacks lately, though, obviously she was
wrong.

Deena mistook Nikki's flabbergasted expression for shock
at her backstabbing behavior. Nikki was really blown away by
the fact that she had been played like a fiddle by Yvette.

"Hey, it wasn't my fault that he liked me better than he did
her," Deena replied. "She's been jealous of me ever since."

Just then Yvette walked by their table and said, "Ladies."
She then covered her mouth. "Ooops, I meant to say Deena,
and what's your name?"

Nervously Nikki extended her hand. "Nikki," she nearly
whispered. At that moment she wished that she could be swallowed up in the leather sofa.

"It's a pleasure to meet you, Nikki," she said, glaring directly at Deena. When Deena turned away, flipping her hair ar-
rogantly, Yvette favored Nikki with a wicked conspiratorial
wink. That was when Nikki realized that she had been playing
way out of her league.

31

A WRONG TURN

Since the day they'd run away from the small house in Buffalo, Jonathan had been even more of a nervous wreck than usual. He'd become convinced that Mallory and the detective she hired were planning to show up with the police. So the day before they were supposed to meet, he packed up their few belongings and hightailed it to the outskirts of town. There he managed to rent a seedy pay-by-the-week one-bedroom apartment on the second level over a small grocer.

As much as he would have loved to get rid of the kid to lighten his load, he hadn't figured out a way to do it, especially knowing that there was no way that Linda would turn the boy over to a stranger. He was beginning to realize that the chances were slim that she'd ever turn him over to anyone, even Mallory. As if all that didn't keep him up at night, lately he'd been seeing a blue Honda in his rearview mirror whenever he ventured out of the house.

Because he didn't know whether this was the Feds or the mob, his imagination was driving him to drink. Though he used to be a batch-brew-bourbon kind of guy, he was now reduced to rotgut whiskey. As bad as it was, it did help to calm his increasingly jittery nerves. If he drank enough of it, the alcohol also helped him to sleep, which he didn't do easily of late.

Like tonight. While Linda and Dylan lay sound asleep in

the bedroom, Jonathan was sprawled out on the couch, nursing a half-empty bottle of Four Roses. He finally got up, walked over to the window, and peeled the dingy curtains back a few inches. Across the street, parked under a gaslamp, sat the same Honda that had been tailing him lately. A man was sitting inside, watching him. It had to be the mob coming in the middle of the night to do him in. He was sure of it. He took a swift swallow of the bad whiskey to steel his nerves. There was no way he'd remain sitting like a duck, waiting to be taken out.

He hurried into the bedroom and shook Linda urgently. "Get up now. We've gotta go. The mob is waiting in front of the house." Thank God he'd parked their car in the rear. They could sneak out the back entrance of the apartment without being noticed.

Linda sat up in bed quickly. "Wh-what are you talking about?" She reached to the nightstand for her glasses.

"We've got to go. Quick, get up and get the boy ready. We've got to get out of here!" He grabbed the suitcase that held the sum of their belongings and headed to the closet for their overcoats.

Fighting a haze of confusion, Linda stood up and threw on her clothes. Grabbing the slumbering Dylan, she wrapped him tightly in her prized hand-sewn quilt. They were out the back door in two minutes.

Once they reached the car, Linda quickly buckled the sleeping child into the car seat in the back. The moment she hopped in the front, Jonathan peeled away from the curb.

"Slow down," she urged him.

Jonathan had his eyes trained on the rearview mirror as he headed down a hill leading away from the apartment building. "Oh, shit! He's behind us."

While she fumbled for her seat belt, Linda turned around in her seat to see a pair of headlights approaching in the darkness of the night.

Jonathan gave the car more gas, determined to lose the other car. He had to get away. His eyes were glued to the rearview mirror as he heard Linda scream at him, "Watch out!"

He managed to get only the briefest glimpse of the ominous curve that had suddenly materialized. He slammed on the brakes. Skidding wildly on the icy road, the car careened off the road into a thicket of pine trees. The headlights shone closer and closer to a massive trunk, and thoughts of his family, his first car, and his mother flashed quickly before Jonathan's eyes. Then the car crashed with a terrible scream of crushed metal.

Linda's last thought before falling into utter blackness was of her son, who lay fast asleep behind them.

32

BABY'S DADDY

Since returning from the weekend in Miami, Saxton had had a tough time regaining his focus. The time with Mallory had forced him to recalibrate the compass of his entire life. Nothing seemed clear to him anymore. What had once seemed so wrong suddenly seemed right, and what had once seemed right now appeared to be horribly wrong. For Saxton, who had always been so clear about his direction in life, this new development was very disorienting. It was as though a whole new way of viewing the world had been presented to him.

To see it clearly, he only needed to close his eyes. By doing so, he could relive every scintillating detail of that magical night with Mallory, and if he tried hard enough, he could even recall her intoxicating taste and smell.

When he imagined making love to her, a powerful feeling washed over him, one he'd never come close to feeling with Deena. Sure, they had sex, and if he was with the boys, he would really break it down and say that they fucked, but given what had happened with Mallory, he now knew that they had never truly made love. Afterward, he and Mallory had slept in each other's arms for the rest of the night. Occasionally he'd woken up to make sure that it hadn't all been just a dream.

Early the next morning he kissed her softly on her slightly parted lips before heading to his own room to dress for the last day of seminars. He didn't remember what they were about and didn't care. When they all boarded the Gulfstream for the return trip to the city, minus Deena, it took every ounce of self-control he had to keep from sitting next to Mallory and holding her delicate hand and whispering sweetly into her ear. The weekend left him in a euphoric state—that is, until he walked through his apartment door to find Deena on the other side of it. She quickly snapped him back to reality.

He was only thankful that he'd arrived home late and they could go straight to bed without having to spend much time talking. When she climbed under the covers next to him, he rolled over to his side, not wanting to touch her or her to touch him. He couldn't shake the feeling that if he did it would somehow soil him, leaving a stain on his memory of the night with Mallory. After Deena had drifted off, he looked over at her prone figure and almost wondered aloud how he could have ever thought that he should marry her. Then he had lain awake the rest of the night and most of the following one, trying to figure out what to do about the mess that he'd made of his personal and professional life.

He was on his third cup of coffee Tuesday morning when Cindy did something that was totally out of character. She came bursting through his office door barely knocking, nearly out of breath, calling him by his first name. "Saxton, you've got to see this," she panted, waving a newspaper frantically in front of his face. Whatever it was, it was not good news. That much he already knew.

"What is it?"

"Just read it," she insisted, dropping the paper on his desk as though it were a piping-hot potato.

When he finished reading the type that she pointed to, he was more confused than he was before. It was a "Talk of the Town" column.

Baby's Daddy?

We all know how fashionable it is in the notorious rap community to be a Baby's Daddy, but who knew that Saxton McKensie was a bona fide member? We all thought that hanging out with SamTheLover in Las Vegas was just a lark.

Well, you know what they say: birds of a feather do flock together. Hint: the Baby's Momma is not his fiancée, the picture-perfect talk show host Deena Ingram. I guess her next television segment could be: Women who keep men who cheat and why they love them.

Saxton looked at Cindy for an explanation she was obviously unable to give him. As he sat there stupefied, his office door swung open again, but this time the force behind it caused it to ricochet off the back wall.

"What the hell is this?" Deena demanded. She was so angry that her blood had boiled to the surface, turning her light brown skin a crimson hue. Cindy turned tail and slunk from the room.

"Deena, calm down," Saxton said. His own voice was remarkably calm, in spite of the turmoil that had swept without warning through his door.

"What do you mean, calm down?" She put her hands on her hips. "And where is that bitch anyway?" She looked around as though she expected to find Mallory naked, splayed out on the couch.

Saxton looked at Deena like she had just sprouted a set of horns. "Who are you talking about?"

"Mallory. I know about you and Mallory," she said in an accusatory tone.

For a second he was taken aback. How could she possibly know that he and Mallory had slept together Saturday night? "Deena, I don't know what you think you know, but you are off base."

"Are you telling me that you didn't have a little boy with Mallory Baylor?" She crossed her arms tightly and glared at him through squinted eyes.

He cocked his head to one side. "A little boy? Since when did this fictitious child get a sex?"

He didn't know, she was sure. That left the question of how she did? Deena stammered, "I-I was just guessing—that's all."

"Or making it up, just like this Yvette woman. I would have given you a lot more credit than that."

"Are you telling me that you didn't have a child with Mallory?"

"That's exactly what I'm telling you." He met her stare head-on. "Who are you going to believe, me or some gossip column?"

She was in a quandary. How could she tell him that she knew the truth without giving away her double-dealing? She decided that it was best to retreat on this subject, at least for now. "I'm just sick of having your skeletons walking out of the closet and landing right in the middle of the scandal sheets."

"You're sick of it?" He threw his arms into the air and raised his voice. "I'm fed up to here," he said, chopping his hand over his head, "with your selfish concern for your own precious image. That's all you ever think about, isn't it? You are so quick to believe whatever this woman writes. Don't you think that if I had a child that you'd know about it or, better yet, that I would?"

She swallowed the ironic fact that she did in fact know, but sadly, he did not. "It's just that this is such a crucial time for me. I'm under a lot of stress," she said, switching gears. "I am barely hanging on to a slight lead against Gina Davis, and any slipups like this could cost me—no, us," she corrected herself, "everything that we've spent the last five years building." She softened her voice. "And besides that, it hurts me to hear that you may be involved with someone else."

"Do me a favor, the next time you hear or read anything that concerns me," Saxton said, heading to his desk chair. "Before you go flying off the handle, check with me first. I promise that I'll let you know if you have any cause for concern." He sat back down and determinedly resumed his reading, leaving Deena standing ignored in the middle of the floor. Something about his simmering calm and veiled warning worried Deena much more than if he'd screamed at her.

Tuesday morning started out with Mallory buried under a ton of editing and tight deadlines. She asked Vickee to hold her calls so that she might find some light at the end of the very crowded tunnel. Her nose was pressed firmly to the grindstone until around eleven o'clock when Vickee came running into her office, barely able to contain herself.

"What's going on?" Mallory paused with her fingers poised over the computer keyboard.

"Cindy just came from Saxton's office, and he and Deena are having it out!" She was whispering excitedly as though they would be able to hear her through the walls.

This, given recent developments, didn't surprise Mallory. She continued to type. "And?" she said. It was common knowledge around the office that their relationship was less than perfect, and of course, Mallory knew firsthand.

"And I'll bet you'll never guess what it was about." Vickee plunked herself down in the chair opposite Mallory's desk, settling into position to drop the latest office bombshell.

"I have no idea." Mallory kept typing; she didn't even bother to look up.

"Well, according to 'Talk of the Town,' Saxton has a secret child, and Deena just found out about it."

Mallory froze in midkeystroke. When her heart finally began to beat again, she stammered, "A ch-child? By who?"

"According to Cindy, the article didn't say, but it did say that it *wasn't* Deena." Vickee gave her that blown-away look that often accompanied the delivery of scandalous gossip.

The shocking news simultaneously stunned and scared Mallory. Were they talking about Dylan? If so, how could anyone know about him? She had never mentioned him to anyone. She suddenly felt a wave of nausea. A violent chill coursed through her body. She couldn't just sit there. She had to get more information about this mystery child.

Five minutes later, she left the building and quickly headed to the sidewalk newsstand next door to pick up a copy of the *New York Gazette*. As a stream of pedestrians whizzed by, she stood transfixed, fumbling through the pages of the paper searching for the gossip column. After reading it, she closed the paper in frustration. She knew no more about the situation than she did before.

She was headed back into the building carrying the newspaper when she ran into Saxton. He glanced at the paper in her hand and looked toward the sky. "I see that you've heard the news, too," he said, "if gossip qualifies as news."

"I did hear," she said, shaking her head. "I'm sorry." What she could not tell him was why she was sorry. How could she say to him, *Oh, you know that kid they're talking about? I happen to know all about it, and oh, by the way, it's a boy.* She was years late with that news flash.

"I have no idea where they get this stuff from," he said, gesturing to the newspaper. "Don't you think I would know if I had a child?"

Not necessarily, Mallory thought, as she held her head down and said nothing.

Not wanting to take his frustration out on her, he backed off. In a quiet voice he said, "So much for my day. How are you?" They hadn't really had a chance to talk since leaving Miami.

"I'm good," she answered, looking up at him.

He sensed her hesitation. Did she have some reservations about their night together? "Are you sure?"

She gave him a smile to convince him otherwise. "I'm sure."

"We need to talk." He glanced around, knowing that this was not the time or the place. "Can we get together, Thursday night?"

Her feelings were torn. As much as she wanted to see him privately, the news of a child definitely complicated things. "Sure, that sounds good," she finally said.

Later that night as Mallory prepared for bed, Nikki knocked at her door. "Come in," she said as she pulled her nightgown over her head and reached for her Nailtiques hand cream.

"Hey, girl, do you want some popcorn? I just made some fresh," Nikki said, tossing a few kernels in her mouth.

Mallory smoothed on her lotion and never looked up. "No, thanks."

Nikki turned around as though she were leaving the room, but then stopped like she'd suddenly remembered something. In between crunching on popcorn she asked, "Hey, what's this I hear about Saxton having a child?"

"Why don't you tell me?" Mallory fixed Nikki with a penetrating stare.

Nikki looked taken aback. She propped a hand on her hip for better effect. "How would I know?"

"That's a good question." She walked closer to Nikki, until she was just a foot away. "It just seems a little coincidental to me that Yvette, who you denied knowing though you spoke to her at Pastis, consistently reports on details—however inaccurately—of my life or Saxton's. So tell me, how is that?"

"I don't know what you're talking about," Nikki insisted,

though a telltale twitch of her eye betrayed her claims of innocence.

"I find that hard to believe."

"Well, believe it." Nikki changed tactics and put on her most innocent expression. "Mallory, you're like a sister to me. I would never do anything to hurt you."

Like Cain and Abel, Mallory thought, as Nikki hurried away to her room.

She had not lain in bed five minutes before a shrill ring at her bedside pierced the quiet. Instantly alarmed, Mallory snatched the phone from its cradle. "Hello?" she answered.

"Mallory?"

"Yes." She sat up in bed, fully alert. It was Mr. Morris.

"There's been a development."

Mallory didn't like the tone of his voice. "What? What's happened?" she said in a panic.

"I'm sorry to have to tell you this, but there was an accident last night." Mallory's blood ran cold. "The Browns were killed, but Dylan is okay," he hastened to assure her.

"Where is he? Where's my baby?" Mallory was nearly hysterical as she jumped from the bed.

"He's fine. He's at a local hospital with social workers."

"I've got to get there." By now the nightgown was off and she was frantically pulling clothes from her closet.

"I know. Meet me at LaGuardia in an hour, and we'll take the first flight to Buffalo. Oh, and Mallory?"

"Yes?" As she cradled the phone between her ear and shoulder, she was reaching for her shoes and bag.

"There was a note in his belongings for you to be contacted through me in case of an emergency. Just thought you should know." He hung up the phone.

33

SPIN CONTROL

The latest ink to drip from Yvette's poisoned pen took its toll on Deena. Her show's ratings had plummeted in the last two days, driven down by the rampant rumors of Saxton's purported infidelity. The juicy gossip spread like kudzu on the Internet. What had started out as a story about a secret love child took on a new life overnight and grew into a full-fledged hidden mistress and a torrid love affair. All of which permanently stained Deena's image as the picture-perfect talk show personality. Even the network bigshots were calling to weigh in with their opinions, and they were not on her side. They were already putting some distance between themselves and *The Ingram Hour*, afraid that the black cloud apparently trailing Deena might head their way.

Thursday morning she and CoAnne were in the publicist's Madison Avenue office. CoAnne did not want to have the conversation she was about to broach to happen anywhere near Ingram Enterprises. She wore a grave expression as she removed her signature square horn-rimmed glasses. "Deena, my dear, this is not looking good," she said frankly.

"No shit! Tell me something I don't know." Deena's nerves were shot to hell. It was painful to sit by and watch while a hundred million dollars slipped through her fingers like finely grained sand. All because of a man who couldn't keep his dick in place, a trifling little slut, and the slut's bastard child.

CoAnne sighed heavily. "Listen, I know you're angry, but emotions aren't what's going to get you out of this mess."

"Oh, do you have some answers?" Deena asked caustically.

CoAnne pulled a cigarette from the mahogany holder on her desk. "What you need now is a brilliant campaign of damage control. In other words, it's time to pull the fat out of the fire because, honey, right now it's damn near crispy."

"I'm all ears." Deena sat back and crossed her legs and her arms defiantly.

CoAnne picked up a crystal lighter and took her time lighting her Dunhill cigarette. "Let's be real here for a moment." She looked Deena dead in the eye. "You are in a pickle because the man that you were planning to marry in order to complete your perfect image is in fact damaged property. So what do you do?" CoAnne took a deep drag on her cigarette and expelled the billowy smoke into the air before she answered the question for Deena. "You get rid of him, honey." She made a stabbing motion with her lit cigarette. "That's what you do."

Deena was genuinely surprised. "What do you mean?"

"I mean, you cut your losses. Kick him to the curb. Cut bait. However you want to put it."

"But how will that help my ratings?" By now the defiant attitude that Deena had walked in with had deflated into bewilderment.

"That's where spin control comes into play. If you act quickly, we can position you as a long-suffering woman who just couldn't take his philandering any longer, but found the strength to pull away." CoAnne was nodding her head, taken with the new idea. "I'm telling you, women will eat it up! What woman can't identify with that story? Believe me, you'll definitely win fans when you start cashing in on the sympathy vote."

This was a huge reversal in strategy for Deena. "I don't know." She ran her hands nervously through her hair.

"Remember Oprah? In the beginning she'd get on TV and tell the world every problem and challenging situation that ever happened to her in her entire life, and with each sad tale, her ratings grew like an athlete on steroids."

"Hhmmmm." Deena's brow was furrowed in contemplation.

"Besides, at this point, honey, I hate to tell you, but you don't have a whole lot of choice. Let's get real. We all know, given recent events, that a wedding in three weeks is not likely to happen, so rather than be embarrassed again by not having the fabulous wedding that you've already announced, you need to preempt that blow by announcing a split from Saxton altogether. We can word it carefully so that he isn't too scarred. We wouldn't want people to question your judgment for being with him in the first place. Right?" She sucked on the cigarette some more, thinking hard, before blowing three perfectly formed smoke rings to the ceiling. "The press release could go something like this: Talk show personality Deena Ingram is announcing that her wedding to entrepreneurial attorney Saxton McKensie has been called off due to unresolved differences. The two remain friends and she continues to wish him well."

Deena sat with her legs sprawled in two different directions. She felt as if she had been hit head-on by a semi. As much as she hated to admit it, CoAnne was right about everything. She had to go into self-preservation mode now—every man, woman, and child for herself.

CoAnne saw Deena's wheels turning and thought she'd help speed them along. "Deena, this is the only chance that you've got to recapture your ratings within the next few weeks. Trust me," she said, snuffing out the cigarette in a Baccarat crystal ashtray. "You don't have a choice."

When Mallory had called the office early Wednesday morning, she'd gotten Cindy's answering machine and left a short message that she'd had a family emergency and would not be in. When Saxton found out, he called her apartment and got no answer. He tried her cell phone, where her voicemail gave him its standard greeting. It was now Thursday, and besides another brief message, there was still no word from her. Now he was beginning to worry. They had a date tonight, and in her message she'd made no mention of it.

"Cindy, could you come here a minute?" he called into the intercom. He was leaning back in his chair, chewing on his thumbnail.

"Yes, Mr. McKensie?" She appeared in the doorway, pad and pencil in hand.

"What exactly did Mallory say when she called in this morning?" he quizzed.

"Not a whole lot really," Cindy shrugged. "She left the message at six, just saying that she wouldn't be in again today."

"Uhmmm." He wondered whether she'd flown to Atlanta. "If she calls, I'd like to speak with her," he said, scratching his head.

Still worried about her, Saxton tried to concentrate on the next meeting with FBC. The thirteen-week ratings period would be up in just three short weeks, and at this moment it was anybody's guess which way the chips would fall.

The Ingram Hour had held on to an increasingly smaller lead on *The Gina Davis Show* for each week leading up to the *Spotlight* premier party, when Deena enjoyed a favorable spike in ratings. But thanks to Yvette Boynton and this week's baby drama, the show had taken a nasty nosedive. Things were not looking good. He needed to meet with Deena this afternoon to come up with a plan of action.

It didn't take that long. Fifteen minutes later, he got a call from Hazelle. "Mr. McKensie, Ms. Ingram would like to see you in her office."

"Sure, I'll be right there." *Perfect,* he thought. Maybe they could come up with a strategy to salvage the next few weeks. Too bad, he thought, that the personal side of their relationship wouldn't be as easy to save.

"Hi, Deena," he said as he entered her already open office

door. She stood in the middle of the room nervously twirling a lock of her hair.

"Hi, Saxton," she managed through a fake, uneasy smile. "Have a seat." She gestured in the direction of a trio of chairs near the window under a three-foot-tall portrait of herself. Sitting across from each other at the desk, she'd reasoned, would have felt too formal, and this was going to be hard enough.

When they were both seated, Deena turned to face him. "Listen, we need to talk," she said, looking toward him over templed fingers. Saxton knew from experience that when Deena's conversations started like that, it really meant that she needed to talk and he was required to listen.

He leaned back and crossed his legs. "I'm all ears." He also hadn't failed to notice that she was wearing her blue pinstripe Ralph Lauren power suit, with a cream silk shell and black pumps. She usually wore this outfit when she wanted to be taken seriously. She was avoiding direct eye contact. He briefly wondered what Deena was up to now.

Even though she'd only just sat down, she stood up again, nervously rubbing her sweaty palms on the front of her skirt. He watched her, perplexed, as she paced the floor in front of him. She finally stopped herself and said, "I really should just get to the point. The reason I wanted to talk to you is because this is just not working." She spread her hands out toward her sides as if summing up everything.

Saxton did not understand exactly what she was getting at. "Yes, I know. I wanted to talk with you about the show. I thought we could come up with some strategies to build up short-term ratings. We should probably call Co—"

She cut him off. "Saxton, it's not the show that I'm referring to. It's us." She stood perfectly still with her fingers lightly clasped in front of her.

Saxton tilted his head back a little as recognition dawned on him. He almost laughed, but managed to catch himself. Since the weekend he'd spent hours trying to figure out how to get out of their personal relationship, and just like that, she did it for him. "Whatever it is that you have to say, Deena, why don't you stop beating around the bush and say it?"

She started pacing again, wringing her hands with each halting step. "It's just that I know something's going on with you and Mallory. Then there're these ugly rumors about some illegitimate child, and of course the coup de grace is this botched FBC syndication deal. I just think that it's best that we call off the wedding." There, she had said it all. She braced herself, waiting for him to explode in anger or beg for her forgiveness.

Neither one happened. "That's probably a good idea," he said, stroking his chin. He wasn't sure what else to say.

She snorted in shock and disgust at the way he so casually accepted the fact that their wedding was called off. It really made her furious. How dared he be so cavalier about her dumping him? You'd think he could plead a little, even if he couldn't manage the tears. Well, if that announcement did not upset him, she had one that would.

"Just one more thing," she said, ascending to her throne behind the desk. "When can you be out of your office?" It may have taken her a moment or two to warm up to her role as a Heartbreaker, but the role of Bitch came second nature.

Saxton wasn't sure that he'd heard Deena right. Surely he must have misinterpreted her meaning. The idea of her firing him was incomprehensible. It would be like Gilligan tossing the Skipper overboard.

"I'm not sure that I understand," he said, with his head cocked to the side. Maybe looking at her from a different angle would help.

"Then let me spell it out for you. You're *fired*," she said coldly.

The impact of her words forced Saxton from his chair. "You can't fire me. I built this company." Flashes of anger lit up his face.

"The last time I checked—which I can assure you was recently—you were an employee here. A well-paid employee, but definitely an employee, nonetheless. Your contract ends in

June, which, by the way, was when we had originally planned to get married. So talk to one of my attorneys about negotiating a settlement. But settlement or not, I want you out by the end of the week." She walked over to her desk, ready for the meeting to end now that she'd had her say.

"What about shares in the company?" A year ago she had offered him shares in Ingram Enterprises, but after they became engaged, they both decided not to bother with the legalities, because after the wedding he'd own half of the company anyway.

Deena sat at her desk and crossed her legs. "I don't know what you're talking about."

"Don't think for one minute that you can get rid of me this easily. You must have forgotten who you're dealing with. I'll sue you and this company for every dime on the books if you try to screw me." Saxton glared at her through blazing eyes. He took a deep breath and lowered his voice, though he was seething. "In case you need reminding, I *built* this company— and you!" He jabbed toward the floor with his extended finger. "If it weren't for me," he said, "you'd still be a struggling field reporter for Channel Seven news. So if you think for one moment that I'll simply stroll away from here with my pockets empty, then you've sadly underestimated me."

Deena was seeing a side of Saxton that she'd never seen before. The spit polish of Harvard was being unseated by grit from the street.

"Trust me, I'll bring this whole place down before I ever walk away from here with nothing." He then calmly turned toward the door, saying, "You'll be hearing from my attorney."

As he walked back to his office, he was bombarded by conflicting emotions. On one hand, he was relieved to be out of his personal relationship with Deena. For a while now he'd been worrying about how to back out of the wedding without looking like a complete jerk. But on the other hand, there was no way that he would ever sit back and let her kick him out of the company that he'd built.

His first call was to his long-term personal attorney, Denise Brown.

"Denise, you're not going to believe what that bitch did."

"Whoa! Which bitch are we talking about?"

"Deena. She fired me and she says I can't have any part of the company. Can you believe that shit?" His anger was burning through the phone lines.

"Calm down, Saxton. Your contract lasts through June. Besides, we have a good case to demand more. So don't sweat it. Come by the office tomorrow. Okay?"

"Sure, I'll be there."

As he was putting the phone back in its cradle, Cindy called him on the intercom.

"Yes."

"A package just arrived by courier from Mallory."

A package? "Bring it in." He met her at the door and snatched it from her hands. Quickly he headed over to the sofa in front of the fireplace. He gently slid the handwritten note out of the folder. It read:

Dear Saxton,

I apologize in advance for not doing this in person. But in the last two days a lot has changed, causing me to reassess my life. Please do not be alarmed. As they say, "It's all good." And it really is this time. . . .

Unfortunately, I will not be able to continue my employment with Spotlight *magazine. But please know that I am forever grateful for the opportunity that you gave me, and I truly enjoyed the job.*

I wish you, Eric, and the rest of the Spotlight *staff much success in the future.*

Warmly,
Mallory Baylor

Saxton sank dejectedly into the deepest folds of the leather sofa. All thoughts of Deena and Ingram Enterprises were set aside. What had changed so suddenly in Mallory's life? Where did it leave them? His head was spinning with questions, but no answers emerged. What was going on with Mallory? Was she sick? Was she dying and didn't want to tell him? Alarmed, he jumped up from the couch, grabbed his coat, and hit the door.

34

CARBON COPY

Mallory arrived home Thursday morning with a sleeping Dylan nestled in her arms. Before opening her apartment door, she turned to give Mr. Morris a big hug with her one free arm. Dylan shifted his weight in his sleep to keep his solid perch, his head resting on her shoulder.

"It looks like you've got yourself a handful," Mr. Morris said, smiling down at the sleeping child.

Mallory smiled, too. "I never imagined him to be such a big boy," she said, gazing lovingly at her son. "I guess in my mind's eye he stopped growing after I got my last picture."

"I've got two of my own, and trust me, it doesn't quite happen like that," he laughed. "Before you know it, he'll be off to college, and he'll be holding you."

Mallory thought about Saxton, as she had so often the past two days, and her heart ached with the realization that she would never be able to join the two people who meant the most to her. At least, she reasoned, she did have warm memories of their night together in Miami to help soothe the ache.

Mr. Morris caught the moment of melancholy. "Are you going to be okay?"

"Yep, I'm just fine," she said, nodding her head adamantly. Though Saxton was her one regret, she knew that she was doing the right thing by keeping him in the dark about Dylan.

There was no way that she could subject this innocent little boy, who'd been through so much already, to the media buzzards who would feed on him merely for existing. Besides, the scandal would also ruin Saxton's career.

"So what are your plans?"

"The first thing I'm going to do is pack up my things as quickly as I can. Fortunately, I don't have a lot. Then we're heading to Atlanta on the two o'clock flight." She checked her watch. "I think it's about time that my family met my son."

"But I thought you loved New York."

"I do, but Atlanta's a much more kid-friendly environment, especially for a single mom." She chuckled to herself when she said this, reminded of her older sister and the suburban moms that she'd sworn she'd never be like. As the saying goes, never say never.

"Well, you should be okay, legally. The note Linda Brown left in Dylan's bag and the will she left with her mother both identify you as the birth mother and the person she wanted to raise Dylan in the event anything happened to her."

Mallory said a silent prayer for the souls of Mr. and Mrs. Brown.

"Well, I'm gonna take off now. Good luck, Mallory."

"Thank you for everything." They embraced again before Mr. Morris headed to the taxi that he had waiting curbside.

Mallory opened the door to the apartment and saw that no lights were on. She came in and gently placed Dylan on the sofa before covering him with a throw from the back of the couch. As she tucked the blanket securely around his little body, she gave another silent player to God for sparing the life of her child.

Dylan had been strapped in his car seat, asleep in the back of the Toyota Camry when Mr. Brown lost control of the car and ran off the road into a pine tree, killing him and his wife instantly. Fortunately, a passing motorist arrived in seconds and scooped up a disoriented Dylan along with the bag next to him before he had a chance to see any of the carnage. By the time Mallory and Mr. Morris arrived at the hospital, he was sitting up alert with only a few small bruises to show for the car wreck. The doctors explained to her that often sleeping kids fared well in accidents, because they didn't have the opportunity to tense up, which would cause more trauma. Rather, they were like limp dolls rolling with the impact instead of absorbing it.

When she walked into his hospital room, Dylan was sitting up in his bed playing with a red fire truck the nurses had given him. "Hi, Dylan, how are you feeling?"

"Okay," he said, though he did turn his arm over to show her the bruise that he'd seen the doctors examine earlier.

"It looks like somebody has a boo-boo," Mallory said, easing over to the bed to sit on its edge. "Dylan, my name is Mallory." She held out her hand to him.

His ears perked up. "You're Mallory?"

Puzzled by his response, she answered, "Yes, I'm Mallory. Do you know me?"

"My mom told me all about you," he said, nodding his head. He resumed spinning the wheels of the truck.

"What did she tell you?"

He stopped spinning. He squinted his eyes in concentration and nibbled on his thumbnail, like he was taking a test. "She said that you were my birth mother." Mallory could tell that he didn't really understand exactly what a "birth mother" was, but she smiled at his seriousness, not missing the fact that Saxton had that same expression when he was deep in thought.

"What else did she say?"

"She said that one day I might meet you. Are you my birth mother?" The truck was forgotten now, and his features took on a more somber cast.

"Yes, baby, I am."

"But where is my mom?" he asked, looking around the small hospital room.

"Your mom had to go away to be with the angels."

"Is she coming back?" Now he was confused.

Mallory folded him in a hug. "No, baby, she's not coming back." She held him at arm's length to look at him. "That's why she sent me to take care of you."

"Is Dad with her, too?"

Mallory nodded her head.

"If they aren't coming back here, can I go see them?" he asked. Tears began to well up in his eyes.

"No, baby, I'm afraid you can't. God and the angels took them away to take care of them, but they left me to take care of you." As tears rolled down his cheeks, she hugged him tight. "It's okay to be sad because you loved them and they loved you." She pulled away for a moment. "But guess what?" she asked, looking into his tearstained eyes. "I love you, too." Then she held him tight and rocked him quietly.

After a few minutes passed, he asked. "Are you my mom now?"

"Yes, baby, I'm your mom now." After all these years, they were together as mother and son.

"Why are you crying?"

"I'm just so happy," she said, smiling through her tears.

A perplexed expression pinched his face. "Why do adults cry when there're happy? I don't get it." When she couldn't reply, he lost interest and went back to playing with his truck.

He was still holding on to the truck as he slept soundly on the sofa. She kissed his forehead lightly before getting up to begin packing. Nikki was out, and hopefully she would stay away until they were long gone. Mallory was not in the mood to explain Dylan to anyone quite yet.

Suddenly, remembering her life that existed before yesterday, Mallory quickly wrote two letters of resignation, one to Saxton and one to Eric, and then sent both by courier to the office.

She dragged all four of her suitcases from under the bed and spread them open on the floor in the living room, where she'd have more space to pack her things. She spent the next couple of hours throwing clothes, shoes, and other possessions into the open cases. She was almost done when she heard a knock at the door. Assuming it was the driver coming to take them to the airport, she ran to answer it.

"I'll need just another fifteen—"

Mallory froze in midsentence as she saw Saxton on the other side.

"Mallory, what's going on?" He quickly registered the stunned expression on her face. He grabbed her shoulders and shook her lightly, hoping to jar her from whatever was going on in her head. His eyes eventually wandered past her and into the living room. Releasing her, he slowly walked through the door. Mallory's hand crept up toward her open mouth.

"Mallory, I—"

That was when the little boy woke up. He rubbed his eyes with both fists and looked questioningly at Saxton. "Who are you?"

Saxton stood transfixed. His mouth opened in shock, and his brow creased deeply. He looked back and forth from Mallory to the little boy on the sofa.

"Mallory, what's going on here?" Saxton demanded. His thoughts were jumbled, clouded by a swarm of facts he couldn't comprehend. He was standing inside Mallory's living room with her luggage packed all around him, and a sleepy little boy who happened to look exactly as he had at that age on the sofa. The child had the same caramel complexion, the exact same thick, dark curls, and eyes that could have been small replicas of his own.

Mallory hung her head low and shook it slowly. At last she gathered the strength to face him. "I just didn't know how to tell you."

"Tell me what?" he pleaded.

"Mom, who is that?" Dylan asked, pointing to Saxton. He was wide-awake now.

Mallory knelt down beside him. "You remember in the hospital you told me how Ms. Brown told you that I was your birth mom?" He nodded his head. "Well, this is Saxton. He's your birth dad." Dylan seemed to consider this latest development, then shrugged his little shoulders.

Even though the physical evidence was right in front of his eyes, Saxton still had trouble assimilating the fact that he had a son. No, that he and Mallory had a son. He was speechless.

Mallory stood and picked Dylan up. "Saxton, I'd like you to meet your son, Dylan. Dylan, this is your dad."

Saxton held out his hand, and they shook hands. Even in his shock, he smiled at the boy. "Whatcha got there?"

Dylan turned the toy truck over in his hands before holding it out to show to Saxton. "It's a fire truck. The nurse at the hospital gave it to me."

Alarmed, Saxton looked at Mallory for an explanation, and she quickly said, "You'll have to show your dad how it works after you've eaten, okay?" She ushered Dylan into the bathroom to wash his hands before taking him into the kitchen to fix a bowl of Froot Loops.

When she returned to the living room, Saxton was standing there holding the toy in his hand. "Mallory, why didn't you tell me?"

"I hardly know where to start," she answered, her head bowed. "I didn't find out I was pregnant until after you'd already left Atlanta, and when I didn't hear from you, I realized that you had moved on with your life, and it wouldn't include me. So I figured that there was no point in telling you." She was wringing her hands and fighting back the tears that threatened to erupt. "Besides, I vowed never to be one of those pathetic women who clung to a man by having his child. In fact, I'd planned to have an abortion, but it didn't happen. So I put the baby up for adoption." Her voice began to crack. "I didn't tell anyone, not my family or friends." She took a couple of deep breaths to give her the strength to continue. Through sniffles, she continued the story. "A few years ago the couple who adopted Dylan, the Browns, disappeared, vanished from sight. That's when I started searching for him. I didn't have any luck until recently, when I was able to hire a private investigator."

By now Saxton had sat down on the sofa, flabbergasted, with his hands clasped between his widespread knees. It was all too much for him to bear standing up. "I wish you had told me." He thought of the little boy in the next room. That was *his* child. A little boy that he didn't know.

The story that she'd kept deeply buried so long continued to bubble out of her. "A few weeks ago, I'd finally found them, but by the time I got to their hideout they'd taken off." Tears began streaming down her face as she relived the nightmare in Buffalo. "I'd given up on ever seeing him again, until I got a phone call late Tuesday night. The Browns were killed in a car accident, but luckily Dylan was unhurt and Linda left a note for the authorities to contact me." By now the tears were running unchecked. Five years of tears flowed by.

Saxton reached out to hold her as sobs began to rack her body. "I am so sorry," he repeated to her over and over again. He remembered the handkerchief in his breast pocket and took it out to wipe away the tears.

Neither Saxton nor Mallory heard Dylan until he was standing before the two of them, wearing a solemn expression. He began patting Mallory's back the way he saw Saxton do. "Does this mean that you're happy again, Mom?"

Saxton picked him up and set him on the knee opposite Mallory.

She smiled despite her tears. For the first time her heart embraced the fleeting hope that the three of them might be together. The tight smile wore thin as she thought of Saxton's fiancée. "What about Deena?"

"What about her?" By now Deena was all but a bad dream to Saxton. He realized without question that where he belonged was right here with Mallory and their son, Dylan.

"She'll never—"

He finished her sentence for her: "She'll never have anything to say about what I do, ever again."

Mallory looked at him, confused.

"Deena and I are not getting married, Mallory. In fact, I'll no longer be working there."

Before Mallory could react to this unexpected news, there was another knock at the door. When she opened it, Greg walked in. "Is everything okay?" he asked. After receiving Mallory's cryptic note, Saxton had phoned him from his cell phone on the way to Mallory's apartment, telling him it might be a medical emergency.

"What are you doing here?" Mallory asked him.

"Who are you?" Dylan asked for the third time that day.

"Everything's fine," Saxton said, not knowing where to begin to explain anything else.

"Can I ask a question now?" Greg asked, looking from Saxton to Mallory, then to Dylan. "What the hell—excuse me"—he put his hand discreetly over his mouth—"what the heck is going on here?"

Mallory took a deep breath and recounted an abbreviated child-friendly version of the story that she'd shared with Saxton. Then Saxton picked up with the story of his breakup with Deena and his firing.

After being ignored long enough during all the adult conversation, Dylan walked up to Greg. "My name is Dylan, and I'm five years old. Who are you?"

"It's nice to meet you, Dylan. I'm your uncle Greg, but don't you ask me how old I am." He reached down to tickle the little boy's tummy. Dylan laughed while trying to curl up to prevent the onslaught.

After they'd calmed down some, Greg said, "I just have one question."

"Only one?" Mallory asked, her head still spinning.

"How did 'Talk of the Town' find out about my little buddy here, if no one else, including Saxton, knew about him?"

Mallory shook her head. "I have a pretty good idea, since

the only evidence was a file that I've always kept in my bedroom."

Before she could finish answering his question, the front door opened again and in walked Nikki. When she saw the cozy reunion set out before her, the hairs on the back of her neck stood up. "Mallory, what's going on?" she asked, but her tone rang off-key, which they all caught. She tentatively walked into the room, not sure what land mines were strewn about, but deciding on the fly to make it quick.

Mallory noticed her unease, plus the silent signals that flew through the room like the telling electricity in *Ghostbusters*. She decided to play it cool. "Nothing really. But why don't you meet Greg? He's a friend of ours." Greg eyed her strangely, trying to place her. "And this is my son, Dylan, and of course you *do* know Saxton."

Nikki gave a round of fake greetings before picking up a bag in her room and hightailing it back out of the front door. After she had beat a hasty retreat, Greg said, "Well, I think we have the answer to at least one question. But there is something else." He scrunched up his nose, trying hard to dredge up a slip of a memory. He squinted his eyes as though it would sharpen the image that was evading him. "I've seen her somewhere before, and it's nagging at me." He slapped his thigh. "I think it could be important."

Mallory was staring at the door Nikki had closed behind her. "I can't believe that she'd do this to me. Why would she do that?"

Saxton pulled her close to him. "Well, my dear, motives are always pretty simple. It's always either love, money, or love and money."

"I live with her, so I know the girl doesn't have any money."

"What about love?" Greg asked.

Mallory shrugged. "I know that she's been seeing this guy named DJ."

"Have you ever seen him?" Greg asked.

"No, but she's always out with him."

That was when Greg's eyes nearly popped from their sockets. "Now I remember where I've seen her before! She and Deena." He stopped abruptly and turned to Saxton. "What's Deena's middle name?"

"It's Jean," he answered as awareness began to dawn on him.

"Aha! Listen to this. On the night of the *Spotlight* party I was walking by one of the staterooms downstairs, looking for a bathroom. It was right after I left you guys. Anyway, I tried a doorknob, but it was locked. As I turned to walk away, who walks out of the room, smoothing out her dress, but Ms. Helicopter-cum-Bond herself along with this Nikki chick. I remember wondering at the time why they were in a stateroom with the door locked, but really didn't think much else about it. I was just trying to get back upstairs to Beverly." He coughed, and Mallory and Saxton exchanged a knowing look. Recovering, he went on. "But I do remember they both appeared a little disheveled. And at the time, of course, I didn't know who the femme fatale was, but there is no mistaking her. Nikki was definitely with Deena the night of the party."

"I wonder what were they up to," Mallory said, frowning.

"I'd guess that they were having a little fun," Greg ventured slyly.

"No!" Saxton and Mallory exclaimed at the same time.

Dylan looked from one adult to the other, not understanding what the fuss was about. Shaking his head, he returned his attention to the Duplos that Mallory had pulled from the tote bag.

Greg said, "This may come as a surprise, especially to you," he said, motioning to Saxton, "but I think it's safe to say that our two friends are best described as lovers."

"Wow!" Mallory was blown away. "That explains so much," she said as the pieces began to fall into place.

Saxton and Greg turned to her with questioning expressions.

"It's just that now I know why she insisted that I take the

job. I think she wanted me to come between Deena and Saxton so that she could have Deena all to herself. She's got to be the one who leaked the *Heat* information and the piece that identified me as an ex-girlfriend of Saxton's. And after she found the adoption papers, I'm sure she couldn't wait to tell Deena, but not before she leaked it to the press behind her back."

"Who's Deena?" Dylan asked, looking from face to face for an explanation.

"Did you read *Snow White and the Seven Dwarfs*?" Greg asked.

Dylan shook his head.

"Well, Deena would be like the Wicked Witch. Your mom is Cinderella, and your dad is Prince Charming."

"Greg, I think you need to brush up on your fairy tales."

"I know, but he's a smart kid. He'll get it."

Saxton was still digesting this latest bombshell.

"Well, I'm glad that someone has it all figured out, because I'm still trying to put the pieces together. I'm meeting with my lawyer tomorrow. I've got to figure out a way to keep Deena from taking the company from me."

"Leave it to Uncle Greg. I might just have an idea or two up my French-cuffed sleeve." He smiled conspiratorially.

Saxton realized his friend was on to something. "Keep those ideas coming, because I am quickly running out of time, especially now that I have a family to take care of," he said, scooping up Dylan and placing him in Mallory's arms.

Mallory planted a flurry of kisses on Dylan's forehead, and he wiped them away with a devilish little smile. When she kissed Saxton, he mimicked the boy, with large comic brushes of his hands that made the child laugh. "Like father, like son," Mallory said, hugging them both.

35

SEX, LIES, AND . . .

Deena and CoAnne were camped out in Deena's office, going over the details for the press release to announce her breakup with Saxton. They planned to get the press release out that afternoon so the weekend papers could play it up without additional comment from the parties involved. Readers would be left to believe exactly what was in print and, hopefully, have sympathy for Deena, the victim.

"Do you think this is going to work?" Deena asked, worried. Now that she had pulled the plug on Saxton, she was a little nervous about how fast the water might flow down the drain.

"It's too late for the jitters now," the pragmatic publicist said. "Our only problem is the fact that you had to go and fire the man." She continued to wordsmith the document on her laptop computer.

"You told me to ditch him," Deena whined.

"No, honey. I told you not to marry him. No one ever said that you should fire him. Who's gonna run the company now?"

"I'll do it," she said bravely, "until I can find someone else. Besides, who knows me better than me?"

"Good luck," CoAnne snorted, never looking up from the computer screen.

Deena persisted stubbornly, "It can't be that difficult."

"Running the company isn't your biggest issue right now. What you need to be worried about is the fact you've got a really pissed-off man ready to wring your neck, and in your position the last thing you need is more enemies. I think you've got enough of them as it is."

"Gee, thanks," Deena said sarcastically, rolling her eyes.

They both looked up when a tall familiar figure barged in with Hazelle hot at his heels, saying, "Ms. Ingram, I'm sorry. I tried to stop him."

Both women sat with their mouths agape as Saxton strolled in. CoAnne gave Deena a see-what-I-mean look.

"That's okay, Hazelle," Deena said, and the frazzled assistant glared at Saxton and reluctantly left the room.

"What a cozy pair," Saxton said as he calmly sauntered to the chair behind Deena's desk. "I hope that I'm not interrupting any more of your devious schemes that might involve me." After he sat down, he said, "But please continue. Maybe I can help you with some of the fine points."

CoAnne turned beet red and snatched her huge eyeglasses off her face, but she couldn't come up with a reply snippy enough.

After Deena picked her face up off the floor, she said, "Saxton, what are you doing here?"

"Oh, I didn't say, did I? I just thought I would save you a little extra humiliation," he said, drumming his fingers on the desk.

"If anyone should be concerned about being humiliated, I think that would be you."

He turned his head, perplexed. "Why would you think that?"

"Well, you *are* the one with a bastard child who was fucking his employee. Or was that your evil twin?" Venom dripped from her every word, but when her dig didn't bring the desired result, concern cracked Deena's veneer of arrogance.

"I wouldn't worry myself with that if I were you. You've got some problems of your own to deal with."

"Whatever it is that you have to say, I suggest you say it quickly before I call security. We have work to do here."

"Oh, don't worry. I'll be quick. In fact, I'll save us a lot of time. After all, a picture is worth a thousand words." Saxton stood up and headed over to the entertainment center on the far wall. He pulled a videotape out of the portfolio that he had brought with him. "Seen any good movies lately?"

"What are you doing?" Deena challenged.

Intrigued by this development, CoAnne put her glasses back on the bridge of her nose. She didn't want to miss this.

"Just came across this interesting tape recently, and I was sure that you'd want to know about it. So you can consider this a private screening. The public premiere can be scheduled for later." After he inserted the tape, Saxton picked up the remote control and took a seat on the sofa, crossed his legs, and pressed PLAY.

Deena was making her way to the VCR to stop his nonsense, but before she could reach it, the image that appeared on the big-screen TV stopped her dead in her tracks. She and Nikki were shown in living color embroiled in a torrid lip-locked embrace, with Nikki's hands busily exploring beneath Deena's evening gown. CoAnne's eyes grew as large as her frames, and her Chanel-red mouth hung open in astonishment.

Mallory had worked with Caché on many of the details for the *Spotlight* premier party, and she remembered Morgan, the owner of the event-planning company, telling her that transforming images to big screens throughout the boat wouldn't be a problem, since the yacht's owner, a security nut, had the entire boat covered in video surveillance. Greg and Mallory then placed a call to Morgan, who then phoned Mr. Ventura, the boat's owner. She begged him to let them go through the video footage from that night. And since Morgan had scheduled several expensive bookings for the boat, he agreed. After two hours of viewing, they hit pay dirt.

Saxton sat lazily swinging his crossed leg, and on the screen, Nikki slid to the floor and under Deena's dress for a muff dive, while Deena threw her head back in unabashed ecstasy. Deena later returned the favor with just as much zest.

"I only wish," Saxton commented mildly, "you'd shown as much interest in me."

Deena, stunned, sat in shock watching her reputation and career swirl down the toilet right before her eyes. Before the tape was finished, Saxton walked to the VCR to retrieve it. "I'm sure you get the point," he said.

Enraged, Deena ripped the cassette from his hands. Hysterically she yanked the tape in streams from the casing. "You bastard!" she screamed, nearly foaming at the mouth. CoAnne looked on in horror.

Saxton calmly shook his head. "I hope that made you feel better, since it does nothing to help your sordid predicament. You must know that I have several copies of that, and unless I have a cashier's check for my half of this company's net value within forty-eight hours, you and your precious viewers will get to see an instant replay in its entirety on NBC, ABC, CBS, FBC, CNN, and any Internet site with streaming-video capability." He turned to leave.

"You can't do this to me," she shouted.

"Watch me," he said. "You went too far this time, Deena. Just consider this payback." He turned and left the room.

After he was gone, Deena crumbled to the floor in tears.

CoAnne walked over and patted her back. "Well, honey, now you've got some real problems," she said, "and unless you want them played out on the six o'clock news, I'd suggest you make a beeline to accounting."

36

RINGS AND ROSES

It was a beautiful early-spring day, one made expressly for brides by God himself. He even held the famous Atlanta humidity at bay for the occasion of Mallory and Saxton's wedding. The excitement in the Baylor house was tangible as Dr. and Mrs. Baylor raced around putting last-minute touches on the house and garden. Mallory was in her bedroom with her sister, Judith, both fussing over her hair, makeup, and the drape of her cream net veil. She still wore a silk robe, waiting for the last possible moment to put on her dress. Dylan and his cousin Owen had been banned from the living room and the garden, where the wedding would be held in thirty minutes. To occupy each other they headed downstairs to the playroom and pulled out every toy they had between the two of them, trying to remember not to muss their handsome cream tuxedo jackets, which they wore over black pants, cream shirts, and black ties. They each had white boutonnieres affixed to their lapels.

Mrs. Baylor walked into Mallory's bedroom and inhaled the smell of her daughter's happiness. "Mallory, you look beautiful."

"Thank you, Mom." She ran to the door to hug her mother. This was the most wonderful day of her life. She couldn't stop counting her blessings and thanking God for each one.

"Mom, don't mess up her hair," Judith fussed. They all

laughed and held back the tears that threatened to ruin perfectly applied makeup.

Suddenly there was a knock at the door. "Mommy, can I come in?" It was Dylan.

"Yes, sweetie."

He walked in with Owen in lockstep. "Would you tell Owen that I'm the ring bearer and that I have the most important job today?" His honor was at stake, and he needed a little backup.

Mallory knelt to his level. "Absolutely. Without you bringing the rings down to Reverend Kimbrough, your dad and I wouldn't be able to get married. So I'd say that's pretty important."

"See, I told you." And both boys raced out the door.

"Mallory, he is adorable," Judith said, "and so is that fiancé of yours. I am so happy for you." She gave her sister a hug, too, careful to avoid the well-coiffed hair.

Mr. Baylor stuck his head in the door. "Okay, ladies, our guests are starting to arrive."

After he closed the door, Judith and Mrs. Baylor held the delicate butter-colored satin wedding gown with a princess-cut bodice, while Mallory stepped cautiously into it. After they had her zipped, buttoned, and smoothed, they stepped back to admire the most beautiful bride they'd ever seen.

Fifteen minutes later, thirty guests—including Beverly, Eric, Saxton's sisters, Cindy, and Vickee—were all seated in white wooden chairs in the midst of Mrs. Baylor's English-style garden. As a lone harpist strummed exquisite chords of music, Mrs. Baylor walked down the aisle to take her seat in the first row of chairs. Judith and Owen walked together and stood on either side of the rose-covered arbor. Next Saxton, Greg, and Reverend Kimbrough walked to the center of the aisle.

As Mallory appeared in the garden, Jennifer Freeman sang the opening chords of "Ave Maria." Every guest craned his neck to get a better view as she walked down the aisle with her father on one side and her son on the other. Dylan wore a smile that was as handsome and engaging as his father's. The specialness of the fairy tale–like occasion didn't escape a soul, as dry eyes began to mist over. Everyone was touched and charmed by Dylan, but none more so than Saxton, who could not have been happier. He felt like the luckiest man to ever walk the earth, to have a beautiful bride he loved beyond life and a handsome, bright son who stole his heart more and more every day.

The trio reached the arbor, and as Dylan was handing the rings to Reverend Kimbrough, he whispered, "Mom, it looks like everyone here must be happy." Mallory smiled through tears of her own.

EPILOGUE

Chad was leaning back in his desk chair, feeling like the king of the world. Raymond had just completed the sale of *Heat* magazine to a concern called Wanderlust Enterprises. Rumor had it that the principals behind the company were relatively new to publishing, so as far as Chad could see, he was sitting in the catbird's seat, since he would be bringing years of experience to the table. He figured that he was in an excellent position to negotiate not only a healthy raise but a lofty title and a corner office to boot. And from what he'd been told, money was no object with this company.

Wanda, his latest office victim, buzzed him through the intercom. "The executives from Wanderlust are here."

"Great, show them to the conference room." He would make them wait a little while to better establish his position as the one in charge here. He daydreamed for a minute or two about the decor for his new office. He would definitely want a newer, larger couch, maybe even one that pulled out. The one he had now had seen better days—and nights. Straightening the knot of his tie, he stood up and stuck his chest out. When he was satisfied with himself, he strutted out the door and headed down the hall to the conference room.

He walked through the door ready to put his most charming self forward. "Welcome to—"

The bullshit got caught in his throat when he came face-to-face with none other than Saxton McKensie and Mallory Baylor, the new owners of *Heat* magazine.

Mallory stood up from the head of the table. "Long time, thankfully, no see," she said, making her way to within inches of him, hovering over him the way he least liked.

"M-M-Mallory, I had no idea," he stumbled.

"You never did, now did you?" she said. "I think you know my husband, Saxton McKensie, but I'd like you to meet someone else." She gestured over to Eric. "Meet Eric Handley, your replacement."

"B-b-but . . ." This wasn't going at all according to his plans.

Mallory pressed a button on the intercom. "Wanda, would you please send in security?" She then sat on the edge of the table and said evenly, "In case it's not clear to you, your services won't be needed. So please be out of your office within the hour." She, Saxton, and Eric headed for the door, but then she stopped short. "Oh, and by the way, you can take your couch with you."

When the taxi pulled up in front of a nondescript building, Anton said, "This is it?" Looking at the building, he scrunched up his face as he got out of the taxi.

Jimmy took a crumpled piece of paper out of his pocket and read the address he had scribbled down. "Yep, this is it."

"With his money, I'd think he'd be livin' large," Anton said, looking up at the chipped paint on the ceiling.

Jimmy didn't comment on the condition of the building, because he had seen far worse. When he reached apartment 5B, he rang the bell and impatiently waited for an answer.

"Well, it's about time."

"Excuse me?" Jimmy asked the woman who greeted them. "Uh-uh, I must have the wrong apartment," he stammered and stared. Standing before him was over six feet of beauty. Her rich auburn hair was blunt cut and dusted her shoulder blades; her makeup was flawless, enhancing sculptured features, making the overall effect . . . magnificent. "If I were straight, I'd be all over her," Jimmy thought. He then turned to walk away.

"Hey, where are you going?" asked the woman.

Jimmy looked perplexed, "Is this apartment 5B?"

"Yeah, fool, get in here. It's me."

Jimmy's jaw nearly dropped to the floor as he and Anton said in unison, "Tyrone?"

"In the flesh," he said. "I'd like to introduce you to Contessa Aventura Dubois," he laughed, spinning around so that they could get the full effect.

Anton and Jimmy walked into the loft in a state of disbelief. Of course they knew about Tess, but seeing her up close and personal was shocking. There were no traces of Tyrone, not even a hint of testosterone. He was all Tess. "Damn, I got to give it to you." Jimmy slapped him five. "You all that, and some cream."

"Glad you approve," Tyrone said, leading them into the loft.

As Anton was busy checking out the decor, Jimmy was checking out Tyrone's transformed body. "Man, where'd you put the beefcake?" he asked, noticing there were no traces of Tyrone's manhood poking through the black jumpsuit he wore.

"It's tucked away in a safe place," Tyrone chuckled.

Anton slowly walked around the room in amazement. Tyrone was indeed living large. Everything from the drapes to the furniture seemed to be custom-made; Anton's initial sentiments about the shabby building quickly dissolved as he surveyed the well-appointed loft. "Is this silk?" Anton asked, fingering the throw on the back of the sofa.

"One hundred percent, imported from Bali," Tyrone said with arrogance oozing from every syllable. "So you must be Anton?"

Sensing the hairs rising on the back of Anton's neck, Jimmy walked over and put his arm around the other guy's waist. "Tyrone, this is my new man."

"Charmed, I'm sure," Tyrone said, sinking into the cushions of the sofa and crossing his long legs.

Jimmy sat across from him on one of two oversized chintz ottomans as Anton continued his inspection. "What this set you back?" he asked, referring to the Bang & Olufsen stereo system mounted to the wall.

"You don't even want to know," Tyrone said, evading the question.

"I bet it was more than four G's," Anton said with disdain, "and speaking of four G's, where's our money?"

Tyrone patted an envelope on the cocktail table. "Your two thousand dollars is right here."

Jimmy reached for the package. "What about that bonus we talked about?" he asked, thumbing through the bills.

"Oh, that's right. I completely forgot." After liquidating Edmund's assets, Tyrone had promised to give Jimmy an extra bonus for helping him create Tess to begin with; after all, if it weren't for the hormones that Jimmy had stolen from the doctor's office, Tyrone wouldn't have been around to collect all those millions.

"I just bet you did," Anton hissed.

Jimmy shot Anton a look, as if to tell him to play it cool. "No problem. I know you good for it," Jimmy said.

"I don't have much cash in the house, can I . . . ?"

Anton bristled and was set to pounce. "Why don't you take yo a—"

But Jimmy stopped him short. "It's cool, man. We can wait until tomorrow." Jimmy didn't have to face Anton to know that the other man was sneering and giving him menacing looks behind his back. Jimmy didn't want to wait any more than Anton did, but what choice did they have? "I can go to the bank with you in the morning," Jimmy offered.

This time it was Tyrone who bristled. "Who said I'm going to the bank?"

Anton butted in. "You just said you didn't have any money in here."

"Before you cut me off, I was going to offer you a check."

"We ain't takin' no check. We want cash."

Tyrone dug deep into his pocket and threw a few crumpled bills on the table. "Here's your damn cash."

Jimmy looked at the money and counted three hundred dollars. Clearly this wasn't what he had in mind. The bonus he envisioned came with a few more zeros than that. "Come on, y'all. We ain't goin' argue over no money. We'll take a check"—he gave Tyrone a knowing look—"but you know cash'll be better."

Tyrone cut his eyes at Anton, then turned his attention to Jimmy. "Call me tomorrow, Jimmy, and I'll give *you* cash. I gotta run." He stood up and walked to the door.

Jimmy followed closely behind, but Anton lingered, reluctantly walking to the door. "Okay, I'll see you tomorrow," Jimmy said.

"I know one thing. Jimmy better check that Negro," Tyrone said to himself once they had gone, "coming in here eyeballing my shit and demanding *my* money." He slid the wig off and fanned it in the air. "I need a drink after all that drama."